# PRAISE FOR *ORIGIN OF PARADISE*

ORIGINAL, COMPELLING, AND LEAVES YOU WANTING MORE." -JOANNE G

"WONDERFULLY WRITTEN...INTERESTING CHARACTERS AND THRILLING STORYLINES." -REBECCA S. MULLINS

"FAST PACED AND WELL WRITTEN." -M. HENNY

"AMAZING IN ITS USE OF FACTUAL INFORMATION COMBINED WITH SUSPENSEFUL TWISTS AND TURNS." -D. ZEILER

"VERY EXCITING...EXCELLENT STORY TELLING AND MYSTERY!" -MICHAEL A. DAVIS

"KEPT ME ENTHRALLED...COULDN'T PUT IT DOWN AND THE END CAME WAY TOO FAST!" –LORNA

*ORIGIN OF PARADISE*

PART ONE OF *PARADEISIA* BY B.C.CHASE

THE *PARADEISIA* TRILOGY:

*ORIGIN OF PARADISE* (PART ONE)

*VIOLATION OF PARADISE* (PART TWO)

*FALL OF PARADISE* (PART THREE)

B.C.CHASE is the internationally bestselling author of *Paradeisia: Origin of Paradise*, *Paradeisia: Violation of Paradise*, and *Paradeisia: Fall of Paradise*. His titles have consistently reached the number one slots of science fiction, thriller, women's adventure, and medical bestseller lists. He is regularly found on Amazon's top 100 author lists for science fiction and action and adventure. His mastery of combining hard science with edge-of-your-seat suspense has earned him a reputation as an author of authority.

Kinkajous are not a domesticated species: they are wild animals and are suitable as pets perhaps only for a handful of extremely dedicated individuals. Please do not allow my story to encourage you to make a commitment to an animal with a twenty-five-year lifespan if you are not absolutely certain it is a commitment you can keep.

**EXCLUSIVE INTERVIEW WITH THE AUTHOR
AND CHARACTER LIST ENCLOSED AT END.**

In Memoriam

J.M.C.

# 4085 Woodbridge Street

Wesley Peterson woke up, his heart pounding. He was wet and his sheets were soaked from a cold sweat. A shatter on tile broke the dark stillness. He reached for her, but she wasn't beside him. "Sienna!"

There was no reply, but there was panting and a whimper. The panting was heavy and strong. The whimper was his fourteen-weeks-pregnant wife.

His pulse was throbbing in his neck as he quickly drew his handgun from the nightstand drawer. A surge of adrenaline sent tremors through his hands as he tried to load it. He couldn't get the magazine to slide into the well. He tried to force it until he realized a round was protruding from the top. He slipped it in with its brothers, jammed up the mag, and cocked the slide to chamber the bullet.

He tracked toward the partly open door of the bathroom, feeling the sickening sensation of sticky-wet carpet under his feet.

He was afraid his 9mm wasn't sufficient.

He dashed his fingers inside the door frame to flip on the light and flung the door open, aiming inside. It took a second for his eyes to adjust to the blinding luminance, but what he saw made him stagger backwards.

His young wife was alone, spread-eagled on the floor in a pool of blood. He moved down to help her, but she pointed behind him and let loose a nothing-held-back, bloodcurdling scream.

# ORIGIN
OF
# PARADISE

# International House of Bacon

The blonde stared dismally at the tip she had just received. *Couples with small kids were the worst. The messiest and the smallest tippers.* Her cell rang from her apron where she stood at the server's station. She wiped the sticky syrup off her hands and dashed around a corner. "Hi," she answered.

"Aubrey, it's Maggie."

"I'm at work—what's up?"

"You know the job I told you might open up eventually if you were really, really, *really* lucky?"

"Uh, yeah. You told me *yesterday*."

"It's available! If you make it to La Guardia in an hour you'll get an interview!"

"An hour? I couldn't possibly make it that fast. I don't even have my resume ready." That's what Aubrey said, but her heartbeat accelerated with hopeful anticipation.

"That's okay! I'll send a limo for you—don't worry!"

"A limo? I'm in my uniform. And besides, I couldn't wing an interview for that job. I don't even have any experience!"

"I'm sending a limo now. Just get in and I'll take care of everything else."

Aubrey stepped forward from behind the corner and gazed at the floor of the busy restaurant. She had dreamed of leaving this world of bacon and pancakes for a long time; in fact, pretty much from the moment she arrived.

"Brie, you there?"

"Yeah, I'm—" Aubrey could see the black form of a limousine pulling up outside the frosted glass. "Maggie, the limo's already here."

"Already?" Maggie voice sounded a little anxious, "Wow! The driverless ones are getting *so* fast! Hurry and get in or you might miss it."

Uncertainly: "Maggie?"

"Hurry!"

"But Maggie . . ."

"Aubrey Vela, I'm older and I've lived way longer than you, so listen. Most people only get one chance to change their lives forever. This is your chance. Get in the car."

She paused a moment, pondering her choice and trying to calm her nerves. Finally, she said "OK. I'll be there."

Although her heartbeat was fluttering with excitement, her stomach was queasy as she slipped her phone back into her apron and walked slowly past the piles of plates . . . the screaming kids . . . the pots of coffee . . . and out the door.


## La Guardia


When the limousine pulled up to the departures platform Aubrey spotted Maggie standing at the TransPacific Airlines kiosk, rubbing her own shoulders for warmth. Maggie ran up to the limo and opened the door for Aubrey exclaiming, "I'm so glad you made it in time!" As Aubrey emerged, Maggie clutched her around the waist and manhandled her into the busy airport—almost like a porter with a piece of luggage. When they were inside, Aubrey broke free and protested, "Now you didn't tell me why I had to come to the *airport* for the interview. Why so fast?"

"Yes, well, we have to leave just as soon as he's seen you. He's just taken on a new company from England and we're flying out right away."

"So wait. You're telling me that if I'm going to accept this job, I have to fly out today, right away, without any warning at all?"

Maggie admitted, "Uh. I mean, yes. That would be a yes. I wish I could give you more time. But this is urgent."

"Maggie! I don't have anything with me except what I'm wearing!" Aubrey's mind and emotions were in a whirlwind.

"I know, sweetie. I know. But we'll get you new things."

When this didn't alleviate Aubrey's baffled expression, Maggie added, "Better things than you had before."

Aubrey wasn't impressed. She drew a long breath and exhaled fast, trying to compose herself. "How long will we be gone?"

"I don't know."

"Can you estimate?"

"I frankly have no idea. That's the name of the game here. But I know you'll love where we're going."

"How do you know that?" skeptically.

"Because it sure as heck won't be the International House of Bacon. Now let's go."

They rushed so quickly past the iris scanners and through the terminals that, before Aubrey knew it, they were outside again and at the steps of a screaming white jet the size of a commuter airliner. It read, "INTRAWORLD CAPITAL" on the side in black letters. The smell of jet fuel was strong despite the chill of the air.

Maggie was halfway up before Aubrey's protest came from below, "Maggie, I don't have a passport."

"What?"

"I've never flown before," Aubrey said sheepishly.

"Sweetie, I know you're naïve, but gosh, nobody needs a passport anymore! You got your USID card like all of us, right?"

"Yeah."

"They scanned your irises. That's your passport. Now get up here!"

So Aubrey dashed up the steps and entered the cabin, greeted by a rush of cool air.


## Jet


Inside, Aubrey hardly had time to take in the surroundings as she was whisked through the plane, and although she hadn't ever been in one before, she knew this didn't look like anything people usually flew in. There was a lounge with supple, leather wrap-around sofas and sleek-looking armchairs, a conference room where several men sat at a rich wooden table, and a hallway with wood paneled walls—one side lined with doors and the other side arching down and dotted with the small, round windows typical of airliners.

They stopped at a door in the hallway and Maggie quickly looked Aubrey over and batted some dirt off her skirt, saying, "You look good enough. You're definitely pretty enough."

"Uh, what if he asks me about my experience. I don't have any at this kind of job."

"He won't."

"What do you mean? Doesn't he care?"

"He's too busy to care." Maggie knocked on the door. An immediate, baritone response came from inside, "Come in."

Motioning for Aubrey to wait, Maggie stepped in and closed the door behind her. Aubrey heard her muffled voice, "Your new personal assistant is here, sir."

The reply came in a rich, Anglican accent, "Show her in, Maggie."

The door opened and Maggie's hand appeared around the door frame, making two quick motions to usher Aubrey along.

She stepped around the corner into what was a contemporary, but elegant office; there was a modern sofa against one wall and two chairs facing a glass desk. Behind this sat a strongly-featured man, breathtakingly handsome, but austere in expression, with eyes fixed on a screen that he held between both hands.

Aubrey stood there before the desk, waiting, but the man didn't even lift an eyebrow. She cast her eyes at Maggie, searching for some kind of guidance, but Maggie motioned for her to wait. And so she did . . . for at least two minutes.

Finally, the man raised his eyes and, as if he were surveying a new suit, fleetly looked Aubrey over. He then nodded to Maggie, "She'll do."

Aubrey's jaw would have dropped, but Maggie didn't give it a chance to, pushing her straight back into the hallway. After the door was closed and they were a safe distance away, Aubrey protested, "*She'll do*? What kind of an interview was that?"

"We're departing soon; he doesn't have time to do a full interview. You're actually lucky," Maggie laughed nervously.

"I don't know if I feel lucky or insulted!"

"Trust me, you're lucky. Now let me show you where you'll sit for the flight."

Maggie led her back through the aircraft to an area directly behind the cockpit where there were three sections; one was a galley, one had bunk beds, and the last had rows of seating. In one of the seats was a sixty-year-old looking woman with bright red lipstick. She had big curls that were dyed golden and she held a long-stemmed glass of sparkling champagne in one hand. Maggie introduced her as "Lorraine, the stewardess." She then directed Aubrey to sit in one of the seats and dropped a cell in her lap. "If this rings and it says, 'Henry Potter,' that means he needs you for something. Go find him and ask him what he wants—politely. I'll be back later." Maggie left them alone.

Aubrey felt a tingle of excitement when the plane began to move. Despite the strange "interview," she felt pride at having been granted the job. She had, after all, dropped everything to come here at a moment's notice. Few people would have had the nerve to do that, she surmised.

"So you're Henry's new personal assistant?" Lorraine asked, not bothering to hide her skepticism.

"Yes."

Snickering: "Well good luck."

"Thank you." Aubrey said, her satisfactory feelings now giving way to dubiety. "Why would you say that?"

"Oh, no reason. It's just that his last personal assistant left this plane about two hours ago. And she had only been with him for five days."

"Oh really?" Suddenly the pieces began to fall into place. The urgency, the limo, the lack of an interview . . . . Maggie had been on the hot seat for a new PA, pronto, and she'd capitalized on Aubrey's ignorance.

Lorraine chuckled hoarsely, and broke into a cough. When she recovered, she said, "Oh yeah, I've been on Henry's planes since the first time he had one, and I've never seen him keep a personal assistant longer than three months."

"Oh . . . *really*." Aubrey's disappointment was betrayed by her voice.

"Sorry kid, but Henry Potter is a first-class jerk, at least when it comes to his PA's," Lorraine said. "This new job of yours is going to be hell on earth."

The engines fired loudly and the plane started to accelerate toward takeoff. Lorraine raised her glass jovially, "Champagne?"

The cell rang. It was Maggie, "Come down to the conference room as soon as we're in the air."

"Why?"

"Just do it."

## Antarctica

Having not seen the titanium submersibles in over a month, Zhou Ming-Zhen, PhD, cringed at the sight of them now, lined up on a platform in the drilling station. They were identical: eleven feet tall, twenty-five inches wide, tubular, and topped with an acrylic glass bubble. Hidden inside the edge on the bottom of each was a propulsion fan. Two buoyancy bladders were inflated.

Members of the international press had congregated around them. Some were snickering to each other. There was no getting around what the machines looked like. They had even received an endorsement offer from a condom manufacturer. Given the preeminent importance of the endeavor, China had gracefully declined.

Back in the East China Sea, Doctor Ming-Zhen had spent hours under water in order to master his claustrophobia and learn how to maneuver them. Conditions inside were atrociously confined: it was like being in a metal coffin. To say he was relieved when training was over was to put it mildly.

At the insistence of his camera crew, he jumped up to pose in front of the subs with the only person who would descend after him: Doctor Ivan Toskovic.

They made an odd pair, Doctor Toskovic winking with triumph at the journalists and Doctor Ming-Zhen staring straight-faced and anonymously into their lenses. The two wore tight wetsuits; Doctor Toskovic's accentuating his muscular physique and Doctor Ming-Zhen's emphasizing his skeletal smallness.

After the photo op, the first vessel was prepared for descent. Two hooks at the end of a steel cable with a $Y$-split were attached to a small u-bar protruding out on each side. The cable slowly tightened and lifted it up onto a platform above the steel-rimmed borehole. As it came down to rest with a clang that echoed up the ninety-foot tower, the press shuffled, murmuring in expectation.

Doctor Toskovic shook Doctor Ming-Zhen's hand, saying, "Are you ready, my friend?"

He nodded a reply. "And you?"

Doctor Toskovic smiled with a shrug, "I like dark abyss, I like certain death." He motioned to the sub, "I like to drive giant penis. So, I love this mission!" He grasped a compass hanging by a chain from his neck and kissed it, "Besides, I have lucky compass. We will be A-OK."

Doctor Ming-Zhen knew that he carried the compass with him at all times. It was a matter of pride for the Russian after he had been lost in the Arctic wilderness while working a remote drill site. Placing a hand on Doctor Ming-Zhen's shoulder, the Russian said, "I see you on other side of ice, eh?"

Practically blinded by a hundred camera flashes, Doctor Ming-Zhen walked up the steps to the platform and entered the doorway on the side of the upright submarine. Inside, he climbed two notches in the white, round wall up to a spot with stirrups for his feet. Then he buckled a vest around his chest and placed his forehead against a brace. When he pushed a button, the vest, the brace, and the stirrups all tightened so that he was firmly buttressed within the machine.

He pushed another button and the door swung in and clinched shut with a suction sound. There was a hiss which he knew to be the chamber pressurizing.

He was now totally sealed in. He started to feel a wave of panic, but he took a deep breath and closed his eyes. *Claustrophobia.* It quickly subsided.

Opening his eyes, he said, "Ready for descent."

"Have good trip," Doctor Toskovic's voice said over speakers in the cabin.

"Acknowledged," he said.

He heard operators talking over the speakers: "Ready for descent. Releasing submersible, opening hatch." Doctor Ming-Zhen knew that much of this was actually automated; the operators were mostly there for dramatic effect—for the journalists.

He slipped a picture of his wife and daughter out of his sleeve. Fastening it to a rim below the glass, he said a quick prayer mantra.

His stomach lurched as the machine took a sudden two-foot drop. He heard some members of the press shriek in alarm, but he knew there was no reason to worry, at least not yet. The platform had simply given way and the submersible was swinging mildly from the steel cable like a giant pendulum. He folded his hands over his chest and took another deep breath. There was a loud metallic twang from the tower and he felt the machine beginning its descent.

Doctor Zhou Ming-Zhen was now forty-two years into his paleontology career. His last educational acquisition had been his second PhD, this one in Ecology and Evolutionary Biology from Stanford, awarded over twenty years ago. He was now head of the Chinese National Academy of Sciences Institute of Vertebrate Paleontology and Paleoanthropology.

His childhood, burdened by heavy expectations, had done little to contribute to his success in the field. His late father had been a Communist Party official in a smaller town, relatively poor compared to the officials in Beijing. His mother, still living and now placed in a monolithic assisted living facility housing thousands of the elderly, had been a homemaker. The two of them had presented a dichotomy of nurturing values: on the one hand he was coddled and spoiled as the lone child, but on the other he was chastised and scolded with the constant weight of the family's success on his shoulders.

When Ming-Zhen secured a scholarship to attend university through outstanding academics, his parents dispatched him with the anticipation of greatness. None in his family had attended higher education. But when he chose Paleontology as his course of study, his parents were devastated, even angry. How could he improve the family fortunes by scratching the ground for old bones? He was a fool, his mother said. He shamed his family, said his father.

And now, forty-two years later, he agreed with them. He was known the world over not merely as a paleontologist, but as the greatest fraud in the history of paleontology.

This came about through a chance discovery in the Gobi—during a routine fossil dig two years ago. What he and his team of students found there in the desert was something so astonishing that all his years of study and practice could never have prepared him for the firestorm that it unleashed.

As he descended down towards the deep interior of the ice, he desperately wished he would never have stepped foot on the Gobi, that he had listened to his parents and become an engineer. But here he was, dropping into the dark unknown, not knowing if he would return at all.

## Gobi Desert, Inner Mongolia

Unlike many deserts, the Gobi was cool in the summer and outright cold in the winter. His team of students wore jackets as they worked. Dealing with finger-numbing winds on a dig was not ideal, but, in Doctor Ming-Zhen's mind, anything that drove others away served to save more fossils for his teams.

They had so far exposed two twelve-foot skeletal forearms. The expectancy of his fledgling team was palpable. Veteran that he was, even he had some trouble containing his anticipation. Such a find was extraordinary even if the arms were not attached to anything.

One handsome member of the team, named Chao, was "studying" to be a paleoanthropologist[1], though from what Doctor Ming-Zhen had seen he had not exhibited any discipline, spending his time at the Academy in revelry and womanizing. His wealthy parents had paved the way to his success with golden bricks, paying for a lavish lifestyle at the Academy and bankrolling any project he undertook there, notwithstanding this dig in the Gobi.

Since the moment they had arrived, Chao had treated Doctor Ming-Zhen more like an employee than an esteemed professor. Now, with a tone of authority, he asked, "Are you able to identify the dinosaur from these bones, Ming-Zhen *jiàoshòu*?" Chao spit the respectful salutation out like a sour grape.

Doctor Ming-Zhen arose from his crouched position and asked the rest of the team, "Is anyone ready to venture a guess?"

His team squirmed. He repeated, "Anyone?"

A young woman on her knees grasping a dental pick looked up. She speculated, "Well, *tarbosaurus* was discovered in this area, but these

---

1    A paleoanthropologist specializes in fossilized hominids.

arms have three fingers, so we know it is not a *tyrannosaurid*."

Doctor Ming-Zhen nodded with approval, "Very good, Jia Ling." Of all the students he had ever guided, she had been his most promising; not because she was necessarily smarter than any of the others, but because she had shown the most patience. Probably the best example of this was her endless dedication to the hunks of earth they brought back after the excitement of digging them up was over.

Whenever possible on a dig, a large fossil was lifted away by heavy machinery as part of the sediment in which it was contained—as a giant, multi-ton chunk of plastered earth. Loaded onto a huge truck, it was carried to a museum or other facility where the sediment was meticulously drilled, air-blasted, chipped, and brushed away until the fossil was fully exposed and analyzed. This process often took months or even years of exhausting, tedious labor.

For Jia Ling, though, it was the thrill of the hunt. Long after all the other students had bored of this mind-numbing work, she would toil into the nights, picking away endlessly under hot overhead lamps.

As a result of her tenacity, she had once discovered a cluster of eggs within a six by six rock that they had thought only to contain a fossilized adult. These eggs had revealed several interesting aspects of behavior: among them that the dinosaur had carefully laid its eggs in a spiral, and that the young would be born with fully functional claws and teeth, quite ready to kill.

Doctor Ming-Zhen rewarded her dedication by taking her under his wing and devoting special attention to her welfare. She came from a poor family and her father had died in a construction accident when she was young so she had no money to visit her mother in distant Chengdu. At Doctor Ming-Zhen's invitation, she frequently spent evenings at his home with his wife and pre-teen daughter. Doctor Ming-Zhen and his pupil had become very close. So close, in fact, that Jia Ling was a second daughter to him in everything but law.

"Could it be a *carcharodontosaurid*?" another student asked.

Jia Ling said, "No, these arms are too long."

The other student shot back defensively, "There isn't a fossil of carcharodontosauridae with arms, so how would you know?"

Jia Ling looked down, defeated, "Well, in the depictions I've seen I think it has shorter arms."

Doctor Ming-Zhen contributed, "Actually, the holotype[2] of the most famous carcharodontosaurid, *tyrannotitan*, has a partial ulna and a scapulocoracoid[3]. The depictions are based on that."

Jia Ling asked, "What about an *ornithomimosaur*?" Ornithomimosaurs, known casually as "ostrich dino's" were small headed, frequently sporting beaks. They were known for their long arms, though most of them were small.

Doctor Ming-Zhen said, "I believe you are on the correct course." He said this because he actually recognized these fossilized limbs: he had seen a matching, eight-foot pair before, in a Barcelona museum. With three two-foot-long fingers tipped by gigantic claws, the fossil at the museum presented such a frightening prospect that the original discoverers had given the new dinosaur the Greek name for "terrible hand." He provided his students with a hint, "What other dinosaur was discovered in this province, something *terrible*."

Jia Ling smiled, "*Deinocheirus!*" She pronounced it dino-KY-rus.

Doctor Ming-Zhen said, "You are correct."

Jia Ling leaped into the air and jumped up and down with a squeal of excitement. Chao embraced her and kissed her soundly.

Doctor Ming-Zhen shot Chao an icy stare, clenching his jaw in anger. The most recent target of Chao's philandering had been Jia Ling, and she had thus far ignored strong warnings to avoid him. Doctor Ming-Zhen was not sure how far their relationship had gone, but he knew one thing for certain: Chao wanted her for only one thing. He was not going to get it while Doctor Ming-Zhen was around.

Chao returned Doctor Ming-Zhen's gaze by cocking his head in triumph and planting another kiss on Jia Ling's mouth.

Doctor Ming-Zhen's blood boiled as he stepped forward.

## Pleasant Plains Elementary School

---

2    A holotype is an original specimen on which a species was recognized and named.

3    A scapula is a shoulder blade, coracoids are bones connected to the scapulae in front of the ribs.

Wesley was sitting at the front of the third grade classroom. His forty-five students were taking a test. To pass the time, he turned to his phone. Innocently, he sent a text to Sienna:

u bored like me?

Her reply was quick:
y these emails nver end!

He responded:
was just thnking how much I love u babe
so glad u said yes

*blushing

u know wht I want?

wht?

i wnt to pick u up

a date? cool

seafood?

perfect. thn wht?

a movie

cool, thn wht

home

and? ;)

whtver u wnt

i wnt to make ur baby
com get me

He felt a rush, looked up from his desk at the kids. Cute little things had no idea how their little lives began.

Of course he didn't leave the school right away because he couldn't. But he was practically breathless by the time he did reach home. She was waiting for him.

That's the way it had been since their wedding day. After the rings went on, the gloves came off. It was mind-blowing, marital Shangri-La. They were desperately, passionately in love, and their youthful sexual energy had exploded like a piñata. They had fun, tried everything, drank deep of love.

But it didn't work.

This time, like every time, the test showed negative. As she stared at him sadly from the toilet, the stick in her hand, Wesley said quietly, "It's been a year now." He swallowed, "I think we need to see a doctor."
She wiped a tear from her cheek.
"I'm sorry, baby," he said. But he couldn't bear the look on her face. He wanted to fix this.

An x-ray and some tests rendered the verdict: it was impossible for them to conceive.

Their perfect American dream had come crashing to a halt.

So, like true Americans, they sought a quick fix. This landed them at the sleek, modern office of a fertility MD, who wasted no time in unleashing an onslaught of probes, collections of fluid, and tests. Then, they met him one day to hear what he had to offer. He said simply, "I can get you pregnant, and I bet I can do it within a year."
Wesley looked at Sienna, shocked. Then they both exhaled with a relieved laugh. Wesley asked the doctor, "You're sure?"

"Oh, yeah. That's not the question. The question is *what kind of baby will you choose?*"

The Doctor's name was Kenneth Angel. He looked no older than forty, though they knew him to be in his seventies. Barrel-chested, he wore a tight-fitting shirt with mini sleeves to show off his biceps. He had a deep, baritone voice and spoke with authority, sounding almost paternal, "These days infertile couples have options. A test tube baby isn't just a test tube baby anymore. Now it's a test tube baby on steroids."

He smiled, "We can perform all kinds of amazing miracles now, so much so that we are helping everyone make babies, not just the infertile. In fact, I would say thirty percent of the couples I help do not have any fertility issue at all. They just want me to work my magic."

"Those are probably people who have a lot of money," Wesley commented.

"Maybe." He leaned forward, "Or maybe they are people who don't want to leave their child to chance, they want to choose their baby—and they can. You can . . . .

"Listen, if you went to buy a car and the salesman said 'pay me 16,000 dollars and we'll bring you a random car from our lot,' you'd say he was crazy, wouldn't you? So why would you come in here and be happy if I gave you a random baby from your genes when it's totally within our power to choose what's best for your family—and most important, what's best for your child?"

Wesley and Sienna stared at him blankly.

"Okay, I can tell this is a little abstract for you, so let's talk specifics.... We could choose mom's or dad's eye color. Sounds simple, but let's say you want more options. Not a problem. I could even let you choose from a range of color options, free of charge." He held his hands out, "The possibilities are limitless. Of course, eye color is a matter of preference, but eye *shape* is what determines attractiveness. If you want this boy—"

Wesley interrupted, "Who said it would be a boy?"

"Sienna said so, on the phone."

"But isn't sex a roll of the dice?"

"Of course not," Doctor Angel replied, deadpan. "Those are *choices* now: male or female, homosexual or bisexual. Your pick." He shrugged with annoyance, "Now, what I was saying was, if you want this boy—or whatever you choose—to have really beautiful eyes, there is an array of shapes we can choose from—and they don't even have to derive from either of you. Right now almond-shaped eyes are all the rage, but if you want him to have the more bulgy, surprised look like you, dad, we can go with that.

"And dad," he chuckled, "I don't want to get personal here, but have you been entirely happy with . . . size?"

Wesley blinked, "What size?"

"You know, downstairs. Now let's be honest here, no keeping secrets from your doctors these days. I know you're only average, a little smaller than average, actually. I have the numbers right here. But wouldn't you like to give your son the opportunity to really impress in the bedroom? Don't you want his girlfriend to be wowed in the bedroom? Why let him be average when he could be more than average? You wouldn't want to condemn him to disappointments in the bedroom, would you? The truth is size does matter."

"I haven't had any disappointment," Wesley asserted with confidence.

Doctor Angel rolled his eyes, smiled, "Despite what you might have been told, the truth is size has a lot to do with performance. A lot. Studies prove it." He shrugged, "But the point is that this is just one of the things we can help your son with now, before he becomes sexually active; *before he is even born.*"

Suddenly a gigantic screen inlaid in his desk flashed to life. At dizzying speed, he tapped through a number of scenarios with a program called "*Conception.*" By selecting different physical traits, he showed them examples of what their baby could look like at birth and what he could become as he grew.

Wesley thought it was like playing a computer game, creating an ideal character—only the character would come out of his wife's body. Surreal, in an unsettling way.

When Doctor Angel was done toying with their son's aesthetics, he moved on to brainpower. He showed them what a likely IQ for their child would be without gene selection. It wasn't good. With a wink, he said, "We won't blame that on mom or dad." He arranged some new options for them, boosting their child's IQ by double digits. He went through different possible skills: mathematical abilities, creativity, artistic aptitudes and so forth. He probed psychological traits and reviewed sixteen possible personality types.

After stupefying them with these prospects, he dramatically switched to scare tactics. Wesley and Sienna's genes, it turned out, had a terrifying number of lurking dangers. He gave them an example of what their offspring could be without any gene selection at all: a cancerous, diabetic, and morbidly obese wretch suffering from migraine headaches, incontinence, addiction to alcohol, and high blood pressure.

"Now you know the government keeps a record of every child's DNA. If you think they won't use it to price his insurance, then you've got another thing coming. Let me tell you, with health problems like this, his healthcare costs are going to be unbearable."

Doctor Angel told them that clearly, *ethical* parents couldn't allow themselves to produce such a burden to society. Moral parents would spend the extra money to abolish at least a handful of these dreadful genes.

"Let me be honest with you guys. Gene selection is the new norm; hardly anyone will be making babies the old-fashioned way, no matter how much fun it is. Performing a little gene selection now is like paying your kid's college tuition in advance—only these are guaranteed results. If you want your children to be able to compete in this world, you have to give them this head start. It's survival of the fittest."

Wesley asked quietly, "How much does this cost?"

"Oh, well beyond the cost of getting you pregnant, the choices we're talking about would start at 20,000 and go up from there. But we'll work with you."

Sienna protested, "We don't have that kind of money."

"How much did both your cars cost?"

"Uh . . . ."

"You financed your cars, am I right?"

"Yes."

"And how much do you owe on your house? Just a *little* bit?" he squeezed two fingers together, smiling wryly. "Look, guys, we work with banks all over the country. We can finance anyone, no matter their situation."

Wesley hesitated, "I don't think we'd want more debt."

Doctor Angel leaned back in his chair, folding his hands on his chest and adopting a sage expression, "You financed those temporal things, but you wouldn't finance your child's future? Wesley, you're young so I'll cut you some slack, but you really have to ask yourself about the wisdom of that kind of thinking. I mean, if you don't do it now he's just going to have to pay for all this stuff later in gene therapy treatments. That is *way* more expensive than what we're talking about here. And because he can't get a job and has such high health insurance costs, guess whose door he's going to be knocking on for money. That's right. Yours; Mommy's and Daddy's. The people who didn't invest in his future when it really mattered." He sighed, "Frankly, if you can't do this for your child, it might be time to talk about whether you guys are ready to be parents. Are you responsible enough?" He tapped closed the "Conception" program and glanced over his e-mails. "I don't remember off the top of my head, but I'm not sure your metrics on 'planning' were very high. Procrastinators, both of you."

He looked up, "So, what do you say?"

Like they had learned to do at any car dealership, they left to talk it over before they made a choice.

They were overwhelmed by all the miracles science could work. What should they do? What was the *right* thing to do? Should they do anything at all?

In the end, it was all irrelevant. Shocking Doctor Angel, Sienna missed her period and turned up positive on a pregnancy test the next day. An intuitive distaste for Doctor Angel led her to return to her original doctor, Richard Kingsley, while she brought the baby to term.

So this night when they had slipped into bed, they were happy. She had a decent-sized baby bump; fourteen weeks. All was well.

Wesley spun around to where Sienna was pointing, expecting to face an intruder, but there was no one there.

"Please look! He could be alive on the bed!" she screamed. Turning back to her, he saw that she had knocked a vase off the tile surrounding the bathtub. His heart sank with a sudden realization: her stomach was conspicuously flat.

There was no intruder. She had lost the baby.

After all they had been through he couldn't believe it. As he stepped back toward the bed, he thought about the last maternity checkup. Doctor Kingsley said everything was progressing just fine. That was four days ago.

So what had happened?

Wesley approached the bed and was sick at the sight of a little lump under the white comforter.

It definitely wasn't moving. Then again, he didn't expect it to be; he was pretty sure a baby couldn't survive a miscarriage at fourteen weeks. The duvet was draped off the side of the mattress and was dripping blood. Wesley had never felt so sickened in all his life. He didn't want to uncover the lump in the covers. He didn't want to see their baby like this. He wondered if it would be best just to call 911.

"Wes?" Sienna cried weakly. "Is he . . . . . Is he alive?"

Wesley closed his eyes and jerked the cover off the lump. Slowly, his stomach in a knot, he allowed his eyelids to open.

Nothing.

The baby was not there. The lump under the duvet was nothing but a sheet wad.

Wesley checked the path back to the bathroom again. There was no fetus on the floor, only blood. He checked through all the covers, searched under the bed. Nothing. He went back to the bathroom and looked at his wife's surroundings. The fetus wasn't there. He opened the lid of the toilet, just in case.

"What are you doing?" his wife asked.

"It's gone. There's no fetus."

"Don't call him a fetus."

"Did you go anywhere else but the bathroom?"

"No, I . . . I came right here." She was pale and looked weak. Then she gasped, clutching her stomach, where the baby bump had clearly disappeared.

"Bad pain?" Wesley asked.

She nodded, her eyes squeezed shut.

"I'm calling 911," Wesley said, concerned that she had lost so much blood.

But as he walked out into the living room to retrieve his phone, something told him that he should also be worried by the fact that their baby had totally and completely vanished.

# United Nations Security Council

Doctor Matthew Martin was sitting at the front row of the vast audience that had gathered at the United Nations Security Council chamber. The chamber was airy, expansive. A large painting ornamented the front of the room with a giant semi-circular desk situated below it. The top of the auditorium was circled with blacked-out glass from where Doctor Martin knew an army of the international press was busy broadcasting the event to the world. The fact that he knew the event had garnered so much global attention made him all-the-more nervous.

When he had received the call from Secretary General Kwame Aidoo, he had scarcely been able to believe it. His work of the last eleven years had received positive attention mostly only from the lunatic fringe. Now was the chance to provide his discoveries with the mainstream exposure they deserved.

Science had been meddling with the tinker-toys of the universe; physics, biology, anthropology and the like, he thought. Now it was time to move beyond that. Now, it was time to play with the big boys. And he, Matthew Manley Martin, was going to be the harbinger.

He was scared senseless.

Sitting next to him, his fiancée squeezed his trembling hand. "How are you?" she inquired, her voice smooth and controlled, as always.

"Developed a bit of a stomach upset, I'm afraid," he replied.

She shook her head, trying to hide a grin, "Have you, pet? Shock me." Then she said, "You're quite pale."

"Am I?" he inhaled fretfully. "Well, we can only hope they listen to my words rather than critique my appearance."

"I'm sure that they will," she said. She patted his cheek, "Don't worry." She raised her hand, displaying a diamond ring, "Your powers of persuasion were convincing enough even for me."

He grinned, "As I recall, you did not require much persuasion. You've always been a bit of a dominatrix, haven't you?"

"Have I?" she asked, biting her lip and touching a finger to her chin.

From the front of the gigantic auditorium, the gavel made an unceremoniously tinny clang as a gray-haired man struck it three times. He was seated at the giant circular desk with at least twenty other men and women, each with small plaques in front of them. His read "AUSTRALIA—PRESIDENT."

Adjusting the microphone, the man said, "The 7,402nd session of the General Assembly is called to order. The provisional agenda for the session is before the assembly in document S-AGENDA-7593 which reads, quote, 'Evaluation of Key Events and Phenomena Relevant to Awareness, Felicity, and Security.' Unless there is an objection I will consider the agenda adopted." He banged the gavel, "Adopted." Bowing his head for a moment, he said, "Before we begin, I would like to take a moment to declare our compassionate solidarity with the United States in this time of tremendous difficulty. We express our deepest condolences. Our thoughts and prayers are with you." He nodded to the representative of the United States, who acknowledged.

"I would now like to welcome the distinguished heads of state, the representatives, and the Secretary General to this meeting. Thank you all for coming. This meeting will be somewhat unconventional, but as you are all well aware, the topic is also unconventional. And now, without further ado, I would like to welcome the first member of our witness panel, Doctor Matthew Martin."

Doctor Martin had not expected it to happen so quickly. He was frozen in his chair. There was supposed to be some long introductory speech, some politicians were supposed to wax eloquent for far longer than anyone had the forbearance to listen. Then, when everyone was properly stupefied, Doctor Martin thought, he would be called upon to take the chair. Not like this: not the opening act.

"Doctor Matthew Martin?" the Australian repeated, staring at him.

His fiancée gave his hand another squeeze and he regained control of his body. He reached down for the pile of paperwork underneath his chair and, rising, stepped up to the front, feeling every eye upon him.

The auditorium was engulfed in total silence and his footsteps echoed off the giant walls. He reached the tiny desk that sat facing the large circle of representatives and set his papers down, one fluttering off to the floor. The audience laughed. Paper was so rare that, apparently, its appearance floating in the air was amusing to the modern imbeciles, Dr. Martin thought. As he knelt to retrieve the stray sheet, the gray-haired man said, "We can provide you with a tablet."

"Yes, thank you. I prefer good old paper." The chair behind the desk squeaked as he sat in it. He cleared his throat and stared up at the circle of power-brokers.

Suddenly, he was frantic. His eyes darted from person to person. *Where is she?* He spun around and found her. In the mass of humanity, he found His fiancée smiling encouragement from the front row.

Somehow, the longer he had known her, the more dependent upon her he had become. In a way, it was odd. In another, disconcerting. All he really knew is that this woman had suddenly appeared in his life just when he needed her, and without her he was nothing. He couldn't help but love her, whether she was in charge or not.

He turned back around and hesitantly tapped the microphone. Hearing the loud reverberation it caused, he leaned forward and spoke softly, "Thank you, Secretary Kwame Aidoo, for inviting me to this pivotal meeting. As you know, when I spoke at TED my talk was censored, that is, removed, so I am grateful for this opportunity. Thank you, members of the Security Council, for indulging me with your time. And thank you, all of you who are here or watching remotely, for lending your ears to this subject, a subject which is quite certain to turn your little worlds," he giggled, wiped sweat from his forehead, "upside down."

The Australian representative said, "May you state your name and position for the record, sir?"

The professor adjusted his feet under the desk, and replied. "My name is Matthew Martin, I am a professor of biology of at the University of Cambridge, England."

"Thank you, sir. Now, please proceed with your testimony."

Doctor Martin felt himself calming. This was no different than a lecture at the university, he thought. His tone was even as he said, "Many of you might have sensed throughout your lives that there was something beyond what you could see or touch; that there was a power or presence, if you will, beyond the physical world. You might have heard of psychic phenomena such as fortune-telling or mind reading or telepathy. You might have seen these things for sale, perhaps at a fair or on the internet. You might have experienced certain strange feelings or thoughts that you could not explain. Feelings such as déjà vu or premonitions. You might have sensed that ideas were placed in your mind. You might believe that you were contacted by something or someone. You have heard of 'out of body' experiences and find them either unsettling, or empowering. You might have been frightened, even terrified at times and not known why; for example, in the dark.

"If any of this is true of you, then rest assured, you are not alone. I have also experienced some of these things, and so have eighty percent of the world's population, according to research.[4] And I believe," he chuckled, "that the same is true of this as it is about the study on men and masturbation: ninety-nine percent of men admit they have masturbated, and the other one percent are lying.

"Now, these phenomena are so common and so pronounced, in fact, that religions are founded upon them. When looked at as a whole, the fact is that, for better or worse, the 'spiritual' or 'psychic' side of humanity has been the greatest force for change acting on the world since the beginning of recorded history."

He shifted his feet again. "In dealing with these phenomena, let us call them 'psychic phenomena,' you will fall into one of nine groups. In the first group, you find them so overpowering that they become the focal point of your worldview and you ascribe powers of good or evil to them, devote significant amounts of your time trying to appease them, and do a great deal to convince others to do the same. This would be most of the population who strictly adhere to a religion of some sort.

"Second group: You believe they are real and are forces to be harnessed for your personal benefit and advancement. This would also

---

[4] Mail & Guardian. "Out-of-this-world response to online ghost hunt." 11/16/2006. http://mg.co.za/article/2006-11-16-outofthisworld-response-to-online-ghost-hunt.

be many religious adherents, such as charismatic Christians, Krishna Buddhists, and so forth.

"Third group: You believe they are mostly evil and, as such, should either be ignored or warded away through the use of incantations, good luck charms, evil eyes, or other means. This would include many Native American faiths and superstitions of the American Ozarks in the nineteenth century.

"Fourth group: You do not know what to think, so you think nothing.

"Fifth group: You believe they have something to do with outer space and are at risk of becoming fixated with UFO sightings, crop circles, cattle mutilations, abductions, and other phenomena. Once a firm believer, you may become convinced that you have experienced sightings or abductions yourself. The British UFO Association is a glorious example of this.

"Sixth group: You are skeptical. You think that in cases where subjects are not fabricating information, psychic phenomena are always explainable by science. They are contrivances or afflictions of the mind; for example, they take the form of mental illnesses or randomly firing neurons, as in dreams. Most of these phenomena, if problematic, can be dealt with through the use of drugs. Psychologists make billions of dollars every year treating their patients from just this mindset.

"Seventh group: You are curious, you want to know more, but you have not learned enough yet to form an opinion or belief, and you don't find it to be worth your time. You are lazy, qey sera sera, that is all.

"Eighth group: The implications of these 'psychic phenomena' frighten you so much that you refuse to ascribe reality to them despite being knowledgeable enough to know better. You are in denial. Take Richard Dawkins as an archetypal example of this."

He sipped some water, then continued, "In the ninth group, you are unaware, and therefore have yet to form an opinion. Less than one percent of the population can honestly claim to be in this group.

"If you are in group six, if you are a skeptic, I am now speaking to you. I was also in group six. I believed psychic phenomena were fodder for the weak-minded.

"One day, eleven years ago, I had an experience that changed my mind. It was the worst experience of my life, and it forced me to move into group seven; I now want to know more. I will now relate what happened to me that induced this change."

# Jet

Maggie met Aubrey outside the now-closed double doors of the jet's conference room. "Henry said he would like you to sit in on this meeting, but they're about to start. If you listen, you might *learn* something." She led Aubrey into the room where they took seats against the wall, off to the side of a table where there were seven men in suits, including Henry, and one elderly woman in an elegant-looking emerald-green pantsuit. Seated at the head of the table, she had a hawkish nose, but this feature was grandstanded by her large, piercing eyes.

"Are we quite ready to begin?" she inquired impatiently. Receiving nods from around the table, she tapped her hand and said, "Good." Then she declared, "Let me be abundantly clear: What we have received for our trouble is an utter catastrophe." Her small lips curved downward into a sneer of disgust, "When my feckless nephew came to me and asked for a considerable investment in this scheme, I didn't have the foresight to cast him from my threshold like the black cat he was. His sales antics were far better than his business acumen proved to be. So, alas, I invested. And when that investment was brought to nothing, he exploited the good faith I had placed in him to bewitch all of you," she motioned to the men around her, "who invested. And when that was lost, and he had the nerve to come cooing around my doorstep once more, what do you think I did?" She waited expectantly for an answer.

Henry Potter, resting his chin on his hand with one elbow on the table, raised his other hand and offered, "Invested again?"

"No indeed I did not! Merciful heavens," she scowled at him. "I plucked the toy from the infant's grasp and took up the chairmanship of this miserable board." Her comment received looks of gloomy agreement from the men.

"Unfortunately, I was far too late," she continued. "Waste, exorbitance and no plan whatsoever to earn a single farthing back has been our return on investment. This aircraft itself—" she made a sweeping motion to their luxurious surroundings "a corporate jet the size of a commercial airliner—is evidence of my nephew's excesses.

"Now for your part, Mr. Potter," she fixed her eyes on Henry in a stony glare, "your miraculous history of resurrecting corporate debacles seems too miraculous to be true. But our expensive consultants have told us that you are the man of the hour. So here we are, throwing ourselves upon your mercy.

"We have contributed our largest and, I expect, last infusion of currency to keep the fiasco afloat for now. Please accept my sincerest wishes for your success. So tell us, what is your plan?"

Aubrey watched as Henry sat there for a moment, listlessly gazing out the window. Then, clearing his throat, he straightened his posture and said, "Lady Shrewsbury, you call your nephew feckless, but in fact it was *you* who was feckless."

She hardly had a moment to take offense before he continued, "Had he ever done anything positive with money before he came to you for it? My guess is 'no;' otherwise he would have had no need for your patronage. Yet you knowingly shared your considerable wealth with him. Without any logical evidence that his proposition was worthy of the slightest consideration, you invested. This, this was feckless indeed. So do not castigate your nephew for doing what anyone would have done in his shoes. Everyone spends money freely that is freely given. Now *you* tell me, am I mistaken?"

Lady Shrewsbury looked aghast, "You have stinging words for your new employer. I suppose you've never heard the phrase 'do not bite the hand that feeds you,'" she stared directly at Henry, "lest you be flung from the jetliner."

Henry appeared fatigued, like a professor with a classroom of unmotivated students, "I ask the question, my feckless Duchess, because in order to be entirely motivated to redressing your mistake, you must, entirely, take the blame for it.

"Time and time again I've seen it. Every person in your situation begins with the same problem: they blame others for their errors. 'My accountant wasn't paying attention, politics got in the way, I had twins, the bank wouldn't give me a loan, my father was abusive, I ran out of cash, my wife divorced me, my partner was an idiot, there was a drought, my parents died . . . .'" He looked the duchess directly in the eye for his next sentence: "'My nephew was feckless.' These are all wonderful sentiments if one wants to sooth feelings of self-loathing, but they do nothing to fix problems. So I ask you again, do you want to fix your mistake? Were you a feckless duchess?" He swung his finger like a conductor, "Say 'I was a feckless duchess.'"

"I will not soil the honor of Shrewsbury by including my title in the matter. However, I will acknowledge that my actions were unseasonable."

Henry raised a single eyebrow, unimpressed, "And do you agree that your nephew cannot be blamed?"

She grinned patronizingly at Henry, "I think you will discover, as I have, that my nephew is extraordinarily gifted. Regrettably, his gift is not making people money; it is in making people smile." She raised herself up in her chair, "So, to the extent that I placed my trust in him for the wrong reason, he cannot be blamed."

Henry mumbled, "I'll accept that."

She said, "So, my nephew makes people smile; you make people money. The question is, will combining your gifts produce results we can all smile at. This, Mr. Potter, is my chief concern."

She leaned back, her nose upturned slightly, a coy grin playing on her lips, "I am placing my good faith in you. And make no mistake: I will be watching, I will be listening, I will take note of every whisper that I hear. For the first time in my very long life I have been made a fool, and if I come under the slightest impression that you could turn once into twice, let there be no doubt:" her eyes grew large, "hell has no fury like an old woman scorned."

When the meeting adjourned, Aubrey returned to her seat. She had hardly sat down when the cell in her lap buzzed again. The screen said "Henry Potter." She answered it, "Hello?"

His sharp voice came on the other end, "When I call you, it's not because I want the latest gossip. It's because I need you here, now. In the future, don't bother answering, just get over here. Is that understood?"

"Uh, yes."

"And I'm certain Maggie would have explained this to you."

She was silent. Aubrey wasn't sure if this was a question or a statement.

"Didn't she?"

"Yes, she didn't. I mean no, she did. She did." She waited for a response, feeling foolish.

The response that came from him shocked her:

"Idiot."

And the call ended.

After she recovered from the surprise, Aubrey was mad. She was just mad. Maggie had manipulated her into this job and now she was trapped on a plane with a new boss who was clearly a British jerk. And, to make things worse, she didn't even know where the plane was going! She decided she would find out. But first, she was going to give this Henry Potter a piece of her mind.

She swung open the door to his office. And immediately all her bravado disappeared. She couldn't explain it, but just something about the man standing there behind his desk disarmed her. It could have been his suit. It could have been the lavishness of his office. It could have been something within her that longed for approval; but whatever it was, she froze.

Henry shook his head impatiently and said, "Okay, here you go again. What does one typically do when entering a room?"

Aubrey's head spun. She couldn't think. What had she done wrong now?

"Merciful heavens. What rock did Maggie find you under? Aubrey: one knocks. So go out and knock on the door." Henry was rubbing his temple in exasperation.

Aubrey backed out, feeling dismayed, absurd, and angry all at once. After the door was closed, she raised her hand and paused. This was really going to be difficult to do. But she just couldn't deny this inexplicable urge to please him. She knocked.

"Come in."

She opened the door and entered.

"Let's not have a repeat of this lesson, shall we? Knock next time."

"Yes."

"Now, I called you here because I like to personally explain how things should be done. First, we'll go visit the closet so you can familiarize yourself with my mode of dress. Come along."

As he walked past her, Aubrey couldn't believe what she had just heard. Did he actually say "visit the closet?"

From the hallway he called, "Do you expect me to whistle at you like a bitch? Come along!"

He led her to one of the on-jet suites where there was a queen size bed, armchair, and generously sized closet, all surrounded by mahogany walls. He proceeded to elaborate on every facet of his attire, from which suits matched which shirts to what socks he preferred to wear with which shoes (shoes he expected to be polished and at-the-ready all the time). He expected her ironing to produce "creases sharp enough with which to shave." He had a large collection of ties, each one especially selected for specific outfits.

Her head spinning at the flurry of instructions, Aubrey blurted, "I can't remember all this!"

"No, I suppose you can't," Henry said, eyeing her with resignation. "Lucky for you, it's all on a chart in your cell."

They moved on to his toothpastes, mouthwashes and other toiletries, which he expected her to keep in stock. He had exacting procedures for sanitizing and storing all of his morning accoutrements.

Then it was his phones.

He had three phones, each the same exact model. In the morning, he required the first to be neatly wiped and ready for his use. Mid-day, he anticipated to switch to another polished, print-free phone. And in the late afternoon, another. He demanded that they be wiped, first with Windex and then an isopropyl alcohol solution (to kill any and all microorganisms, he said).

And so it went. Every part of his day spelled out, no detail overlooked. To Aubrey, it was readily apparent that obsessive-compulsive didn't even begin to describe him. In fact, he was practically like a baby in the extent to which he demanded his needs be met. The longer he went on and on, the less intimidating he became until Aubrey concluded that Henry was not a first-class British jerk at all; he was just a moron.

"Aubrey, are you listening?" he said, apparently perturbed by the far-off look in her eyes.

She smiled with the patronizing gaze of a mother and replied, "Yes, of course I'm listening, Henry."

As he continued, now spelling out the importance of keeping her skirt free of lint and her general appearance tidy, she realized that this was not just a job; this was a higher calling: this man needed to be rescued from himself. He was an imbecile, incapable of doing anything.

That's what she thought, at least, until he dropped the bombshell.

"Of course I'll expect you to undergo gene replacement therapy," he said.

"Huh?"

"I'll cover the cost, but there are two things with your appearance that don't meet my approval."

"Oh, really? What are those?" Aubrey said, her eyes narrowing. She had never heard any complaints before. "First, your hair. Either you can have gene replacement if you want a long-term change, or you can simply dye it. I don't give a damn. But it cannot stay blonde."

"You want me to change my hair color?" Aubrey exclaimed.

Henry explained, "Studies have shown that blondes are not as respected as brunettes. If you're going to be by my side as I do business, I need you to be as respectable-looking as possible. If you want to be more respected for the rest of your life, allow me to pay for a treatment."

"And what's the second thing?" she inquired suspiciously.

"Bust reduction."

Aubrey was aghast, "You've got to be kidding me."

"Not that I need to explain this to you, but countless studies have shown that women with smaller busts are perceived to be more intelligent. As much as my work relies on intellectual prowess, aptitude, and experience, the plain fact of the matter is that I am a brand. You are part of that brand. Maggie is part of that brand. Everything we say and everything we do must convey competence, confidence, and success. I'm offering this change to you charitably, as a treatment that would be to your benefit long-term. You would want to be seen as intelligent as possible, wouldn't you?

No, he didn't need rescuing after all, Aubrey thought.

He was just a jerk.

Suddenly Maggie interrupted them, "Sorry to intrude, Mr. Potter, but we're almost there."

"EPU-1350," Henry said, rising from his desk. "Count on a dozen governments to come up with a name like that. Let's see if it's worth my exorbitantly valuable time."

## 4085 Woodbridge Street

Wesley knew something beyond the miscarriage was happening to his wife, now leaning back against the bath surround. The whites of her eyes had turned sallow. This terrified him, but he went into a total panic when they began sporadically rolling up in her head. Every a few seconds, her head dropped to her chest and he found himself shaking her to wake her. He cried her name to her face, but she was disoriented and breathed, "Our baby . . . ."

Wesley lifted her up and laid her on the bed, the only thing he could think to do. To his relief, the blue and red lights of the police sent shadows across the bedroom walls, and he left her to let them in.

When he returned with them, she was slumped over the side of the bed, her head and arms dangling. She had vomited on the floor, and now she was unconscious.

It was surreal to him, like a nightmare. He felt oddly disconnected from the events around him, as if this just wasn't happening. It *couldn't* be happening.

But it was.

The paramedics came right behind the police and rushed into the room to transfer Sienna onto a stretcher. He was powerless and lost as he followed them out the door and down the driveway to the ambulance. Then they were in the ambulance, siren blazing down the road.

The paramedics asked him a flurry of questions about her medical history as they worked, and he answered in single words.

Then he was there by the stretcher, his face near hers, and she was awake again, saying "My baby! My baby!" through breaths but in a horrifying world of her own. He touched her cheek, but had to jerk his hand back. She was boiling. She turned her face to him and met his gaze.

"Wes," she breathed. "I'm sorry . . . our baby . . . ."

"It's not your fault," he said.

"No, I wanted to make a baby for you," she strained to speak. A tear formed.

Wesley had no words. He wanted to say something, but he couldn't find a way to say what he felt. All he could do was gaze into her eyes, which were flaming yellow now. She raised her head back up and gasped as if in terrible pain. Her skin was pink. Blood seeped over the white of one of her eyes as her body arched in a convulsion.

He touched her again; she was blazing hot. This was a fever out of control. Wesley was horrified as he saw her arms beginning to tremble and her chest literally, violently pounding with a powerful, rapid heartbeat. The paramedics were a blur of chaos around her feminine form. She was scalding hot; her breaths were coming out as vapor in the cold air, ever more rapidly.

Until they stopped.

"SIENNAAAAAA!" he screamed.

She was in cardiac arrest. All the paramedics' efforts to revive her were meaningless.

She was dead. The baby was gone.

As he stood in the ER watching her body being rolled away on the stretcher, Wesley could not believe that his small family had been taken from him in a single night.

## St. Joseph's Medical Center

"You were aware of the fetus's condition," Doctor Richard Kingsley said, a statement, not a question.

"It was healthy." Wesley said, his black-ringed eyes belying the lack of sleep and tremendous stress he had endured over the night.

"Yes, but I mean its genetic condition."

"Yes."

"Sometimes the mother's body senses that there is a problem, even if it won't show up until later in the child's life. So it expels the fetus. In a way, it's Mother Nature's way of preventing suffering." Doctor Kingsley sighed, "I am very sorry."

"But if she had a miscarriage, where did the baby go?"

"I'm sorry, Mr. Peterson, but, from my perspective, there is only one possible explanation. And I know you're grieving now and it's hard. But your wife must have disposed of the fetus," the doctor placed a hand on Wesley's back.

"But I told you, she didn't know where it was. She thought it was in the bed. She told me to look for it."

"She was in a state of horrible shock." Doctor Kingsley said quietly, "Most women who endure a miscarriage suffer denial, in the beginning."

"Well I checked the toilet myself, if that's what your suggesting," Wesley's voice was testy. "It wasn't there."

The physician appeared about to say something, but then sealed his lips.

"You think she flushed it, don't you?" Wesley accused.

"I'm terribly sorry, Mr. Peterson." He looked empathetic, paternal, "It was small enough."

"She knew what was going on, and she said it was on the bed. She didn't start losing consciousness until later," Wesley said loudly.

The doctor simply nodded sympathetically. "I am so very sorry. My advice is not to obsess over what happened to the fetus. Seek some counseling. And rest. You need to rest. It would help if you realize that, at fourteen weeks, it's only a fetus, incapable of surviving outside the womb."

Wesley was angry. He swore, "Don't call it a fetus! It was our baby."

Doctor Kingsley stepped back. "I apologize."

"I'm going to find out what happened to my son!" he spun around to storm away.

Doctor Kingsley shook his head sadly as he watched Wesley go. He called after, "I'm here if you need anything. Please take care of yourself,

Mr. Peterson!"

Doctor John Burwell, pathologist, and his technician, Sarah Rodriguez, had received the latest cadaver with the following notes:

```
-Miscarried 14 weeks approx. 04:00

-TOD 04:40 en route to St. J's due to miscarriage

-Paramedics report could not perform CPR-high fever

-No success with AED

-Tried to vent via trachea
```

"Could not perform CPR-high fever?" Doctor Burwell said to Sarah. "That doesn't make sense... Who were the bozos on that ambulance?"

"I've never liked paramedics. They always seem so cocky." Then she said quietly, "They're not like you." She didn't look up at him. She just said it into the corpse, as she always did when she dropped a compliment.

Even though he noticed these little hints and even though he found her brilliantly attractive, he could never bring himself to reciprocate. The only time they really spent together was in the lab, cutting open cadavers. It just didn't seem right to make plays at her in that environment, especially since he was her superior. And he never saw her outside the morgue. So even though they hadn't exchanged romantic conversation, there had been plenty of romantic tension over the last eight months.

Doctor Burwell unzipped the body bag, revealing a woman with one eye wide-open, jaundiced, and staring at nothing; the other blood-red. Her throat had been slit, probably by the ER surgeon who had tried to get air in through her windpipe: clearly the situation had been desperate.

If a patient was unable to breathe via mouth because of an obstruction or fluid, it was sometimes possible to insert a tube directly into the trachea. Called a cricothyrotomy, this procedure was performed only on extremely rare occasions due to how dangerous it was. But Dr. Burwell was puzzled. He thought this patient had died in the ambulance. Surely the paramedics had not attempted a cricothyrotomy. Only experienced surgeons were qualified.

Her skin was pink, but upon closer inspection, he realized that this was because of millions of tiny blood spots that had come to the surface. Rupture of the capillaries. Doctor Burwell knew that this could occur in cases of untreated diabetes. He noted the symptom.

Even through his gloves, he could feel that the skin was warm. They had taken the body from the refrigerator. Five hours later, and still warm? The other tech must have left it sitting out of the fridge and then, noticing his mistake, slipped it in right before he and Sarah showed up. Gross incompetence. The kind of incompetence that deserved termination. That guy was getting more and more careless. Just last week he had—

"What the heck," Doctor Burwell said, distracted from his thoughts. As he raised the body to look at the backside, something very strange became apparent. Although the time of death was over five hours ago, rigor mortis had not yet set in: the appendages were loose. He made a note of this and then, turning the body back over with Sarah's assistance, proceeded to make an incision on the front, down from each shoulder, to the sternum.

Next to no blood seeped from the tissue because there was no blood pressure: the heart wasn't pumping. From the sternum, he cut all the way down to the pubic bone. All the organs had the same red spotting that he had seen on the skin.

He used a special blade to saw off some of the ribs and began the methodical process of extracting the organs. As always, he would have to remove the throat and tongue by going up from the chest: families at the funeral didn't like to see their loved ones with stitched chins.

As he began the procedure, he noticed a major problem. The thyroid gland was missing. A butterfly-shaped organ that wrapped around the throat, it produced the hormones that regulated everything from metabolism to growth and development. But it simply wasn't there.

Perhaps she had been born without one. Congenital hypothyroidism occurred in one of 4,000 babies. If so, she would have been taking thyroid medication since birth.

However, when he further inspected her throat, it he realized something he should have in the very beginning. There was no blood at the site of the thyroid incision. These cuts had been made postmortem. No, the missing thyroid was not congenital. The gland had been removed, and recently.

Doctor Burwell shook his head. This was the most bizarre autopsy he had ever performed, without a doubt.

Doctor Burwell turned to Sarah, "I know I'm supposed to be the one with the experience here, but have you seen anything like this before?"

She shook her head an emphatic "no."

He continued extracting the other organs. And as he did so, it became more and more apparent that, aside from the other strange findings, something was very, very wrong.

The note had said "Miscarried." But Doctor Burwell was dumbfounded. Normally after a miscarriage, the cervix would have been open to allow the tissues to pass, but the uterus was empty, and the cervix was closed. There was no remnant of amniotic fluid, no sac, certainly no fetus . . . nothing. In fact, with the exception of Montgomery's tubercles around her nipples, there was no obvious evidence that this woman had been pregnant at all, and certainly not that she had miscarried.

## Gobi Desert, Mongolia

His fingers trembling with fury, Doctor Ming-Zhen growled, "This is a scientific excavation, not a party."

Jia Ling backed away from Chao, her head down, "Yes, Ming-Zhen jiàoshòu. Sorry, we are just so excited."

Doctor Ming-Zhen nodded, "I'm sure you are." At least even if Chao didn't have any sense, his Jia Ling apparently yet retained some of her faculties. He straightened his shoulders, "Now, let's see what else we can find."

The skeleton was lying belly up, as if it had rolled onto its back when it died. They dug down past the coracoids to the upper ribs, and were now busy clearing out the chest cavity. Doctor Ming-Zhen was eager to see if the spine was there, because if it was they could trace it up to the head.

Most complete dinosaur skeletons that had been found exhibited opisthotonus, or the "death pose." Head thrown back, tail raised up, as if in agony, the "death pose" occurred in any creature that died of brain damage, asphyxiation, or drowning, including humans.

So if they did find the head, it would probably be behind the vertebrae of the back.

Now, though, they unexpectedly ran into a round dome-like fossil within the lower rib chamber.

As his young students chipped away at the debris around the domed fossil, Doctor Ming-Zhen watched closely to be sure they didn't damage it. They were using dental picks and brushes, but fossils were very delicate and you couldn't be too careful.

It was definitely a domed skull from something; most likely the deinocheirus' last meal. This was exciting because it could reveal something about the extinct creature's diet, but at this moment he couldn't remotely identify what it was from.

They continued to work, and by the time the forward facing eye sockets, nasal cavity, and top row of teeth were revealed, the truth was so obvious that Jia Ling dropped her pick with a sudden gasp, pulling away in revulsion.

Evident even to an untrained eye, this was the skull of a mammal, a primate. And not just any primate. The familiar, disconcerting gaze which stared back from the gaping eye sockets conveyed the irrefutable truth to every person staring back: this was *Homo sapiens.*

From his knees where he had fallen, Doctor Ming-Zhen gazed at the long-dead human and was overcome with a strange horror. Flashing through his mind was a giant, long-fingered hand clutching a man, the claws curled around to gore him through the chest, and immense jaws swooping down towards his head.

But this was impossible, he thought. Dinosaurs and man were separated by millions of years of evolution.

His mind spinning, he remembered that a team of his colleagues had identified a cat-sized mammalian fossil that contained a tiny dinosaur in its stomach. At the time, scientists the world over had admitted that it overturned the premise that early mammals of the Cretaceous had been timid little animals that lurked in the shadows of the much more advanced *dinosauria*. This premise had of course been based on the necessity of evolution taking time. The cat-sized animal provided an image of a more powerful, more evolutionarily advanced Cretaceous mammal.[5]

Even so, a small mammal here or there did not equate to a human being. Not by a long shot. This was impossible.

And yet, here it was, before their very eyes.

Still gazing at the fossil, he said quietly and slowly, "It is fortunate that you came, Chao. It seems we require the expertise of a paleoanthropologist after all."

*If only he really was an expert*, he thought with repugnance.

## China Academy of Sciences

Doctor Ming-Zhen and his team made the journey back to Beijing as soon as they had completed excavating and packing all the large chunks of earth. Then they began the painstaking work of cleaning the rock from the fossilized bone. Jia Ling, of course, devoted more time to this than anyone. One day as he entered the lab, he caught her quickly stashing something in her pocket. He approached her and her eyes shifted away from him.

"Ming-Zhen jiàoshòu. Isn't it exciting?" she said with a high pitch, staring at the fossil.

"Yes, it is," he replied. "Is everything going okay?"

"Yes," she nodded emphatically.

"Not that you would think of doing this, but you do know it is illegal to take pieces of the fossil for your personal collection."

---

[5] Hu, Yaoming; Meng, Jin; Wang, Yuanqing; Li, Chuankui. "Large Mesozoic mammals fed on young dinosaurs." Nature. 2005/01/13.
http://dx.doi.org/10.1038/nature03102. 10.1038/nature03102 10.1038/nature03102.
http://www.nature.com/nature/journal/v433/n7022/suppinfo/nature03102_S1.html

"Oh, yes," she said. "I know."

"Very good," he said.

"It's a picture of Chao," she said. "In my pocket. I know you don't like him."

"I want the best for you, Jia Ling. He is not worthy of your trust."

"He does respect you."

"Does he? He doesn't show it very well."

"But he does. He is insecure, is all."

Doctor Ming-Zhen raised his eyebrows. "Be very careful. You have very much promise. I would hate for him to distract you."

"I will."

When every last bone had been cleaned and studied, they began work on a paper for publication. Knowing that their discovery would likely attract a great deal of scrutiny, they left no stone unturned and took a full year to document the find.

When they had finished clearing the stomach cavity, every piece from the unfortunate human was accounted for. It appeared the dinosaur had swallowed him in three chunks; fairly dainty dining for something with a ten-foot mandible. And the evidence was proof positive that the deinocheirus had swallowed the man: the teeth of the dino perfectly matched indentations on the human's bones.

As for the deinocheirus itself, the truth of the creature proved paleontology to be totally mistaken in its classification as an "ostrich dino."

Representing an amalgamation of features from several dinosaur families, the complete deinocheirus skeleton defied belief. Its head was nearly twice the length of tyrannosaurs, and the jaws contained an extremely formidable set of teeth; the longest tooth measuring in at over a foot from jaw line to tip. It turned out to be the largest carnivorous dinosaur ever found; sixty-five feet in length.

Clearly, t-rex was going to fall to be bottom of little boys' toy chests. This skeleton had proven deinocheirus not only to be the new "king" of the dinosaurs, but also, given the contents of its belly, the king of men.

They documented all of it, every last detail.[6]

But it was all for nothing. In the end, he wished he never would have found it.

## 94 Golfpointe Road

Wesley's eyes opened. He couldn't believe he had actually been sleeping. It had been two days since Sienna died, and he hadn't slept a wink until now. He brought the recliner upright and yawned, orienting himself. He was in the sitting room of his mother's house, a five-bedroom, lakeside colonial. In the room was a sandstone fireplace surrounded by white shelves filled with those bounded vestiges of the past that nobody knew how to get rid of.

For a few moments, Wesley just stared at the flames as they licked off the logs. Why his mother had a fire blazing in near-summer weather, he didn't know. Probably just the ambiance. He almost felt like he might doze off, but then it happened again.

A memory.

They were at the department store exit, sunshine glistening off the pavement outside the glass doors. He was pushing a cart with the new crib and a couple of baby supplies. She was scampering in front wearing little shorts and a carefree t-shirt. The doors slid open and she spun around with a smile, "This is going to be one spoiled baby!"

"You've got that right," he said, laughing.

And the memory froze as he felt a sharp pain deep within him. That sweet smile, radiant with her sparkling eyes.

Dead.

---

[6] This was written before the more complete fossils of deinocheirus were discovered. Additional information is available in the author's notes in Part III, *Fall of Paradise*.

But the memories. They were alive and well. Each one brought a new kind of pain, laid another stone on his monument of grief.

His cell phone rang. The caller ID read, "CDC 202-342-3993." He welcomed any distraction, so he answered immediately.

## St. Joseph's Medical Center

"So what's our verdict, John?" Doctor Kingsley asked into his phone. "What does the lab have for us?"

Doctor Burwell had been receiving calls like this from Kingsley ever since the Sienna Petersen case had come down to the morgue. Kingsley had been the woman's OBGYN, so it was understandable he was concerned. Doctor Burwell said, "Whatever it was, it wasn't good; they sent it to the CDC."

"They did *what?*" Doctor Kingsley's voice was suddenly tense. Then, "I'm sorry, where did you say they had it sent?"

"They sent it to the Centers for Disease Control. Her death was definitely not related to the miscarriage."

"Are you sure about that? Miscarriage can cause all kinds of secondary problems."

"Well you know what I said about the miscarriage. She didn't have one."

"I know what you said, but you know there's no other alternative."

"I sent pictures to a friend. A gynecologist."

"You could have sent them to me."

"I'm sorry; I know she was your patient. I didn't want to upset you."

"What did your 'friend' say?"

"He said never. He said that, as recent as it was, the cervix would have been open and there would have been some blood at the very least."

"Hmm. Well, I still think she flushed it," Doctor Kingsley asserted. Then he changed the subject, "So admin is sectioning off the fourth floor?"

"Yes, they're putting Sarah and me in quarantine. They asked us to go voluntarily until the Maryland authorities decide what to do. They also said the CDC would need an executive order to enact a quarantine. You know how bureaucracy is."

Doctor Kingsley grew serious, "But John, this is ridiculous. The woman had a miscarriage and died. There isn't any kind of pathological threat. You're seriously not going to stay there are you?"

"Yeah. I am."

"I'm going to fight this for you. It's not right."

"Richard, I know you're upset. This was your patient. You feel responsible. But it should make you feel good to know she didn't die of a miscarriage. She was sick."

"You know I think of you as a son. You've been my protégé around here. But I'm telling you, she miscarried and died. And I'm going to tell the CDC, too."

## 94 Golfpointe Road
## Travilah, Maryland

"Is this Mr. Wesley Peterson?"

"Yes."

"I'm Doctor Phillip Compton, Director of the Centers for Disease Control. I wanted to speak with you personally because I want you to know how seriously the CDC is taking this situation. I understand you lost your wife unexpectedly and I know that this must be a very terrible time for you. Please accept our condolences."

"Thank you," Wesley said, a little surprised at the call. The man's tone said 'I am important, I'm used to being in charge.'

"I am very sorry for your loss, as is everyone here at the CDC."

"Thank you."

"And I know our people have held interviews with you, to get information about her case . . . but has anyone given you her cause of death? Anyone from Maryland, I mean?"

"No."

"Okay, well, while I cannot give you any specific information, what I can tell you is that it was not the miscarriage which caused it. It was a disease."

Wesley was incredulous. While he agreed it wasn't a miscarriage directly, a "disease" seemed awfully far-fetched. In fact, to Wesley, this sounded like some kind of cover to keep him from the truth. "A disease? She was fine until that night."

"So I understand. However, a disease definitely was the cause of death."

"What disease?"

"That I cannot say."

"You don't know or you cannot say?"

"I know more than I can say, but I don't know everything—far from it. And that is partly why I am calling. Between then and now, whom have you had contact with?"

"Well, I'm staying with my parents. I drove over here from Towson."

"Did you stop anywhere along the road? A toll booth or anything at all?"

"No."

"Didn't even go to the bathroom?"

"No."

"And you haven't seen anyone else?"

"No, I just drove straight here."

"Okay, thank you. It would be wise for you to isolate yourself until we find out more about this and you can be tested. Since we don't know everything, we need to stay on the safe side."

"Yes, so I've been told. What about my mother? Should she be quarantined, too?"

"At this point, I cannot impose a quarantine on anyone. It will be up to your local authorities in Maryland to determine that. And I also should stress that there has been no evidence that this has spread to anyone beyond your wife. However, you might think it wise to alert your mother that she should stay out of contact with others."

"So we had a funeral scheduled in two days. What about that?"

"I would cancel it."

"What about her body? The hospital said they won't sign the death certificate until they can put a 'cause' on it."

"I'm afraid that her remains will not be accessible to you for the time being."

"I see. So if I cancel the funeral, people are going to ask why."

"Tell them something they will believe. Even at the risk of looking selfish: 'I can't handle a funeral now' would do. Just please don't tell them the true reason. I don't want to cause undue alarm."

Wesley suddenly wondered if this would be good person to relate his assessment to. He was eager to talk with anyone who would listen and possibly help. "My wife didn't have a miscarriage, you know."

"You mean she wasn't pregnant?"

"Oh no. She was fourteen weeks pregnant. What I mean is that her doctor told me that she flushed the baby, but I was there that night and she didn't. She thought the baby was on the bed until I saw that it was missing."

"Okay . . . ."

"So she didn't flush it, but it was gone."

"Hmm," Doctor Compton sounded patronizing.

"Hear me out, please! The baby just disappeared. I'm telling you this because I don't know who else who might be able to help."

There was silence on the other line. "So what do you think happened to it if she did not miscarry?"

"I don't know."

"Well, in my mind, the only other alternative would be that someone came into your home and took the fetus from your wife, unbeknownst to her or to you. How would you propose that happened?"

"All I'm saying is that the baby disappeared, but she didn't flush it!"

"I'm sorry, but I have to side with the doctor you spoke to. She must have flushed it. I know you'd like to believe differently, but we must come to terms with reality sometimes, even if it's uncomfortable."

"Yeah, okay," Wesley said, but his feelings did not agree with his words. Wasn't there anyone who would listen to him, even if he sounded crazy?

With a little introspection, he realized that he wouldn't.

"Mr. Peterson?" Doctor Compton said.

His reply came out sounding defeated, "Yes."

"Missing children in any state fall under FBI jurisdiction."

"Oh?"

"If I were in your shoes, I would contact the FBI and report your child as missing."

"Thank you."

"Best of luck to you."

"Really. Thank you," Wesley's voice cracked. He was overcome by suddenly having a slight suggestion of hope.


## China Academy of Sciences


Oddly, Doctor Ming-Zhen's paper on the man-eating deinocheirus had been easily approved for publication in a prodigious journal by the anonymous scientists who peer reviewed it, yet became the subject of unrelenting castigation and dismissal from everyone else. Peer review was an excellent system by which academics could either anonymously censor others with whom they disagreed, or hide from controversy after they signed off on truth that the public couldn't stomach. In this case, none of the original reviewers of the paper came forward to support Doctor Ming-Zhen. Not one. The journal, however, issued a retraction.

No one believed that he and his team had found Homo sapiens within the belly of a deinocheirus, especially a deinocheirus that was so complete in its preservation and so surprisingly menacing in its construction. The whole thing simply seemed so entirely implausible, and even with all the evidence, no one was willing to recall Sir Arthur Conan Doyle's adage, "Once you eliminate the impossible, whatever remains, no matter how improbable, must be the truth."

Before long, Doctor Ming-Zhen was horrified to hear many calling his discovery an absolute hoax, from the human remains to the deinocheirus itself. As this line of thought gradually came to be accepted by the media and, with them, most scientists, he was angered not only because of how unjust it was for him personally, but even more so because of the damage it did to his team of pupils.

Then, the unthinkable happened.

One evening he was watching the news on a large screen, his wife standing behind him, when two of his students appeared on an interview. Undoubtedly buckling under the tremendous pressure brought to bear and determined to salvage their own careers, they told the world that the fossils were a chicanery and that their esteemed professor was a fraud.

One was the carouser Chao. The other, his precious Jia Ling.

His wife placed a hand on his shoulder. "I am very sorry," she said.

He could not muster a response. He was utterly devastated, and he was filled with a terrible rage against Chao, who had doubtless pushed Jia Ling into this treachery.

In short order, Doctor Ming-Zhen was labeled the greatest fraud of paleontology.

After that blow, the issue became a simple matter of faith, with a very small number of his closest friends and colleagues quietly accepting Doctor Ming-Zhen's testimony (because they knew his character), while the rest of the world chomped at the bit in zealous outrage, practically ready to have him hanged for scientific heresy.

Because he was the head of the Academy of Sciences Institute of Vertebrate Paleontology and Paleoanthropology, the institution itself was castigated. Calls were made for his resignation. He found himself shunned at the institution by all but a handful of professors.

Because he did not resign, the Academy of Sciences, and, by virtue of equivalence, all of Chinese paleontology took the fall. There were many claims from the rest of the world that this was only the pinnacle in a series of fallacious discoveries. Papers were rejected for publication on the basis of mere suspicion. New discoveries were ignored, scrutinized to the point of exhaustion. It was a catastrophe for Chinese science.

Doctor Ming-Zhen suspected a sinister reason for all the uproar against Chinese paleontology.

Before he published his infamous paper on the man-eating deinocheirus, China had swiftly risen to prominence as the epicenter of paleontology, with more, better-preserved discoveries surfacing there than anywhere else, and more experts in the field than any other nation. Because China now had such a large and thriving crop of its own homegrown paleontologists, scientists from the outside were rarely admitted to partake in the abundance, and if they were, they were mere spectators or dirt-pushers. For this reason, the rest of the world was dripping with envy, and Doctor Ming-Zhen's supposed fraudulence, and the Academy's silence on the subject, gave them the perfect excuse to shut China down. The ire was nothing more than basal human jealousy, he thought.

Regardless of the cause, he wondered what he possibly could do to redeem himself and his few perseveringly loyal students.

And then he received a call from his mother at the giant assisted living facility. She demanded an immediate visit. She did this very frequently. At first, he told her now wasn't the time, but she would not accept "no" for an answer.

So when he arrived at her tiny apartment and sat down beside her, she said, "I've seen you on the news. It seems," she coughed, "you've run into some trouble."

He hung his head.

"Zhou, you know we did not support you becoming a paleontologist." She took his hands in her withered ones, "But we could not deny that you became a good one. Before he died, your father told me that he was very glad that you had not become an engineer, after all. You made us more proud as a paleontologist than you ever could have as an engineer." He felt like a child as tears welled up in his eyes. Though he didn't know it before, his whole being had been yearning to hear this.

She said earnestly, "You can prove to them that you are who we know you are. You are not a liar, you are a man of character and honor. You can prove to them the truth." She firmly shook his hand between both of hers, "You only need to go and do it." She then straightened in her seat, frowning, "And besides, it will keep your mind from negative energy." She looked out her window absently for a moment, appearing to have a senile moment. Then she turned her head slightly and jumped in her seat at the sight of him. "You're not gone yet?" she clucked. "Now go!" she waved her arms. "Go show them!"

His mother's little pep talk ultimately gave him the encouragement he needed to dismiss the uproar around him and to return to science for the evidence he needed.

It was when he was in the middle of this research that he was called to the head of the Academy's office.

Yue Zhang, the *Xiàozhǎng* (head) of the China Academy of Sciences, was an impatient man, prone to fits of anger when things were not going according to his timeline. But he was also sensible, highly intelligent, and equitable. He had been a near-failing student in school himself, and did not possess a PhD in any field, but his aptitude at management was second-to-none. It was for this reason that he had led China's most venerable science institution for the last ten years.

Short, with a round face and piercing black eyes under thick eyebrows, he looked down at Doctor Ming-Zhen from an especially large desk and tall chair. Zhang said, "I am sure you have heard of the calls for your resignation."

Doctor Ming-Zhen looked down, "I have considered resigning myself, for the sake of the Academy."

"And what has stopped you?" the superior inquired sharply.

Doctor Ming-Zhen looked up and said calmly, "I did nothing wrong."

Zhang took a deep breath, casting a glance out the window as if he longed to be somewhere else, and said, "Now you know you have already tried everything. No amount of photographs, documentation, radioisotope dating, or remains will satisfy them. They've taken thousands of samples of the fossils and done their own studies. It's all come to nothing. You cannot prove it to them."

"You are correct that they will ever accept the original fossils as genuine. But I can prove what the fossils prove."

"Which is?"

"That Darwinian evolution over vast amounts of time has not occurred."

Zhang raised a skeptical brow, "And how could you prove that?"

Doctor Ming-Zhen sat back in his chair, "Antarctica."

Zhang furrowed his thick eyebrows, "Antarctica? What relevance could that possibly have?"

Doctor Ming-Zhen explained, "Once, many years ago, I assisted a colleague at San Diego State University in documenting fossils from the Hell Creek formation. It covers parts of North America; Montana,

North and South Dakota, and Wyoming. It is notoriously fertile."

"Yes?"

"Hell Creek has yielded a treasure trove of all varieties of dinosaur fossils over the years. Tyrannosaurus, triceratops, and ankylosaurus, for example. You've heard of all of those, I assume?"

"Yes."

Doctor Ming-Zhen said, "Well, the fossils my friend from San Diego State University and I cataloged were not dinosaurs at all."

"No?"

"No." The paper that resulted from their efforts was published in the *Journal of Vertebrate Paleontology*, and quickly fell into obscurity.

Thousands of representations of all kinds of animals were discovered at Hell Creek, including modern and extinct ones: all manner of amphibians, reptiles, fish, and birds (including many species still alive in modernity). Hell Creek also contained a wealth of plant specimens, ninety percent of which were *angiosperms* (flowering plants), a type supposedly in its evolutionary beginnings. In the words of one professor of paleontology, "If you've ever wondered why so many prehistoric animals are dated sixty-five to seventy-five million years ago, in the Cretaceous, it's because most of them were discovered in Hell Creek."

Also found there were over 1,000 mammalian specimens, and it was precisely these which Doctor Ming-Zhen and his colleague documented.

Spreading his hands, Doctor Ming-Zhen asked, "You tell me, what was such an abundance of mammals doing in a place of history where they were allegedly in their infancy?"

"Weren't they all just little rats?"

"No," Doctor Ming-Zhen said, "They weren't." He cleared his throat, "There were primates. Tree-dwelling primates."

Zhang leaned back with a look of surprise. He blinked, "You cannot be serious."

Doctor Ming-Zhen said, "Oh, they call them 'primitive' primates."

"Why haven't I ever heard about these Cretaceous primates before?" Zhang asked, clearly bedeviled.

Doctor Ming-Zhen shrugged, "Everybody wants to hear about the dinosaurs, so we paleontologists don't talk about the other animals we dig up."

"So you think this lends credence to your discovery of the man in the dinosaur stomach? I really don't think that's enough to—"

Doctor Ming-Zhen interrupted him, "There's more to it than that. Because most of the Hell Creek formation was originally dated to the Cretaceous, in the early 1900's, as more and more fossils of more and more different species were unearthed, it sent the evolutionary timeline back to the drawing board continuously."

"There's nothing wrong with that. It is the way honest science should work."

"Yes. As species were added to the Cretaceous epoch, science was forced to depart from what I was taught in my early days in the field: the old textbooks explained matter-of-factly that the amphibians led to the reptiles (which then included dinosaurs) which led to the mammals and the birds. In some cases, the mix of supposed dinosaur (supposedly Cretaceous) and mammal (supposedly Paleocene) remains was so jumbled that it presented a seemingly insurmountable problem for the timeline. Bug Creek (part of the Hell Creek formation) is a perfect example. Everyone had to breathe a sigh of relief when a solution was found to this problem. The new term '*reworked fossil*' was coined, and it was easily concluded that many fossils had been moved into place and re-fossilized—by some artificial means such as erosion. This is such a problem that, in order to boost credibility, studies sometimes must specify that the age of the rocks is 'undisputed.'

"Now, the textbooks have a convoluted version of history that varies from textbook to textbook but generally refers to a giant burst of life in the Cretaceous followed quickly by a mass extinction (somehow survived by many mammals)." Doctor Ming-Zhen leaned forward, "My question is now: was it possible that the variety of animals at Hell Creek represents not the population of an era, but rather the same type of species localization one would find in any modern environment? At some point, it isn't enough to keep revising the timeline. At a certain point, one must question the entire paradigm."

"I'm not sure I understand," Zhang replied, shifting uncomfortably.

Doctor Ming-Zhen explained, "For example, a child can name the animals typically found in the savannah, and the same child can also tick off many of the animals usually found in the Congo. But the lists would always be *different*. Giraffes in the savannah, gorillas in the Congo. Different areas host different species." He waited, allowing his superior to digest his statement.

"So you are saying that the Hell Creek formation could possibly be a representation of a specific environment hospitable to specific animals rather than an era, or a layer, of geologic time?"

"Yes," he confirmed. "To the east, in the Chicago area, mastodons, woolly mammoths, sabre-toothed cats, and other large mammalian bones are found, but no dinosaurs. Not one. Not even a fragment of a dinosaur is found in that area. Why? Was it species localization? In California and in Florida the same list of mammalian bones have been dug up, but not a single dinosaur in Florida and very, very few in California. In Missouri and down to Texas, both dinosaurs and large mammals are found in abundance. In Colorado, at higher altitudes the large mammals, but lower down are the dinosaurs.

"So what if the cretaceous, and all the other epochs with it, did not exist at all? When you're looking at Hell Creek sediments, you don't say, 'Here are the mastodons on top and here are the dinosaurs on the bottom.' If Hell Creek represents a forest environment with frequent flooding, which I suspect it does, then the mammals you find there are suitable to just such a place. Perhaps the simplest way to look at this is the right way to look at it: mastodons are not found in the Hell Creek areas because mastodons didn't like that environment. What if the epochs have nothing to do with time? What if epochs are actually habitats?"

"But what if that area was covered in ice, during the ice age, so that's why the mastodons are not found there?"

"Visible Hell Creek is not a huge vast area: rather it appears bordering a vast area where very few fossils from anything except plants are found, the Fort Union Formation, supposedly formed during the Pleistocene, right after the Cretaceous. So let's assume that, during an ice age, ice was covering this huge Fort Union area as well as the surrounding exposed Hell Creek areas, preventing mammoths from living there. How is it that the ice was there, but it wasn't covering Hot Springs, South Dakota, right nearby; Qu'Appelle Valley, Saskatchewan to the *north*; or New York to the west, all places where mammoth fossils are found?

"And why are dinosaurs so scarce in California? Because it was covered in ocean back then and they were all washed away, as they say? How about because it didn't offer the habitat that dinos prefer?"

Zhang thought for a moment. Then he said, "But don't you usually dig very deeply for the dinosaur fossils, because they are from far back in history and therefore in a deep layer?"

"Another myth. That's how they draw things in fantastical school textbooks. But the truth is, when dinosaur fossils are discovered, it is most often because they are exposed on the surface of the ground, not because they are dug up from deeply within it. In Hell Creek areas, the common method for finding fossils is by *walking around* looking for them, not by digging up vast mines. The same is true in the Gobi Desert here, the Sahara in Africa, and Patagonia in South America. The idea that these layers are perfectly laid down everywhere underneath our feet is entirely false. There are some places where it looks like some epochs might be discerned one on top of the other, in the Grand Canyon, for example. But even in the Grand Canyon, it is a muddy picture, with the highest layer dating to about 250 million years ago."

Zhang scratched his nose. Then he said, "All right, so your major proposal is that mammoths lived at the same time as dinosaurs, but that they lived in separate areas because of the environments in those places. What does that have to do with Antarctica?"

"If we accept that the mastodons and mammoths lived with the dinosaurs, then this brings into question the existence of the 'ice ages;' the times in which the world was supposedly much colder and dominated by them and wooly mammoths. In fact, it would indicate that there has only been one ice age and we are living in it now. If mammoths were indeed contemporary with dinosaurs, could there be somewhere in the world where dinos have been quick-frozen in time, just as the notorious iced mammoths have been—the ones with fresh grass still in their mouths?"

"And you think Antarctica could be the place?" Zhang eyed Doctor Ming-Zhen skeptically, "Zhou, this seems somewhat fanciful."

Doctor Ming-Zhen nodded, "I grant you, it's not a place famous for paleontology, but it has provided a wealth of fossils for those who have the resources to look. They have discovered ancient vegetation so fresh that petrification has not even begun. This vegetation was quick-frozen, just the same way that the frozen mammoths in the north were. They have also found plenty of dinosaur fossils, but only bones so far. So there is proof that dinosaurs lived in Antarctica before it froze."

"So, you really think there could be dinosaurs stopped dead in their tracks with their mouths full of food?"

"Well, no. I'm not thinking of anything remotely so dramatic." Doctor Ming-Zhen explained that, contrary to popular opinion, most of the frozen mammoths or mastodons had not been entombed in ice, but, rather, within the icy soil, with most of them standing upright, as if they had just been pressed down into the earth where they stood. He asked "Now how could that possibly have happened?"

"Am I the paleontologist?"

Doctor Ming-Zhen grinned enthusiastically, "Actually, the answer came from a seismologist."

Unamused, Zhang asked, "And what was the answer?"

Doctor Ming-Zhen explained, "During severe earthquakes, entire cars and even buildings sometimes sink directly into the ground, as if they had been built on quicksand. Why? In areas where the water table is near the surface or where the soil is very porous, severe earthquakes can cause the water to rise and the soil to become so saturated that it becomes a soup, a process known as liquefaction. It was recognized that the mammoths must have been trapped by this process—thus they were standing upright with food in their mouths when they sunk into the soil and were frozen."

Doctor Ming-Zhen placed his hands together, toying with his thumbs, "There were thousands upon thousands of these mammoths; entire herds of them. They were so numerous and so fresh, it was said that wild wolves regularly fed on their carcasses in Siberia."

"And you expect to find herds of dinosaurs in Antarctica?"

"Certainly not. I only need one."

"One?" Zhang questioned, surprised. "How would *one* help?"

"Well, besides the obvious wealth of answers it would provide to the unending questions we still have about dinosaur physiology, a frozen dinosaur would provide DNA—fragments potentially complete enough to compare with other animals, such as mammals. DNA," Doctor Ming-Zhen said, "would kill the evolutionary tree of life once and for all and show that our discovery of a deinocheirus feeding on Homo sapiens was perfectly plausible."

His superior slouched, "You had me interested with the frozen dinosaurs, but now I'm at a loss again. How in the world could DNA possibly help?"

"Have you heard of the duck-billed platypus?" Doctor Ming-Zhen asked him.

He replied impatiently, "Of course I have. But I don't see what relevance—"

Doctor Ming-Zhen pressed his palms on the desk and stood, "When you have it figured out, give me a call."

And, turning on his heels, he walked out the door.

## Babraham Road
## Cambridge, England

Doctor Matthew Martin easily followed the familiar countryside road outside Cambridge. He had just passed the roundabout and was well on his way towards the city. It was a cool, black night and his windshield wipers easily kept his view clear in the light drizzle.

Despite being home to the park and ride, the road rarely had traffic; especially after dark. But Doctor Martin slowed as he saw brake lights ahead. Coming to a stop behind the line of cars, he squinted, peering into the darkness to try to see what caused the standstill. He could see a hunk of metal off the side of the road not too far ahead. *Must have been an accident.* The whole road must be blocked, he decided, noticing that the opposite lane was vacant.

After a few moments of impatience, he got out to go see if it would be necessary to turn around. The rain seemed to get heavier just as he stepped out of the car.

Nearing the mass of metal in the grass, he could see that it was a mutilated car. The roof had been peeled up off the top like the lid of a can. Blood was flowing over the matted hair and down the body of a figure that leaned forward against the seat belt. The head hung limp on the steering wheel.

He breathed, "Oh God" to the dark sky as he quickened his pace. Blood had spattered the dash, the steering wheel, the ventilators . . . . The victim was a middle aged woman. She did not move. He grasped her right shoulder and pulled her back. When her head moved away from the steering wheel, a section of her skull flipped down over her forehead and bloodied, globular tissue swelled up from the skull. Reflexively, he jerked his hand away and he stumbled back, an agonized moan escaping his lips.

He knew this woman.

## United Nations Security Council

Doctor Martin blinked away the memory, returning to the present. He stared up at the faces of eager listeners in the circle above him. "I was driving on countryside roads on the way back from a visiting lecture. At a certain point in the route there was a roundabout, with two roads to take, both of which would eventually lead me to Cambridge. One was shorter than the other. I naturally always took the shortest road. But on this night, as I came to the roundabout, I had this sudden, foreboding feeling. I had the sense that I should take the long road, that I *must* take the long road instead of the short one.

"Now, I am not a person prone to superstitions or premonitions or any of these sorts of things. I like to think of myself as quite rational. So, of course, I ignored this sense and took the short road. Just a brief drive down the road I saw brake lights ahead. Stopped traffic, of course.

"I waited there for only a brief moment or two while cars lined up behind me. I could see something on the side of the roadway in the distance. I thought of my premonition, and something in my rational side made me determined to prove it wrong. So I left my car and marched over to see just what was going on and see if, perhaps, I could get things moving again.

"There had been a horrific accident, a fatal accident. An entire family had lost their lives; mummy, daddy, and three little ones. I saw their bodies strewn all over the place. Totally, dreadfully mutilated. The driver of the truck that hit them was also in a bad way, but he, at least, was still living.

"Worst of all was that I knew these people. Intimately, I knew them. It was—" he swallowed a sudden frog in his throat. With white-knuckled fists he gripped the edge of the desk. His voice faltering, he said, "It was my very dear sister and her family." He paused, closing his eyes and swallowing, regaining control.

"So when I did get back to Cambridge, I mulled the incident over in my mind, as I have a tendency of doing. Why and how had something told me not to take the short road?

"There were two very disconcerting things about this question. The first was that the premonition did not seem to come from events which had already occurred or which were occurring at that moment. No, this was a premonition about a *future* event." He allowed the audience to digest that for a moment.

"The second was the fact that I felt the premonition in response to a human fatality, indeed, the fatality of someone who was very close to me.

"You often hear about 'life-force' or some interconnectedness between us. Of course it all sounds like so much rubbish until something like that happens. Then you begin to wonder.

"Well, eventually I had more or less concluded that there was nothing to it but a simple and conceivable coincidence and that, whatever the case, there was nothing I could do about it even if there was something to it.

"I went on with my life as if nothing had happened. And then, I was slapped in the face with something. And I was no longer able to rationalize my way out of it. No, rather, it became my life's work and a complete and total obsession. A miserable obsession," he giggled oddly "you might say."

## The White House

Doctor Karen Harigold, Secretary of the United States Department of Health and Human Services, was furious.

"Why can't I see him?" she shouted down at a man in a motorized wheelchair.

The man, Abael Fiedler, Chief of Staff, had a horrible knotted scar on his face from his forehead across his eye to his cheek. And although he was seated, he was hunched over. There was a grotesque, boney hump in his back, and even his arms were gnarly with bulges and juts like the roots of a tree.

Karen knew why he looked this way: he suffered from *fibrodysplasia ossificans progressiva*, an extremely rare genetic disorder in which bone grew anywhere there had been even a slight injury, and sometimes just appeared randomly. It was a long, tragic disease that started in early childhood and grew progressively worse until mobility was increasingly impaired. Anyone who had it wasn't expected to live past forty. Most died much earlier than that.

And yet Abael Fielder was forty-one. Karen knew that virtually every minute of those forty-one years had been painful, cruel and horrific. She wondered if that's what had turned him into such a power-seizing, conniving devil. He had survived, but it was clear: time was running out for him. For Karen, it couldn't come soon enough.

For now, though, he was here, and he didn't flinch under her rage. He spoke steadily, "The President is with his family."

"Like hell he is! You know as well as I do he hates his family. We're facing what could be the worst health crisis since 1918 and I can't even see the President?" She knew she might be exaggerating, but it was worth it to try to get this guy's attention.

"Karen, he'll be back in an hour or two. I'll have him sign it then. I'll even have him call you."

"Right, as if *that* will happen. Just like he was going to show up at the last *six* cabinet meetings, you—" she swore at him.

"Cabinet meetings have no real value. A simple publicity stunt is all."

"They're as good as gold if I'm stonewalled by his Chief of Staff and he doesn't return calls, doesn't respond to emails, and doesn't even bother to see me when I come all the way down here to talk to him!"

"Karen, the truth is I will decide when and if he sees your request, so you really should treat me better."

"Who are you to wield that kind of authority?"

He cocked his head in an eerily reptilian way. "I was chosen," he said, his voice hollow. The corner of his mouth turned up slightly in a disdainful smile. With his black eyes leering up at her and his body as still as a snake, Karen half expected a forked tongue to project from his thin lips.

Of course that didn't happen; he just stared at her with his usual condescension. She swore a final time and spun around to stomp back down the marbled hall.

When she was gone, Abael Fiedler lifted the paper from his lap. It was an executive order for the quarantine of anyone potentially exposed to a virus of some sort. As he did with any new piece of information he received, he studied it carefully. Then he wheeled himself into the empty Oval Office, placed the paper on the President's desk, took one of his pens, and signed the document in the President's hand:

*Robert Surrey*

Abael then wheeled himself out of the Oval office and into a corridor to a door on the left. He knocked.

A reply came from within. He opened the door to reveal a small office. The President, wearing a jacket and slacks, reclined in an armchair with his legs propped up on an ottoman. He looked up from the screen he was reading.

"How may I help you?" the President said.

"Karen just came. She had an executive order she wanted you to sign. Another health scare. I signed it for you so we can give it back to her tomorrow."

"Thank you, Abael. You know how busy I am."

"Yes, I know, sir. The world will look to you, you know."

The President sighed and shook his head, looking distant, "And they don't even know what's coming."

## EPU-1350

Aubrey heard the mechanical clunks as the landing gear descended. She was in her seat beside Lorraine, gazing out the window, and in spite of Henry, she felt a flutter of excitement in her chest at what she saw outside.

Bright blue sky was punctuated with small fluffy clouds, and in the distance far below, the sparkling ocean was interrupted by a round white beach of cresting waves. A vast expanse of flat land blanketed with grass, shrubs and the occasional palm tree spread out from the beach. Then a cascade of tropically canopied green ridges rose up to a grand vista of lush mountains. Far in the distance were two peaks towering magnificently above it all, wisps of fog billowing near their crowns.

Lorraine was clearly as moved by the sight as Aubrey, and breathed, "My word. It's beautiful."

"But where are we?"

"Paradeisia," a voice behind them said. It was Lady Shrewsbury. She pronounced the word pair-ah-DAY-sya, and her face bore a pleasant, though mysterious, expression. "137 square miles of tropical paradise."

Aubrey posited, "So it's an island."

"Yes, part of the Lesser Antilles to be exact." Receiving a blank stare from both Aubrey and Lorraine, she clarified, "You know, Guadeloupe, Dominica, Martinique, St. Lucia. Several years ago, we purchased this island for an outrageous sum of money from France. Of course, back then it was a secret. They called it 'EPU-1350.' Now, it's the largest private construction project ever undertaken. And, so far, still a secret."

Lorraine inquired, "What did they build?"

Lady Shrewsbury raised an eyebrow, "It's not so much what was built as how deep."

"How deep?" Aubrey asked.

"Yes, many of the islands here produce oil. The government intended to extract it from this one by excavating via the empty magma chamber of the volcano. Only they didn't find what they were hoping for. No, they found something quite unexpected."

"What was that?" Lorraine asked.

Lady Shrewsbury drew a quick breath, a hint of a smile gracing her lips, "Well, I'm here for the adventure as much as you. We shall soon see the place together, shall we not?"

The pilot's voice came over the intercom, requesting everyone to be seated. He intoned, "And, please, buckle up. This is going to be a rough landing."

Lady Shrewsbury departed, saying, "I'll see you on the other side, ladies."

As Aubrey turned back to the window, she was surprised to see how close they had come. A myriad of details had now become visible. There was a port with two long piers stretching out from the coastline. A monstrous cargo ship with the words IntraWorld Logistics printed on the bow was docked at one of them. Containers with large white print that read "WARNING: LIVE CARGO" were being swung by a crane from the vessel toward a dock where rows of semi-trucks waited and tiny workers milled about.

Situated on the plain that stretched out from the coast toward the mountainous ridges was what Aubrey recognized as their target: the airport. There were several runways with a maze of asphalt between them. These were edged by a shiny glass terminal.

As the plane circled over the mountainous ridges to align with the runway, it began to shudder, first one wing raising up and then the other. The bumps and jolts of descent became so bad that a knot formed in Aubrey's stomach.

She was thrilled.

The airport was obscured by a ridge ahead. They passed over so closely that the sound of the jet engines reverberated off the rocks and it looked like the tree branches would strike the bottom of the plane.

Finally, the wheels bounced on the runway and Aubrey loosened what she realized was a white-knuckled grip she'd had on her armrests. The plane pulled toward the terminal and then stopped about three plane lengths away, the scream of the engines slowly winding down.

When the door opened, a blast of warm, salty, tropical air blew into the cabin. Before long everyone had exited the plane down a flight of steps to sit on a waiting open-air shuttle. Aubrey breathed in the scent of the sea in the wind that whipped her face as the shuttle sped them toward the terminal.

The shuttle rolled through a large opening in a glass wall. Soaring 100 feet above was a glass roof supported by a network of triangular trusses. Reaching up towards the ceiling was a row of thin-trunked, erect palm trees that lined a platform where the shuttle came to a squeaky stop.

Music with an African chorus, brilliant trumpets, and a strong jungle beat echoed from hidden speakers. A sonorous voice spoke over the music, "Welcome to Paradeisia:" the voice paused for emphasis, "Eden on Earth."

Suddenly, the same sonorous Anglican voice, but very close, very cheerful and no longer echoing, said, "At long last you've finally arrived! I thought you'd never get here, and by 'never,' I do mean not ever."

## CDC

Doctor Compton sat at a large conference table in a room that was packed full of people, some seated, but most standing. The person at the head of the table was Karen Harigold.

Karen spoke, "So explain what's going on, Phil."

Doctor Compton began, "Well, I don't know how much everyone here knows about viruses, I'm assuming you're all fairly well-versed. But just in case, let me explain. A virus is a core of DNA or RNA that's usually coated in protein. Very simple. So simple, it's not even classified as life.

"Now because they are so simple, viruses are parasitic. They must have a host to reproduce, in other words, viruses must infect living cells to reproduce. It is inside these cells that they replicate their DNA and produce new, infectious viruses.

"Now an interesting facet of this process is that more than one virus can replicate inside a single cell at the same time. When the virus replicates, transcription errors can produce mutations that can sometimes be beneficial to it, but it can also pick up genes from its host or from other viruses in the cell. So, what the virus ends up being is an amalgamation of the genes that were useful, both from random mutations and from its hosts or even from other viruses it might have met inside its host.

"Viruses also pass pieces of their DNA *into* their hosts, which then can be passed on to successive generations. The fastest-replicating viruses are RNA viruses. Influenza is an RNA virus. Because it replicates, and therefore mutates so quickly, it has transferred to different species very quickly.

"Now, to get to the point, you all know a mysterious virus killed a woman in Towson, Maryland, and we received samples for analysis. In fact, we now have the whole cadaver."

"Now this virus that we're dealing with here, it's an RNA virus, so the first thing we know is that it has the capacity to mutate very quickly. This means that the way she received it might not be the way it is transferred next time, if there is a next time—God forbid. As it mutates, it might attack other types of tissue.

"We tested the samples and couldn't find a match for any known virus. So we sent samples to some respected labs overseas.

"One of those labs happens to have compared the virus to a database of all known genes. And I mean all known genes from living and non-living creatures. If anyone found a snippet of DNA anywhere, in a bacterium, in a bone, in an insect . . . anything at all, this database has it."

"Yes, it's called 'A.R.K.'. Any lab can freely access it online," Karen said, impatient.

"Yes, that's right. Well, the lab that ran the test just called me." Doctor Compton paused because he knew what he was about to say was going to raise questions. And doubts.

"Well what were their results, Phil?" Karen said.

"This virus is very old."

"Okay???"

"I mean very, very old."

"How old, Phil."

"Ancient."

"So is influenza," she said. "Hippocrates wrote about it. What's the big deal?

"No, I mean before that. Many of the genes from this virus are only shared with . . . ."

Everyone was staring at him in expectation. He couldn't believe that all his study, all his hard work, all the companies he had worked for, his appointment to the CDC . . . everything, had culminated in this: he had to say something preposterous. He finally let it out:

"Sauropods. This virus has genes matching sauropod DNA."

A guy chewing gum and wearing a baseball cap said, "Sauropods? You mean 'stomp, stomp,' 'Welcome to Jurassic Park' sauropods?"

"Sauropods, yes; dinosaurs."

Karen immediately interjected, "But a virus can only be transmitted between *living* things."

"That is correct—well, HIV could survive for weeks in a corpse, and, given ideal conditions, some viruses could even survive for months outside a body, but, yes."

"So whatever gave the virus to the woman must have been alive today."

"Correct."

Karen leaned forward, "What I'm trying to get at is, she couldn't have sat on a rock that a dinosaur happened to have touched a long time ago and picked up a virus from that."

"That is correct.    A virus doesn't sit around for thousands or millions of years waiting to infect someone.  It needs a host.  She probably had to have touched or been in close proximity to the original carrier of the virus."

Karen looked at him with one brow raised.  "Phil, really?  Are you saying she touched a dinosaur?"

"What I mean is she would have had to touch something that was alive today and was carrying the virus.  Not a dinosaur."

Karen sat back.  "Regardless, this sounds impossible."

Doctor Compton nodded.  "It certainly seems like it would be."  Suddenly, Doctor Compton's phone rang.  He looked at the screen and recognized the number.  He apologized, "I have to take this; it's St. Joseph's."

He answered, feeling everyone watching him expectantly while he listened to the person on the other end.  After he hung up, he said, "They say the pathologist's assistant at the hospital has the virus.  It appears our worst fears are true: the virus has transmitted."

There was a hushed silence in the room for a moment.  Then Karen said, "Everyone needs to understand that, so far, the people in Maryland have refused to take this thing seriously.  But, as you've just heard, it's deadly serious.  Unless the President adds this virus to a list for which we can quarantine, we are entirely at the mercy of the states for containment.  Maryland has not reacted with the urgency they should, and that is why I've gone to the White House—to get quarantine authority in advance."

She stood up, and said calmly, "Starting now, we're in national health crisis mode.   This is command central: every piece of information, every directive passes through this gate.  First, I want quarantines.  No one comes or goes from St. Joseph's until I say so. Send a team down there; call the police, whatever you need to do.  And

I want anyone who so much as looked at the original victim within the last week quarantined. This is an unprecedented situation, we are going to take unprecedented steps.

"Now I know you guys are used to doing research, but I want containment. I don't care if we never know how this thing got here as long as nobody else gets it. Flex your muscle first and ask if you had the authority later. There will be hell to pay if this becomes a nightmare on my watch. We must exude confidence. No Ebola repeat. Am I clear?"

Everyone nodded, except for the ball-cap guy, who said, "But we don't know anything about it. We can't really label it a national health crisis until we have done research."

Karen gave him such a severe look that he stopped chewing his gum. "I don't know who you are."

He volunteered, "Guy Giordano."

She rolled her eyes, "And I didn't want to know. But my name is Karen Harigold, I'm Secretary of Health and Human Services, and it's a freaking national health crisis because I said it's a freaking national health crisis. Got it?"

"Yeah," the guy murmured.

"And, Doctor Compton?"

"Yes?"

"Call the news channel. Tell them about the St. Joe's quarantine. Anonymously."

"Just as long as I don't end up with an espionage charge like James Rosen."

"Very funny," she said. "I hardly think you're on the top of the President's hit list." Then she struck out for the door. "I'll be back ASAP."

Doctor Compton asked, "Where are you going?"

She spun around and swore: "I'm going to the White House to get my quarantine order."

# St. Joseph's Medical Center

Sarah Rodriguez and Doctor Burwell sat across from one another at a desk in the quarantine area. They were talking over a meal of hospital food somebody had brought for them. Their first date, really, Doctor Burwell thought to himself. And they were both having a good time, until Sarah suddenly grimaced.

"What's wrong?" Doctor Burwell asked.

"My stomach. I don't think it likes these noodles."

"You want some Pepto? I'll call for them to bring some over."

"Thanks," she managed to smile appreciatively.

Doctor Burwell picked up the phone and dialed four digits. "Hey, yeah. Can somebody send some—" Doctor Burwell stopped.

Sarah cried out, reaching for his arm, "John!"

She had never used his first name before. But now, she was squeezing him with a surprisingly warm hand and gasping in what appeared to be terrible pain.

Doctor Burwell yelled into the phone, "We need help now!"

Sarah's sallow eyes were rolling as her head dropped to her chest. Doctor Burwell rushed around the table to hold her up, but she slipped into unconsciousness. He wrapped both arms under her and lifted her up to carry her to a nearby bed.

Doctor Kingsley entered the area wearing a mask and gown, followed by a team of doctors. Doctor Burwell knew enough to stay out of their way as they flew into a blur of activity. Just as they were attaching the patches from the respiratory monitor, Sarah opened her eyes and cried out in agony, vomit gushing from her mouth and nose.

## United Nations Security Council

Doctor Martin continued, "A neighbor of mine, originally from Russia, told me about something very strange that had happened. Her son was deployed in the navy to the North Sea. He had left his childhood dog at home in her care.

"One day, the dog began to whimper and run back and forth, very agitated. She didn't know what the matter was, so she took it outdoors.

That did not help. It continued in this fashion until she became convinced that it was ill, so she took it to a veterinarian. There was nothing physically wrong with the animal, but upon their return, it simply lay down on the floor and wouldn't move. It stayed like this for days, not eating, just lying and letting out an occasional whimper.

"At the end of a week, she was contacted by the navy. There had been a horrific accident on her son's submarine. The vessel had sunk and the entire crew was lost.

"She told me that the moment the accident happened is the moment the dog became agitated.

"Effectually, the dog *knew*, without a doubt, that its best friend had died, and, by all appearances, furthermore knew the exact moment when the danger first struck.

"As a biologist who has held senior academic posts most of my adult life, I was dumfounded by the refusal of my colleagues in the scientific community to take this seriously. What are we afraid of? Are the implications too terrifying for scrutiny?

"Whatever the case, I proceeded with research. First, I looked into all the information I could on the subject; all the examples of animal intuition.

"It turns out they are everywhere, right before our eyes. You don't have to look at all. Someone simply must give you a tap on your shoulder."

## The White House

"Where is the President?" Karen asked, her hands on her hips.

"He's in his private study, if you must know," Abael replied, calm as always. She strode right past him, but he maneuvered his electric wheelchair around to block her. "I must ask you to stop."

"Get out of my way, you freak," Karen said, stomping past. She opened the door off the oval office and walked down the corridor to the private study. She didn't bother to knock, but swung the door open and stomped in.

What she saw stopped her dead.

The President was sitting at his desk against the wall to the left. He was staring at a large monitor displaying a group of uniformed officers with a Chinese flag in the background and the characters *PLA* in front. The President was obviously having a dialogue with them.

Foreign policy wasn't her area of expertise, but she wasn't an idiot, either. The President was talking with the People's Liberation Army of China, a country with which military cooperation would have been unthinkable due to less than amicable relations of late stemming from friction in the South China Sea.

She said, "Robert?"

The President, looking bewildered, immediately switched off the monitor. "What is it, Karen?"

"There's something . . . I need to show you something." Eying him uneasily, she strode to a screen in the corner and turned it on to the news channel.

On the monitor, the anchor was saying, "--Medical Center in Towson, Maryland, where a quarantine is underway. You can see the police have arrived and, we are told, also the Centers for Disease Control. On the scene now is Fox's Lisa Hamilton. Lisa, what's the situation in Towson?"

"While officials here will not speak to anyone, we have received information from an anonymous source that the hospital is under quarantine due to a virus of some sort. The source stressed that the public should not be alarmed, but that a mysterious virus reminiscent of Swine Flu has turned up there and the hospital has been quarantined. And, while no one will speak to us here, it is quite clear that the hospital will not be accepting any new patients. Police have been cordoning off the area, and it is surrounded—"

Karen muted the television station. "Mr. President, this is an illegal quarantine, but I ordered it. I ordered it because I gave Abael an executive order for you to sign that would have authorized it two days ago. Even though he said he'd send it back to me yesterday, I never got it."

The President looked apologetic, "I'm sorry, Karen. I've been a little . . ."

"With all due respect Mr. President, what could possibly deserve your attention more than this?" she motioned to the screen.

The President took a heavy breath and looked off to the side, appearing solemn. "Preparations."

"For what?" Karen asked almost breathlessly. She was suddenly not feeling nearly as important as she had before. In fact, although she would never admit it, she now felt a little unnerved. Especially when she felt Abael's presence behind her and turned to see him warning the President of the United States with a dark, icy gaze.

The President raised his eyes and gazed directly at her, "You will know. When the time is right, you will all know."

Karen raised her hand to her hairline, gripped by a sudden headache. She lowered her hand and said, "If it's something more important than a national health crisis, don't you think you should have a meeting with your cabinet? Don't you think we should be prepared, too?"

The President nodded slowly. "I have given that a lot of consideration. I certainly would not leave you in the dark unless it was absolutely necessary."

Although feeling less secure, Karen braced herself and demanded, "Why are you talking with the freaking People's Liberation Army? What is going on, Robert?"

Abael interrupted, holding up the signed executive order, "Here's the signed order. I'm so sorry I didn't have this brought over to you yesterday, Karen."

She eyed Abael distrustfully but snatched it from his rigid grip.

The President said, "Thank you for coming over, Karen. Now, please, I was in a meeting."

After she had left, the President turned to Abael, "You know, a man who has only five bucks to his name spends them differently than a man who thinks he has a full bank account. Don't the people have a right to know?"

"You know as well as I do that if they wished to be illuminated, they could be. The truth has been self-evident for all of history, but modern man has decided to turn a blind eye. They choose to be ignorant for the simple reason that *they don't want to know*."

# Paradeisia Airport

Aubrey immediately spotted the source of the voice: a short man, overweight, wearing a beige, short-sleeved safari shirt with huge pockets. On his head was a pith helmet, and he had a giant belt, giant shorts, and giant boots. His face was plump to the extent that he had no jawline, and it was cleanly shaved except for a fluffy, white mustache. His eager, smiling eyes peered out from under huge bushy eyebrows.

The man strode over to Lady Shrewsbury and, removing his hat to reveal a bald head with a crop of white around the crown, gave her a bear hug, much to her consternation. "I've been begging you to come for how long now! And at long last you're here!"

Lady Shrewsbury brushed her pantsuit, regaining her dignity, and said, "Very well, Ignatius. But we haven't come on holiday, you know. We want to see what you've done with this place. But first, you must meet Mr. Potter."

"But yes, yes indeed!" the man exclaimed, eying all the suited men at once.

Henry stuck out his hand, "I am Henry—"

But before he could finish, the man scurried to him and shook his hand very vigorously, "Mr. Harry Potter himself!"

"*Henry* Potter, *Henry*," Henry corrected, being jostled by the energetic handclasp.

"It's truly a pleasure to meet you, my good man! And an honor, too, I daresay, what with your reputation! I hope you have plenty of time over the next week as I've planned a delightful turn around every nook, every cranny, I say, of the island."

Lady Shrewsbury, with a grunt and a slyly raised brow, said, "Mr. Potter, as you've gathered by now, this is my nephew, Fitzgerald Ignatius Jinkins."

Jinkins, who was still shaking away at Henry's hand, turned his face up to him with a childish grin, "The one-and-only, the one-and-only, sir!"

Lady Shrewsbury examined Jinkins closely and said, "Merciful heavens, Ignatius. You are looking very well. I believe you look almost younger than the last time we met."

"Indeed do I? Well that is very good news, very good news indeed!

But not a surprise! Paradeisia is so very invigorating, and by invigorating I do mean like the very Tree of Life!" He chuckled, "After all, it is 'Eden on Earth.' "

Henry said, "Yes, well, I was going to say that unfortunately I will be leaving tomorrow for important business in China, so if you could curtail the tour. . . ."

"Curtail the tour?" Jinkins said as if it was the most dreadful and inexplicable thing he had ever heard. "Oh, but Mr. Potter, this is the most fantastical place in the world—another world entirely, in fact, and it would be—" he interrupted himself, saying with frustration, "Well I couldn't possibly curtail the tour!" His face went pink.

Henry looked up and took an impatient breath, "My visit to China is urgent."

Jinkins looked from person to person, blinking in consternation, until he finally clasped his hands together and smiled, "Well, we'll just take the tour up where we left off, upon your return!" He then proceeded to go around the group and make the acquaintance of every person, including Aubrey, who immediately appreciated his grandfatherly demeanor. Then he stood in front of them, "Now all of you follow me. Since your business is so very urgent, Mr., Potter, the tour begins soon—" he giggled, as he plopped his helmet on, "and by 'soon' I mean now!"

He led them toward a long row of what appeared to be dozens of escalators. As they were all riding up the long length of one of them to the next level, Henry asked, "Tell me about this airport. How much did it cost?"

Jinkins explained, "Aha, well moving people quickly to the fun was one of our primary concerns. We are prepared for passenger traffic of about 69.3 million per annum—and we have allowed for easy expansion."

"How much have you spent?" Henry persisted.

"Oh, it's all in the balance sheets," he chuckled. "All in the balance sheets!" He flitted his hand, "And, you know, I don't really trouble myself with trifles like that—not when so much is at stake!"

Henry shot Lady Shrewsbury an incredulous glance.

She leaned forward and asked, "And what is at stake, Ignatius?"

"That the world experience Paradeisia, of course, and have the time of their lives!"

As they reached the top of the escalator and stepped off, Jinkins said, "What you are about to witness is perhaps one of the greatest technological miracles of Paradeisia: our transit system. We call it the FlyRail, a tourist-friendly term for Suspended Rail System. We think we could easily market the FlyRail to major cities around the world!" Above sliding glass doors was a yellow sign with the words "Anaconda Alley" and a picture of the snake. The doors whooshed open and a burst of warm tropical air greeted everyone as they went through. Outside was a long platform with a railing. Peeking over the edge, Aubrey saw a dizzying drop to the ground below. Across the gap was another platform (for exiting passengers, she assumed), and suspended horizontally over the chasm was a thick, steel, green-painted beam—the rail.

Henry said, "So you said passenger traffic of 69 million? What is the capacity of the island?"

Jinkins replied, "Well, we have 165,000 hotel rooms with more on the way. The retirement community, StarLine Haven, has an additional 5,000 suites. When we are operating at full capacity, Paradeisia will host about 95,000 workers—"

"And that will have to change," Henry said.

Jinkins ignored him, "—or Bwanas, as I like to call them." He chuckled at himself, then said, "Some of them will live on other islands or South America, but about fifty thousand will live here. For them there is a compound, a city, really, on the south end of the island. So, the short answer to your question is that Paradeisia has the capacity, at the moment, to house and feed somewhere around 700,000 happy people at one time if every space was occupied—but of course it won't stop there. Disneyland Paradeisia will be opening in seventeen months. That will add an additional seven thousand rooms."

Henry interrupted, "And Disney agrees to this?"

"Well, we haven't spoken with them yet, of course, because it's still a secret, but once we let the cat out of the bag," he chuckled, "the House of Mouse will be begging our permission to erect one of their little castles here!"

Henry said dimly, "I see. And have you projected an occupancy rate?"

"Occupancy rate? I'd expect 100%, no question. Who wouldn't

come to see the paradise of dreams we have here?"

"Paradise or not, occupancy rate is important to establish. Orlando, for example, is lucky if they get eighty-one percent."

"Mr. Potter!" Jinkins exclaimed, clearly affronted. "I certainly hope you're not trying to compare Paradeisia to Disney World, because there simply is no equivalence. This is the most extraordinary place on earth and, given the chance, anyone staying in *Orlando* would immediately drop whatever silliness Mickey had them doing and jet straight over here!" He moved closer to Henry and furrowed his brows at him, "What they discovered when they were digging is beyond anyone's wildest dreams. I hope you understand, Mr. Potter: I am not toying with some pixy tomfoolery. I am offering people a chance to experience the impossible. So do not compare Paradeisia as if it's like anything else at all. It's not."

Jinkins then cleared his throat and continued, "Now all the projects on the table, including the Disneyland, will expand total capacity to some 180,000 guest rooms—aha. It's coming!" Jinkins smiled, staring down the tunnel in the foliage.

Aubrey could tell that something was coming because a deep rumbling sound rose above the adventurous music that was playing over loudspeakers. Everyone looked down the suspended track in anticipation, and with a blast of air, the gondola arrived, slowing to a stop. It had a sleek nose, tinted glass windows, and a blown-up image of a toucan at the rear. The guardrail on the edge of the platform receded into the floor and, with the sound of escaping air, two round doors on the gondola lifted up.

"Come in, all of you!" Jinkins exclaimed. "There's room for fifty, and by fifty I do mean forty-eight precisely!"

The gondola was cool inside as they boarded. Except for the floor, the entire circumference was glass.

Jinkins commented, "It's acrylic glass, in fact. So the passengers have a 360 degree view! It's so strong you'd be safe from an explosion in here, and by explosion," he chuckled, "I do mean a nuclear blast!"

As everyone found their seats, Jinkins' recorded persona interrupted the music, "Please stand clear of the doors. Smoking is prohibited except in designated areas on Paradeisia." There was an unnatural pause followed by, "Welcome to Anaconda Alley. Our next stop is the FlyRail Hub." The doors closed and the gondola began to move. It gained speed as it cleared the walls of the airport. As it emerged over the foliage, Aubrey held her breath. The gondola was much higher than she had realized. It was a spectacular view: to the left were the tropical mountain peaks and to the right were the coastline and the port.

The resonant voice of Jinkins began again as the gondola ascended a forested ridge, "When visiting paradise, you would expect to ride on the wings of angels. Welcome aboard the most advanced transit system in the world: Paradeisia's FlyRail. The route you are currently taking, Anaconda Alley, is eleven miles long, but at a top speed of ninety miles an hour, we'll reach our destination shortly. Extending a total of one hundred eighty-six miles for your convenience, Paradeisia's FlyRail is one of the most expansive public transportation systems in the world."

Henry muttered, "Don't you mean most *expensive*?"

## Paradeisia

"Certainly not the most expensive, Mr. Potter," Jinkins countered.

"How much was it?"

"Oh, it's all in the balance sheets. The important thing is that our guests will be comfortable and get where they're going with ease."

"The important thing," Henry said loudly, "Is that the balance sheets are not balanced at all."

"How can you quibble about cost when you're riding on the most extraordinary transport system in the world?" Jinkins exclaimed jovially. "There are no wheels here—the tracks and the couplings above us are electromagnetic so they never touch! At any rate, costs such as these were not borne by the company itself. They were subsidized by all of our developers collectively."

"I see," Henry said, not impressed. "And how many developers do we have?"

Jinkins puffed his chest, "Thousands—from all over the world."

"Fantastic, that means thousands of lawsuits if we don't open," Henry said glumly.

Jinkins seemed to not hear the comment, "The developers were responsible for all the different tourist areas. Paradeisia has thirteen unique locales, planned and designed mostly by us but built by the developers. Since our developers are from all over the world, we gave many of the locales an international flair." Jinkins was so enthusiastic that he had to wipe his brow of a sweat that had broken out, "Each area has hotels, restaurants, even rides—the locales are attractions of their own. Nothing, of course, compared to what brought us here in the first place!"

Aubrey marveled at the beauty of the rich green forest that was sometimes beneath and sometimes surrounding the gondola's glass walls as it rose ever higher along the curving ridge. The voice began again, "Now visible to your left, beyond the valley, is Paradeisia's Greece." A cluster of white buildings with blue trim could be seen tucked onto a hillside in the distance by the shore. "The Greek Holiday Hotel—a StarLine resort—offers visitors an authentic Greek travel experience, featuring the finest in Greek cuisine, hospitality, and entertainment. The Olympia restaurant presents a magnificent display of Greek folk dancing several times daily. Adjacent to the Greek Holiday Hotel is Homer's Greece, a delightful entertainment, shopping, and dining district featuring a five-star Hotel and spa. At the Athena Theater, the story of the Trojan War is told nightly through brilliant theatrics and special effects. On special nights, Homer's Odyssey illuminates the stage with all the original splendor of ancient Greek drama. Whether touring modern Greece or taking a trip back in time to the Greece of old, your visit to Paradeisia would not be complete without a journey to the heart of Greek Culture and civilization: Paradeisia's Greece. Get show times or make dinner reservations on your phone. To reach Paradeisia's Greece, take Parrot Path from the FlyRail Hub."

Aubrey noticed that the more the voice spoke, the more fidgety Henry became.

The voice continued anyway, "Coming next year to the area is Paradeisia's Rome. A life-size recreation of the Coliseum will be the staging area for spectacular sporting events, shows and fireworks displays unlike anything you've ever seen."

Jinkins giggled gleefully, "After the Italians heard the Greeks had come, they just had to have their piece of the pie."

"Beyond Paradeisia's Greece is Escape from Atlantis featuring five spectacularly themed restaurants and five award-winning StarLine resorts. Poseidon's Platter, created by world renowned chef Cenon Kyriakou, invites you to dine surrounded by the beauty of the ocean. You might spot a dolphin, a stingray, or even a shark through the glass as you enjoy course after course of delicious seafood.

"Any boaters in the family? Atlantis Bay offers every vessel imaginable from two-seaters to fully staffed yachts. Every night, the bay comes alive with the 'Tale of Atlantis' told through music, special effects, and fireworks including one very special surprise you're guaranteed never to forget. Viewable from the many restaurants, hotels, and walkways that line the bay, 'Tale of Atlantis' is a story you'll be telling your friends about for years to come! Don't forget to obtain show times and make dinner reservations online, at your hotel's desk or at one of the many Information Centers located throughout Paradeisia. To reach Escape from Atlantis, take Parrot Path from the FlyRail Hub."

The gondola steadily moved up to the top of the ridge. On the right side was an enormous forested plain stretching to the coast. The voice spoke again, "Paradeisia is home to two incredible water parks, visible to your right. High Seas Cove recalls the noble (and not-so-noble) seamen of old through six swashbuckling restaurants and three exciting hotels as well as rides and attractions. Captain's Orders is bound to be a favorite with the little pirates in the family as a cast of hilarious sailors show you what life on the High Seas of Hilarity are like through song, dance, and acrobatics. The second water park, Ocean South, celebrates the wonders of life under the sea. At Whalebreach Restaurant, you'll join a school of Orcas on an incredible journey across the ocean as you dine. Also featured at Ocean South is the terrific Ocean Speed roller coaster. You're sure to get wet as this ride sends you soaring like a bird and swimming like a fish through loops and a breathtaking two hundred-foot drop. And don't miss a dip in the world's largest wave-pool: Tidal Beach. Ocean South and High Seas Cove are accessible via Sparrow Speedway."

The gondola continued its ascent up the ridge and the view expanded. "Now visible in the valley to the right is Out of Africa, Paradeisia's authentic African savannah—"

Henry interrupted the voice in exasperation, "Authentic African savannah!?"

Jinkins sing-song laughed to himself and said, "Wondrous isn't it? Just listen!"

The voice: "Stay at any of the three StarLine resorts in Out of Africa, and you could find a giraffe standing just outside your balcony when you wake up. Enjoy breakfast at one of four wildly themed restaurants. During the morning, take an African Safari through countless acres of lush African plains where animals roam freely all around you. In the afternoon, learn about conservation up close and personally with the furriest animals at the Cuddle Club. As the sun sets, hear ancestral African lore told around the mysterious beauty of a campfire. And to close the evening gaze at the stars from your very own watchtower, surrounded by the beauty of the African savannah. There's no end to the fun and adventure at Out of Africa, so don't leave Paradeisia without taking a walk on the wild side. To reach Out of Africa, take Sparrow Speedway from the FlyRail Hub."

The voice paused. "Visible on the coast are India Explorer and ¡Fiesta Mexicana!. These exciting destinations are home to some of the best rides, shopping, and dining options at Paradeisia and have a total of five amazing StarLine resorts. India Explorer boasts the fastest roller coaster in the world, the White Tiger, which attains speeds of nearly 150 miles an hour in six point four seconds. At ¡Fiesta Mexicana!, you'll find the fantastic Mercado Plaza, an open-air shopping and dining experience that immerses you in Latin American cultures and tastes. To reach India Explorer or ¡Fiesta Mexicana!, take Leopard Line from the FlyRail Hub."

Henry spoke again, "How much of this is actually complete?"

Jinkins clapped his hands together and answered, "Oh, only all of it, Mr. Potter! Our developers are already receiving customers at these attractions—mostly yachters who pull in at Atlantis Bay, the occasional cruise ship and so forth."

The gondola rose yet further along the ridge revealing a spellbinding view. A cluster of tall buildings could be seen on the opposite coast as well as a magnificent statue: an elegant female figure draped in a tunic with her arms stretched skyward and her back curving gracefully. A blue sash wound its way up her figure to form a huge arch above her head. "The statue you see in the distance is called the Paradeisia Angel. Designed by the renowned artist Andreas Nikolovski, she was constructed over a period of five years at a cost exceeding seventy million euros."

Henry slapped his forehead with his hand.

"The tallest statue in the world, she dwarfs the Statue of Liberty at a height of one thousand feet. A platform at the crown of her head offers a magnificent view from her eyes—made especially memorable by the nightly CelestiaSky fireworks spectacular." The music climaxed and the voice continued, "The Paradeisia Angel is not the only hot spot in Paradeisia's centerpiece resort area, Living Paradise. Also featured are the Eden Grand StarLine Hotel, the Novae StarLine Hotel, and the Paradise Regal StarLine Hotel, all of which offer heavenly, five-star accommodations.

"Additionally, Living Paradise claims one of the three exciting nightlife districts located on the island. Additionally, a stunning lineup of fifteen fantastic thrill-rides challenge only the bravest visitors. And finally, the Living Paradise dining and shopping district features some of the largest restaurants and stores anywhere including the planet's largest McDonald's as well as nightly performances by world-famous artists. With this much to see and do, a visit to Living Paradise is sure to be at the top of everyone's Paradeisia to-do list. To reach Living Paradise, take Leopard Line from the FlyRail Hub."

"This is indeed a nightmare," Henry said, rubbing his temples.

Jinkins was not dissuaded from his enthusiasm. "I don't understand how you could say such a thing about such marvels. You must admit that this is the grandest place on earth, even without the main attraction!"

Lady Shrewsbury interjected, "Our money has certainly been exploited to grand effect and I'm sure we all appreciate the magnificence of the place, but Henry is here to ascertain if Paradeisia can be *profitable*."

"And profitable it will be," Jinkins crowed, "once we open the doors!"

The gondola was now nearing the crown of the tallest peak. Jagged stone outcroppings projected over the greenery to form a sharp summit. Several miles below the top, between the two mountains, was a gigantic glass building. Shaped like a triangle with one vertical side, the structure was 320 feet tall, 340 feet wide, and 280 feet long. It was made of shining glass supported by huge columns of rose colored stones dwarfing the palm trees planted beside it. Five FlyRail tracks serviced the rear of the structure on five concrete levels. A stream flowed from under the glass in the front and down towards a precipice where it dropped hundreds of feet to a misty pool below.

The voice began, "We are now nearing the FlyRail Hub. Please remember your personal belongings as you exit, and have a wonderful stay in Paradeisia: Eden on Earth." The gondola slowed as it moved underneath a cement floor on the rear of the structure. Sliding glass doors could be seen twenty feet away on the docking platform. Slowing to a stop, the gondola's glass doors lifted open. "Please allow those needing special assistance to exit first. Keep your personal belongings with you at all times."

Everyone stepped onto the platform and through the sliding doors. Inside, the FlyRail Hub was cavernous and light. Signs with FlyRail track names and icons lined the ceiling. Glass elevators overlooked an open plaza containing shops and quick dining options ringing a giant waterfall.

They took an elevator to the ground floor. Their shoes squeaked with the newness as they walked through sliding doors that read, "Parrot Path." Once outside on a platform, it was only seconds until a gondola pulled up.

As they boarded, Henry, looking very grumpy now, asked "And how much did this FlyRail Hub cost?"

"All in the balance sheets!" Jinkins smiled. "Not to worry, I'm sure you'll have a look at them in good order."

"Couldn't we have a look at them now?"

"All in good time, Mr. Potter," Jinkins reassured. "All in good time."

Aubrey heard Henry say under his breath, "And by 'good time,' I suppose he means 'at the last possible moment.'"

Greenery sped by as the gondola emerged from the building. Soaring by the second peak and down a foliage-covered ridge, they moved at the same speed going downhill as they had coming up. The green steel beams that supported the rails above were so high that the coach was above the trees most of the time. Ahead, on a sandy coastline isolated by two forested ridges was a sleek, angular glass tower that stepped up to a sharp, tall spire. The design was inspiring, as if the building itself was reaching for the sky. The voice spoke, "The building you see ahead is The StarLine Paradeisia Hotel. Paradeisia's flagship resort, it is one of the largest and tallest hotels in the world, rising to a height of 1,776 feet. The StarLine Paradeisia Hotel also boasts the largest pool and the most valuable room on earth, the Presidential StarSuite."

The gondola moved over the forest to the colossal building. As the track dipped through openings in the walls, Aubrey gawked up with starry eyes, amazed. Inside, an open atrium rose from the ground floor to the glass roof above. Glass balustrades from each of the 130 floors half-circled the open space. Transparent elevators serviced every floor on either side of a glass wall that rose from the floor to the roof, providing a view of the perfect turquoise water at the beach outside.

The gondola followed the rails behind a waterfall that was surging from the tenth floor balcony into a crystalline pond below. The floor of the lobby was planted with a veritable forest of tropical flora, offset by marble walkways and seating areas. The water from the waterfall followed a meandering route through the lobby under several bridges until it collected in a shell shaped pool edged by beach chairs and a bar. The waterway continued from there to the outdoors where there were waterslides.

Henry shot Jinkins an unhappy glance, then shook his head and said, "I'm not even going to ask how much *this* cost."

"Developers, my dear Mr. Potter! The developers shoulder the heaviest cost."

Lady Shrewsbury said somewhat pathetically, "And yet all *our* money is gone."

The now-familiar voice encouraged the guests to exit carefully and enjoy a pleasant stay at The StarLine Paradeisia Hotel as the gondola stopped.

As they disembarked, Jinkins explained, "Now I realize Mr. Potter is heading to China, but those of you not joining him will be staying here. Luggage is sorted and delivered to the rooms of all guests automatically, whether they arrive by cruise or air. The perimeter FlyRail track, Elephant Express, services every hotel on the island. Luggage is scanned and loaded onto cargo gondolas at the transit points. Amazing isn't it?"

"Expensive, wasn't it?" Henry said, looking like he was about to blow a fuse.

Suddenly, a yapping chirp echoed in the atrium, and when Aubrey looked over she saw a woman cradling a small, brown creature with the face of a Chihuahua—except for small round ears—and the body of a monkey. It jumped down to bound for Jinkins. Its stance was like a gorilla's; hopping on its knuckles, though it was no larger than a kitten. Jinkins knelt down to receive it as it leaped onto his neck. It lathered his face with licks and he laughed, "Now, now, Lucy! Now, now!"

Henry, his expression disgusted, asked, "What, may I ask, is that?"

"It's a—now now Lucy—it's a kinkajou. They're from Central America. They make the most wonderful pets," Jinkins said jovially. "If you'd like I could have one procured for you, Mr.—" then he frowned as the creature had clamped down on his thumb with its little teeth. "No biting, Lucy," Jinkins scolded. The creature furrowed its little brows as it tightened its jaws, grappling with Jinkins' entire arm as if in a death-match. "Now, now, Lucy!" Jinkins said as he struggled with the little beast. "They do like to fight," he explained.

A man in a white shirt and slacks stepped forward with a tray of freshly cut fruit on toothpicks. Jinkins took a pineapple and offered it to the creature, which greedily gripped it with both hands and bit into it. As it munched voraciously, it stared at Henry as if sizing him up as a potential opponent. The man with the tray offered fruit to everyone else as Jinkins said, "I was saying, Mr. Potter, that I could have one procured for you, if you'd like. They do make wonderful pets."

"No, no. That won't be necessary," Henry said, watching impatiently as the creature finished the fruit and grew restless, eagerly searching for more by crawling all over Jinkins.

Henry looked Jinkins in the eye, "Well, it's been an interesting tour, but I'm sad to say the fun is over and the tough choices now begin." Then he cleared his throat and said, "From this moment on, Jinkins, you are here as a subject matter expert only. This means that if I ask you a question, I expect an answer. If you don't have an answer, either find one or find new employment. Is this clear?"

Jinkins' face had gone from bright to overcast in seconds. Even his kinkajou sensed the mood change and stared at Henry in total quiet. "Well, Mr. Potter, I thought that—"

Henry interrupted, "Whatever you thought was wrong. 'Build it and they will come' is one of the most idiotic ideas conceived by man. But I see here you've employed it to its full disastrous potential. So unless you have the fountain of youth here, a new *modus operandi* is required. That is why I'm here—to save you from complete and total ruin, and the sooner you come to grips with that, the better."

When Jinkins stood there in bruised horror, Henry cajoled, "Look, man. Frankly I'm making you a generous offer by allowing you to stay on, so either accept it with dignity, or get the hell out of my way."

Jinkins looked sadly to Lady Shrewsbury for support, but she said, "I am very sorry, my dear Ignatius. But Mr. Potter would only help us with the understanding that he was the law. This is going to be a difficult change for all of us, I'm afraid." She turned to Henry, "But that does not give you the right to engage in rude and seditious behavior! It would behoove you to find a more diplomatic *modus operandi* for yourself, Mr. Potter."

Unmoved, Henry said to Jinkins, "My offer remains. Will you stay on with us?"

His face filled with sorrow, he stroked his pet's head several times and then said, "I couldn't leave Paradeisia, Mr. Potter." It sounded like he was speaking about a child rather than an island.

"Very good," Henry said. "The first thing I must insist upon is that you put your animal away. The next is that you take us down the shaft."

"Portal," Jinkins corrected.

"And the third is that you produce these mythical balance sheets of yours."

And with that, the kinkajou leaped down to the floor and furiously attacked Henry.

# St. Joseph's Hospital

Doctor Kingsley, still wearing his mask, said sadly, "I'm very sorry, John. I know Sarah was special to you." At that moment, two police officers with masks approached.

"Doctor Kingsley? Doctor Richard Kingsley?" one of them asked.

"Not now," Doctor Kingsley said, holding a hand up.

"Sir, this is very important."

"In a moment," he said tersely. The officers nervously backed away.

Doctor Kingsley turned back to all the other physicians who had been trying to save Sarah. They were zipping her body into a bag. The same kind of bags Doctor Burwell opened every day.

Doctor Burwell backed away from the scene and turned around. Slowly, in a daze, he walked through the curtains and out of the area.

When they were done bagging the body, Doctor Kingsley turned around to look for Doctor Burwell. But he was gone.

Doctor Kingsley was stripping off his gloves when his cell phone rang. At that moment, the officers once again approached him, but he held up a hand to take the call. It was his mother-in-law.

"I've been trying to reach you all day but the lines are busy. I'm so sorry."

"Yes, there's a lot going on with this virus."

Her voice was serious, "Rick . . . I'm so sorry. Martha is dead."

He looked up at the officers. In disbelief he said into his phone, "I'm sorry I didn't hear you. What did you say?"

"It's Martha. She's passed away, Rick."

In a daze, he lowered the phone to his side and asked the officers, "Are you here to tell me about my wife?"

One of them looked down at his feet while the other nodded, saying, "She showed the symptoms an hour ago and passed away before they could reach the hospital."

"Where is she?" Doctor Kingsley asked.

One of the officers nodded down the hallway, where a gurney was being wheeled by two people in scrubs.

Doctor Kingsley left the room. He took steps down the hallway, meeting the gurney. He uncovered the body.

Blood was at the corner of his wife's mouth, her sickly yellow eyes open in a gaping stare. Her lips were pale, almost white.

Without a word, he turned around and walked farther down the hall, through a door, down the stairs. He stepped out of the ground floor door and went straight to his Aston Martin. He hated to see it now.

He opened his car door and started the engine.

Leave. He was going to leave this place.

# 94 Golfpointe Road

QUARANTINE

CONTAGIOUS DISEASE

NO ONE SHALL ENTER OR LEAVE THIS PREMESIS WITHOUT
THE PROPER DOCUMENTATION ISSUED BY THE CENTERS FOR
DISEASE CONTROL AND PREVENTION.  (USC 42 PART G)

NO PERSON EXCEPT AN AUTHORIZED AGENT OR EMPLOYEE
OF THE CENTERS FOR DISEASE CONTROL AND PREVENTION
SHALL ALTER OR REMOVE THIS SIGN.  (USC 42 PART G)

ANYONE VIOLATING THIS REGULATION WILL BE SUBJECT TO
A FINE OF NO MORE THAN $1,000 OR BY IMPRISONMENT FOR
NOT MORE THAN ONE YEAR, OR BOTH.  (USC 42 PART G § 271)

That's what was printed on the orange signs posted all over the lawn
and taped to the majestic white colonial on Golfpointe Road.
Cordoning off the lawn was caution tape, and as if that wasn't enough,
someone had painted gigantic red X's on the grass.  Media trucks were
all over the road, and police cruisers were parked at the curb.  Camera
crews with over-made-up reporters were everywhere, jockeying for the
best view of the house.  And the policemen were milling around, bored
to death or posing for the cameras.

Wesley Peterson and his mother, Cynthia, stood by an upstairs
window looking down at the scene.

Cynthia was shaking her head, "I'm not blaming you, of course, but is all this really necessary? Those police are just standing there like homeless people. Susan will never let me live this down." She put her hands out, "I mean look what they've done to the lawn! And all the tape?"

"It's the government, mom. If they can find an excuse for tape, they'll use it," he said. He knew his mother was not really this pretentious. He suspected she was really griping only to downplay the gravity of the situation.

"Our home used to be the pride of the neighborhood. Now it's the *spectacle* of the neighborhood!"

"As soon as my test results come back negative, they'll take this all away."

A silver car suddenly pulled up as close as it could get to the house. A man in jeans and a leather jacket emerged and stood with a phone to his ear.

Wesley's phone rang. He answered it, "Hello?"

It was the man outside speaking: "This is Special Agent Jarred Kessler with the FBI. I need to talk with you."

Wesley's heart jumped, "Great. What's up?"

Jarred's response surprised Wesley: "Have you received any request for ransom?"

"Uh, no. Why?"

"Good. I'd like to speak with you in person. Does this place have a back door?"

"Yes."

"Meet me there."

"You know we're under quarantine," Wesley said.

"Yeah, I know. I'll see you at the back."

Jarred was standing on the large wood patio off the sliding doors at the rear of the house, just as he had promised. Wesley opened the door and said, "I won't shake your hand. Don't want to transmit anything, just in case."

Jarred ignored him, grasping his hand firmly, "I'm not afraid. Seems most men our age are immune."

Wesley led him into the formal living room where they took seats. His mother went off to the kitchen to "get drinks," though he knew she'd be listening closely.

Jarred said, "You probably know I'm not the agent assigned to your case."

"Yes. The last time I heard from him was when I reported it. He didn't sound very interested."

Jarred nodded knowingly, "Ah. Well, I don't want to disappoint you, but I'm not here about your case."

"No?" Wesley couldn't hide the fact that he was disappointed.

"No. But I thought you might have some information that could be helpful to me."

"Okay."

"Now, you've said that your wife was pregnant, and then she wasn't, and that the baby had disappeared. Into thin air."

"Yes."

"What do you think happened to it?" Jarred pulled his cell out of his pocket.

Wesley hesitated. "Well, I guess I think someone took him."

"So here's your challenge:" Jarred accented his words with his hands, "What did your unborn baby have that a kidnapper would have wanted? Every criminal has a reason for what he does."

Suddenly there was a crash and a cry from the kitchen. Wesley leaped up, shouting, "Mom? Are you all right in there?"

His mother cried back, her voice agonized, "Wesley! Help!"

Wesley and Jarred dashed toward the plea. When they went through the doorway, they saw Cynthia laying on the floor, shattered glass and ice cubes catching the light all around her.

## CDC

Doctor Compton walked down the fluorescent-lit hallway, Doctor Guy Giordano at his side wringing his ball-cap in his hands.

Most of the other PhD's at the facility wore lab coats, but Doctor Giordano hated what he saw as pompous bunk. Either you had it or you didn't, and a lab coat didn't prove anything. Doctor Giordano wore what he'd always worn growing up in his home city: a button-up black shirt, jeans, a chain with a crucifix, and a Philadelphia Phillies baseball cap.

Guy said, "Are you sure I should be at this meeting? I don't wanna piss her off again."

"Don't worry about Karen. I have you here for a reason. If you have something to say, say it."

Doctor Giordano snorted with a smile, "So I'm your fall guy."

"You got it," Doctor Compton said. Suddenly, his phone rang. Looking at the ID, he said "Speak of the devil." He answered, "I'm afraid it's bad news, Karen. Very bad."

"Shoot."

"Three new deaths matching the symptoms, and one new case. The new case came from a house we already had quarantined. The cadavers of the other three are being brought to our lab."

"Please tell me they were all in Towson."

"Yes, except for the new case. But like I said that house was already quarantined and there's almost zero risk of transmission from there."

"Quarantine Towson. We have the authority now."

"Already in motion."

"And what's the word on the virus symptoms? Any way to contain it?"

"When you get to the meeting we'll tell you what we know."


# Kinglsey


Doctor Kingsley had stopped at the convenience store and picked up some bottles of something strong. He drove out to the woods by the Loch Raven Reservoir and drank all of them. Then he slipped back into his car and, without buckling his seat belt, floored the gas, pulling onto Route 146. He swerved along the road, passing the acres of wild woodland on either side until he sped onto the Dulaney Valley Road Bridge.

There, against the white backdrop of snow-covered trees, the silhouette of a man stepped from the bridge guardrail into the road.

With eyes that were ghost-white, he looked at Doctor Kingsley and raised his arm out towards him.

Doctor Kingsley swerved just as the bumper struck the man, throwing his body toward the windshield. As if in slow motion, Doctor Kingsley saw the head hit the wiper well and the arms flail as the body cascaded off the left side of the windshield. But at the same instant, he felt the right side of his car lifting wildly into the air.

The car flipped up to jolt over the top of the rail and plunge into the frigid water far below. As the water boiled up all around him, chilling him to the bone he did nothing to try to escape. Doctor Kingsley did not even unbuckle his seat belt. He simply closed his eyes and prayed,

"Hail Mary, full of grace.

The Lord is with thee.

Blessed art thou amongst women,

and blessed is the fruit of thy womb, Jesus.

Holy Mary, Mother of God,

pray for me a sinner,

now at the hour of my death."

## China Academy of Sciences

It took two days, but finally the head of the Academy of Sciences called Doctor Ming-Zhen back to his office. When he arrived, his superior motioned to a chair, "Tell me how the platypus has anything to do with dinosaurs."

"The platypus is local to Australia. That much, I'm sure you know."

Zhang grunted.

"It has the eggs of a reptile, the bill of a duck, the tail of a beaver, the feet of an otter, the fur of a mole, the eyes of a lamprey—that's a blood-sucking fish considered to be extremely primitive—the sex chromosomes of a bird, and a cocktail of venom that includes three proteins all its own. It has mammary glands and produces milk, but is lacking teats so the milk seeps out of its skin and pools in crevices for it's young to lap up. They wouldn't be able to suck on teats since they have bills."

Doctor Ming-Zhen explained that the creature had so many aspects derived from so many different animals that when the English discoverers sent a pelt back to Europe in 1798, it was thought that somebody had sewn the duck beak on as a hoax—they even checked for the stitches.

"But of course no one had sewn on a duck beak. The platypus, as it turns out, derives its DNA from a menagerie of creatures. When its genome was fully decoded, it was found to be only 80% mammalian, and had genes found previously *only* in reptilian, bird, amphibian, and fish DNA."

"What does that have to do with Antarctica?" Zhang asked.

"I'm getting there. But first, let me tell you about another example: the leatherback turtle."

Zhang raised his hand in resignation, "Tell me."

"It has been assumed that sea-going reptiles invaded the water via evolution numerous times, even in prehistory, despite the obvious insurmountable obstacles such as air-breathing lungs and dependence upon external sources of heat. This has been assumed because there are many different types of sea-going reptiles which could not have possibly all evolved down the same tree branch—for example, sea-snakes could not have evolved from sea turtles or vice versa. They would have had to take to the seas independently within their family lines.

"Now the leatherback turtle overcame the heat issue via a simple, but evolutionarily impossible solution; it is the only reptile that possesses fatty insulation known as brown adipose tissue, and the only reptile that regulates a high body temperature. This brown adipose tissue is the expression of the UCP1 gene, and, aside from the leatherbacks, is found only in mammals, amphibians, and fishes. Not one other reptile has UCP1."

"Antarctica?" Zhang said agitatedly.

"Yes, so, I suspect that, if we were to find a fossil or some kind of sample with enough DNA, we could prove conclusively that dinosaurs have no place at the earlier stages of the evolutionary tree. I suspect that they utilized genes common to many different types of animals. For example, what if we find in a dinosaur a gene that is common only to higher primates? I believe we will find such an abundance of commonality and generational skips as to make the dinosaur a clear contemporary to all other life. Dinosaur DNA would conclusively prove that they were not earlier. More importantly, ancient DNA could show us the rate of de novo gene generation."

"Which is?"

"Unknown. De novo gene generation has never been witnessed."

"No, I mean what is de novo gene generation."

"The creation of entirely new genes."

Zhang sat back, contemplating. Then he said, "And you think that the DNA would really survive, and be accessible?"

Doctor Ming-Zhen nodded, "Oh yes. Dinosaur DNA has already been found."

"What do you mean?"

"You haven't heard of Doctor Mary Schweitzer?"

"No," he replied. "I haven't. And let me guess, it has something to do with Antarctica."

"No, not this time." Doctor Ming-Zhen explained, "Many years ago, she was only an obscure scientist, but her mentor was the world's most respected paleontologist of that time, the late Jack Horner. This gave her access to his tremendous cache of dinosaur fossils from Hell Creek.

"She was examining one of his recently excavated tyrannosaurus bones when she found something inside that left her dumbfounded. She was so dumbfounded, in fact, that she called Doctor Horner and verified her procedures with him. When they were confident that she had not made a misinterpretation, they announced her discovery to the world."

"Which was?" Zhang asked, drumming his fingers on the desk.

"She had found the protein signature of soft tissue. *Soft tissue* in something that was supposed to be 65-75 million years old.

"Now, by simple experimentation, it had already been shown that soft tissue could likely not survive beyond 100,000 years. But there it was, the tissue of a dinosaur. And it wasn't deemed to be soft tissue by some molecular analysis; it was recognizable as such by *sight*."

"All right."

"Its appearance under the microscope was nothing to what Doctor Schweitzer found next. Inside another tissue she examined were fragments of actual DNA. In a fossil supposedly millions of years old she found the DNA from tyrannosaurus rex."

"I have never heard anything of this."

"Of course you have not. That's because, at first, we scientists cried foul. But, within a few short years, peer review and independent analysis had proven her analysis to be correct. The world had its first glimpse of dinosaur DNA. Now did the world's museums saw open their bones and see if any dinosaur DNA was in them? No, they did not. Her discovery was quietly swept under the rug. None of us ever spoke of it because we all knew what it might have implied: we were wrong.

"According to the information we had, dinosaurs were not as old as we said they were. She had dinosaur DNA, and it was there despite the simple fact that it *couldn't* be after sixty-five million years: a study from Australia showed that DNA within fossilized bones can survive a maximum, absolute maximum, of six point eight million years before complete and total degradation, assuming the rate of decay is constant. So we were wrong again. Either we didn't remotely understand the rate of decay or the tyrannosaurus was not sixty-five million years old. Not a chance."

Zhang pulled back in his chair, tilting his head skeptically. "You must be joking. You have me wondering if you are not the imposter they say you are. Do you hold nothing sacred?"

"No," Doctor Ming-Zhen said. "I do not. If I did, I wouldn't be a *scientist*, would I?"

After a moment of silence, Zhang asked, "So what is the point of all of this? Do you have an actionable proposal for Antarctica or do you just talk to excess?"

## Paradeisia

As soon as Aubrey and the rest of the group had signed waivers and passed a series of yellow warning signs that highlighted "tremendous gravitational forces," "dynamic atmospheric pressure," and "sulfur hexafluoride," they boarded a gondola which was different from the others. A voice warned them that no personal items could be brought down the portal and that nothing could be brought back. Any material brought back could contaminate the surface, and therefore any such material would automatically be scrubbed. Cameras were not permitted and all film and any memory devices would automatically be cleared.

Roller-coaster harnesses swung down from the ceiling. Attendants strode through and ensured the harnesses were securely latched. Jinkins distributed sticks of gum to help "with the ear popping."

The gondola departed the FlyRail Hub and quickly picked up speed, passing through a forest tunnel around a bend. When it emerged, the track was supported by angular beams bolted into a vertical cliff that formed the edge of a giant crater. The gondola swung out over the enormous drop.

Ahead was a waterfall which surged off the top of the cliff, the glass of the FlyRail Hub just visible gleaming above in the sunlight. The thunderous water caused the gondola to shudder as it passed through. On the other side, the track sloped downwards.

"We'll pick up a few G's on our way down. Nothing to worry about." Jinkins was still standing at the front, holding bars on either side, smiling back at all of them in amusement.

The gondola accelerated towards a mist at the bottom of the crater. The wind rushing by the glass became louder with the descent and made the cabin vibrate alarmingly.

Henry, grasping the sides of his seat with white knuckles, said, "How long till we reach the shaft?"

"You mean the portal?" Jinkins grinned. "Any moment, now."

"And what's down there that could *possibly* be worth this?" Lady Shrewsbury protested, her cheeks jiggling.

At that very moment, the vehicle shot through the mist into quickening darkness and the vibration stopped, a whooshing sound taking its place. Tiny lights flicked on in the ceiling. Lights around the sides of the gondola popped on, reflecting off water far below them.

Everyone in the gondola was startled except for Jinkins. He stood there, still grinning. "No one here has an aversion to speed, I hope," he said, rubbing his hands together and taking a seat. He pulled down his harness and latched it securely.

Aubrey heard Lady Shrewsbury cry out "JINKINS YOU FOOL!" as she eyed a drop in the track ahead of them. As they progressed the gondola took a graduated nosedive, pushing them back in their seats as it accelerated. Some cries escaped from the passengers as they went over.

Aubrey threw her hands up and let loose a scream, giggling like a little girl. Henry shot her a look of disgust, his face contorted with anxiety. She stuck her tongue out at him and smiled, kicking her legs in excitement. She didn't feel like she was free-falling; it was more like being strapped to a rocket due to the extreme speed.

They flew past a rocky outcropping and plunged down beside the gushing waterfall straight towards a watery abyss. Soon they had splashed into the water and all she could see were bubbles rushing by on all sides. A muffled, metallic screaming emitted from under their feet and the vibration resumed.

A voice came from the speakers, "Prepare yourselves for a world beyond imagining." It was barely audible over the noise.

Then the lights went out.

"Jinkins?" Henry's voice shouted.

"Not to worry!" came the reply, "Almost there!" A brilliant spot of illumination appeared before them, fast approaching.

Aubrey saw the sparkle of millions of drops of water all around them, rushing down the shaft, and before she knew it they had reached the opening. With a tremendous whoosh the gondola swept through a gush of water and past a pink fog.

Aubrey's eyes widened with disbelief. The craft was slowly leveling to hover next to the waterfall that had formed from the water as it emerged from the shaft. It seemed that some of the water was dissipating and becoming the fog, or cloud itself. The rest of the waterfall cascaded thousands of feet down, evaporating into nothing. And downward, beyond that was a landscape of ridged peaks separated by vast valleys full of lush gigantic trees that swayed in visibly misty winds.

Water flowed everywhere, toppling off the ridges and flowing all around to pool in huge churning lakes. The lakes glowed with a bright turquoise light from within.

Shooting out of the ground in enormous geysers and cascading off some of the ridges were flows of lava that steamed as they collided with the water. Around the lava, thin whirlwinds frequently developed and disappeared.

The horizon far in the distance was strong white light that was more radiant toward the ground where it took on a pink and yellow hue.

Steam rose from everywhere and settled as clouds in the midst of the air. The clouds at the ceiling jumped up and down in a myriad of pyramids, like the underside of a churning sea.

The harnesses suddenly made a clunking sound and lifted up. Jinkins rose and stood before them, adjusting his pith helmet. "Welcome to Paradeisia. You're not disappointed, I hope."

He said this, but it was clear from the amusement playing on his face that he knew they were not. At any rate, no one answered him because they were all staring in speechless awe.

Finally, Lady Shrewsbury, her fingers covering her mouth, breathed in wonderment, "Jinkins, you *fool*."

Jinkins smiled with pleasure at her remark, saying, "I told you the trip would be worth your while. Paradeisia holds many wonders. We haven't even begun to explore them all."

The gondola was free floating. Now, it turned and began a gradual descent toward the surface.

"Who's driving this thing?" Henry asked.

"It drives itself, following a programmed route," Jinkins said, "but when needs-be, it can be driven remotely at Central Command, in the FlyRail Hub building."

"Drives itself?" Lady Shrewsbury exclaimed. "And just where is it taking us?"

"Over there," Jinkins pointed to a series of nine twisting coils of stone and vegetation that rose high above the landscape, forming vast, thin arches.

The gondola soared on, passing around some of the giant globes of rainbow luminescence along the way. As they passed over one of the lakes, Aubrey noticed that the waves undulated slowly, as if she was viewing them through a slow-motion camera. A myriad of bubbles were rising up to the surface in areas. And in the water she spotted schools of fish. Some of them were very large. And then, to her amazement, she saw something unbelievable.

Jinkins explained, "You would think there wasn't room enough to sustain whales in those lakes, but we believe they are all connected, creating one large sea."

Henry's face had transformed from awe to consternation. "What is the size of this place?"

Jinkins shook his head, "We don't know."

"You don't know?" Henry said skeptically.

"Yes, we don't know. The gondolas can only go so far on their own power, and we spent most of our time building the portal to get them down here."

"And how is it that we are floating?"

"Well that's a question for our engineers, but essentially the same facts of physics that make a hot air balloon float on the surface cause us to float down here."

"Hmm. And yet, I don't see any balloon," Henry said.

Lady Shrewsbury interrupted, "Oh you don't need engineers to explain that for you, Henry. It's quite simple."

"Is it?" Henry asked.

Her eyes twinkling with laughter, she replied, "Oh yes. We have *you* to thank for our buoyancy."

Henry cleared his throat, "And just how is that?"

"Hot air."

Henry was not amused.

Jinkins, looking confused, suggested, "It's actually helium, I believe."

As they approached the arches, the gondola lowered and Aubrey realized that the trees were, in fact, taller even than they had appeared from above. They were as tall as skyscrapers. Some of the leaves were the width of cars. Huge vines grew up around the arches and below them was grass.

The gondola moved down under the first arch and came to land on an area that had a slab of concrete for that purpose.

Jinkins said, "The pressure is going to gradually equalize with the atmosphere. Don't worry if your ears feel a bit funny, and by funny, I do mean ticklish."

Aubrey's ears did feel funny as a whooshing sound came from the floor. But she also noticed that the air became warm and she suddenly felt energized and refreshed, even almost buoyant. Slowly, the gondola doors opened. She inhaled the scent of the organic, misty, fresh air. It was kind of like stepping into one of those rainforest environments at the zoo.

Jinkins led the way out as everyone followed. All the vegetation that surrounded them was huge. Aubrey found that walking was almost effortless.

"So you might be looking at these arches and saying, what magnificent stone formations," Jinkins said, smiling mysteriously. "But I invite you to take another look. There is more here than meets the eye."

Aubrey gazed up at the stone. What she wanted to know was how did each of these arches not come crashing down? They were incredibly thin in comparison to their immense breadth and seemed to shoot up out of nowhere from one side of the valley to the other.

Jinkins pointed out away from the arches. "Look this way."

There was a trail of huge boulders leading out from the arch, all close together and forming a very long line that curved out. Lush brush was growing out of cracks in the stones. At the end, a rock full of cracks and potholes was filled with vegetation.

"This is no stone formation," Jinkins said, very much delighted with everyone's consternation.

Everyone stared at him in expectation, but he just peered at them with a childish grin.

"Well for pity's sake what is it, Jinkins?" Lady Shrewsbury huffed.

"This, my dear travelers, is a fossil. And by fossil, I do mean skeleton."

Aubrey took another sweeping glance and immediately realized that they had all missed the obvious; the arches were ribs and the stone trail leading away was a spine; each boulder a vertebra. At the far end was what must have been a crushed skull. On the other hand, it was no wonder they'd missed it; the ribcage was the size of a stadium.

"Yes," Jinkins said, "This was a very large beast, indeed. And the only way we realized it was a skeleton at all was when one of the scientists hacked off a sample to identify the minerals of the rock."

"So what kind of beast is it? And when did it die?" Henry asked, seeming skeptical that it was a skeleton at all.

"We don't know," Jinkins said, "But we have no doubt it was alive and we suspect it was a marine organism—only a marine animal could be this large."

Lady Shrewsbury piped up, "Well it didn't die recently, I hope." She covered her nose as if to filter a bad smell.

Jinkins chuckled, "Oh no, it's been thousands of years at the very l—" he was suddenly interrupted by a horrific sound echoing across the valley. Everyone froze. The sound was unmistakable.

A man was screaming.

He burst out of the brush near the edge of the bone formation. He was totally bare and his gaunt eyes were open wide with terror. He was stooped over, half lumbering on all fours, and so emaciated that his panting breaths could be seen in his ribs. His hair and beard were torn and thin. Bruises and streaks of blood covered his skin.

When he reached the group, he fell on his knees before Jinkins. Slowly, coughing, he raised his face. His lips looked stretched and were chafed and bleeding; his cheekbones were visible through the taught skin. He raised his eyes to Jinkins.

His voice hoarse, he shouted long and with all the power in his lungs, "*Equo ne credite, Teucri!*" His eyes looked wild.

Jinkins stepped to the man and stooped to one knee, placing a hand on his shoulder. "Andrews?" he said with deep concern. "Is that you?"

## United Nations Security Council

Doctor Martin said, "This ability, or sixth sense, of which I am speaking is very well known and utilized by the security industry. By it they prevent thefts every day all over the world.

"Have you heard the phrase 'mum has eyes in the back of her head?' Well, it is no fallacy. It is true. She did; you simply couldn't see them.

"Each of you, I guarantee, has had the feeling at some time that you are being stared at, and when you looked up, there was someone peering at you. Now women have this feeling more frequently than men because men are usually the ones doing the staring." Chuckles spread across the auditorium.

"We have always attributed this feeling to peripheral vision or some such thing, but this is nonsense. Studies and tests of all sorts have shown that, indeed, people are frequently aware of when they are being looked at, even if they have no physical or natural way of knowing it.

"That is why, in the security industry, it is well known that if you stare at a suspicious person through closed circuit video, they are much less likely to attempt a theft. They *know* you are watching, intuitively. It is perhaps why, when someone is about to tap your shoulder from behind, the nerves have fired in your brain to turn your head before their finger has reached you. This is a verified, scientific fact.

"It is this intuition, 'the sense of being stared at' as I call it, that cannot be explained by science as we know it. Even animals have this sense. Try staring at your cat at home from behind, and it won't take long for him to peep back at you with suspicion, or to slink away in anxiety."

"So what is this intuition? Where does this sixth sense come from?" The vast auditorium was silent; the thousands-strong audience were on the edge of their seats. Now feeling totally at ease, Doctor Martin leaned back in the squeaky chair as he continued, "You all should recall the devastating tsunami in the Indian Ocean. It desolated the entire region, killed over a quarter of a million people, but left very few animals dead. Why did the animals survive?

"Well, when you look at the evidence, a theme begins to emerge. In Thailand, thirty minutes before the tsunami struck, a herd of buffalo looked out at the sea and stampeded up a hill. An hour before the tsunami, elephants at Yala National Park, Sri Lanka, were seen trumpeting and running from the beach. Bats flew inland, dogs refused to go to the beach, flamingos abandoned low-lying areas, and zoo animals rushed into shelters and wouldn't come out. These animals all had one thing in common: they knew the tsunami was coming.

"Extraordinary, you say. Not really. This is nothing new or remarkable.

"The ability of animals to anticipate disasters reaches far back into antiquity. The Greeks and Chinese have historically trusted their animals to warn them of impending earthquakes.

"It is a well-known fact that, during World War II, families relied upon their pets to alert them of air raids long before the sirens sounded. These animals knew that planes were coming when they were hundreds of miles distant, well in advance of their ability to hear them.

"Dogs in London are known to have warned of German V2 rockets, rockets that were faster than the speed of sound. It is a physical impossibility that the dogs *heard* the rockets. So how did they know?

"Well, it seems that these animals have an intuition, a sixth sense, if you will. And they are very well attuned to it. I have recorded 177 cases of dogs responding to the death or suffering of their absent owners and 5,000 cases of similar psychic phenomena in animals of all kinds.

"Among these phenomena, and one which myself and others have tested scientifically through experimentation, is what I call the 'intention effect.'

"We have, in video, documented that dogs at home alone know not only when their masters leave for the house, but when their masters *decide* to leave.

"How do we know this, you ask," he chuckled. "Well quite simply, actually.

"Dogs frequently run to the door or window in anticipation of their owners' arrivals. By setting up situations in which masters depart by various means from various locations at abrupt and unexpected times, we can watch the dogs through video and document exactly when they ran to the door. The statistics show that, overwhelmingly, they run to the door at the moment their masters intend to leave for home.

"So, given this evidence, we come to the inevitable question: How do the dogs know?

"Well, it might be related to this other strange phenomena. Has anyone heard of Moon, the dog?"

No one raised a hand.

"Moon was driving cross country with his master when they stopped for a quick break. Something spooked Moon, and he disappeared in a flash. The master searched everywhere but was unable to turn up his faithful animal. Eventually, the master returned home in despair.

"Now, Moon disappeared seventy-seven miles from home. Between the dog and the house were all manner of obstacles: miles of desert, a rushing river, a mountain range; all of it unfamiliar terrain. Despite this, a week later, Moon appeared in his hometown. How did the canine have the slightest idea where to go?

"Well, perhaps the same way that Skittles, the cat did. Skittles was lost while enjoying a vacation 350 miles from home. When he returned 140 days later, he was skin and bones and his paws were raw. But he made it nonetheless.

"Of course that's nothing to the cat in Russia that traveled 1,300 miles across Siberian wilderness to get back to his family. That journey took three months.

"And what of Smokey the cat of Australia, who was picked up by scoundrels and shot thirteen times in the head and left for dead. He showed up on his family's doorstep a week later, having draggged himself there despite his wounds. Medical care fully restored him to health.

"These are but a few of thousands of such stories, and not only stories about domestic animals, but wild ones. By watching wild wolves, for example, the researcher William Long noticed that the animals seemed to display behavior that was inexplicable by natural means. The animals had an intuition about the others' whereabouts, the sixth sense.

"I propose that we do, too. After all, we use it every day." Responding to the looks of surprise on the representatives' faces, he smiled, "You want to know how. I'll tell you."

Doctor Martin slowly turned his head and searched the audience. There wasn't a single movement, not a single cough. He looked back at the council members and continued, "So to explain the sixth sense, I go back to my original experience, the experience that sent me on the quest for understanding.

"When I had that jolting intuition, that sudden sense that I should take the long way back to Cambridge, was it just a chance whim that happened at that moment? Or was it because I somehow sensed the inevitable truth: that my sister was about to die?

"The one thing that all of these strange phenomena have in common is that, in some way or other, we are linked. All life is linked. We can sense when others are in danger, or have perished. We can sense when others are looking at us. We can sense where loved ones are, and reach them.

"The link between beings is stronger, the more intimate the relationship. That is why dogs can sense when their masters are in peril or returning home, but don't foretell the arrival of a stranger. That is why I had a feeling of foreboding when my sister's life was about to be lost.

"It has often been said that we have souls, that we are not merely physical beings. Well, I propose, in a scientific sense, that this is true. Our existence is on both the physical plain, which we understand to a great degree, but it is also on another, invisible plain, which we do not understand at all."

Suddenly, there was a noise from the council.    One of the representatives was rising to his feet, the one from the United States. Doctor Martin knew him to be Abael Fiedler, chief of staff to the U.S. President.

The man stood from his wheelchair with some difficulty, and, even at his full height, bowed over with a grotesque hump protruding under his suit coat.  From behind, a woman stepped up to assist him, but in annoyance, he waved her away.  He leaned forward to the microphone, yanked it towards himself, and said, "Doctor Martin, if I may say something."

Surprised, Doctor Martin said, "Of course."

"When you began your testimony, you mentioned several different categories into which people fall in reference to psychic phenomena. Whether you are a believer or not, and so forth . . . ."

"Yes."

"Well, I propose that there is a tenth group: those who believe in these phenomena, fully understand them, and use them, or channel them, to their own benefit and the benefit of others."

"Well that would certainly be a hypothetical group, yes. But I fear no such group exists."

Abael stared at him with beady black eyes, his head tilted oddly and slowly sinking towards his chest. Doctor Martin almost thought that the man had fallen asleep with his eyes open, but then he opened his mouth with a pop and said, "Why is that?  Why would you believe no one knows and understands these phenomena?"

"Well because no has come forward with a credible claim.  Those I have seen to date who avow to channel these abilities generally turns out to not have his head screwed on properly."

Abael said, "So to make such a credible claim, a person would necessarily be required to explain what he knows and provide some empirical evidence that he has the power to channel these so-called psychic abilities?"

"Well certainly, yes."

"So you assume that someone in possession of such power would necessarily be willing to share it?"

Doctor Martin took a deep breath, thinking.  He thought he knew where this man was coming from. He said, "If you are suggesting that some government, for example, the United States government, understands and utilizes this power for the advancement of national interest, then you are right. I would not expect that they would be eager to disclose the fact."

Sharply, Abael retorted, "No, that is not what I mean at all!"

Doctor Martin waited for him to explain what he *did* mean, but he made no indication that he intended to do so. Doctor Martin prodded, "What do you mean, sir?"

Slowly, Abael lowered himself back into his wheelchair. He straightened his tie. Then he looked up and said, "I am coming soon. You will see what I mean then."

"Coming where, sir?"

"I am coming soon."

## CDC

Doctor Compton opened the meeting. "So you are all aware that we've had a total of five official cases of the virus. Four of those have resulted in sudden death. The last is in critical condition."

Everyone in the room nodded, including Karen. This time the group comprised more than just those from the CDC. There were representatives from many other branches of government as well.

"Now Doctor Guy Giordano has been heading up the effort at the USAMRIID in Ft. Detrick where they have one of the only BSL-4 facilities in the nation. He has some information to share." He motioned to Doctor Giordano.

Everyone turned to look at the jeans-wearing Italian. When Karen saw who it was, she muttered an expletive.

Doctor Giordano stood. "Thanks, guys," he said, swaying from side to side awkwardly. He took his hat off. It just didn't seem right to speak about something that had killed four people while wearing a ball cap, no matter how much he loved the Phillies.

"What have you found?" Karen asked, rapping her fingers on the table. "Let's keep things moving here."

"Well, some of this information came from other labs—Army Medical will mostly be involved in the effort to stop the virus medicinally. But the biggest thing everyone's noticed about the virus so far is that every victim has been female."

Someone said, "How can that be? I've never heard of a virus that attacks a single sex. Males and females have the same genes, after all."

"Well that's precisely what we thought. So in examining the first victim, we kept that in mind. The original pathologist noted that the body was still hot inside by the time he examined it. So he knew she had suffered a tremendous fever. He also noted something else. She had hepatitis. It wasn't severe yet, but it was present."

"This is just hepatitis?" someone interjected. "All this over *hepatitis*?"

"No, hepatitis just means inflammation of the liver. Her liver was inflamed.

"Now, since the pathologist noted that she did not have a thyroid gland, we looked into it. When we ran her blood work, her thyroid levels were through the roof. So we thought perhaps the missing gland was congenital; maybe she was born that way and has been on pills ever since to compensate and this time she way overdosed. But, wrong. She had no history of problems at all. Was never on thyroid pills.

"So the conclusion is that the gland was removed before she reached the morgue. Now it was noted that the paramedics had tried to administer air directly to her lungs via her trachea. I've never heard of paramedics doing that before, but since they likely did not know what they were doing it's possible that something went wrong there and the gland was disposed of. We are going to hunt them down and talk with them about that.

"When we ran the other victims' hormone levels, though, we found highly elevated serum T3 and T4 (thyroid hormones), but suppressed TSH (thyroid stimulating hormone). So we have this single common factor in every victim: elevated thyroid levels, told us they had all died of the same thing. Thyroid storm."

"What's that?" someone asked.

"It's when your thyroid starts producing so much hormone that your metabolism goes crazy, your heart rate goes nuts, blood pressure shoots through the roof, and you get a deadly high fever. Usually, you get jaundice, which is yellowing of the eyes and skin. Children or teenagers who have a thyroid storm episode often suffer from intense seizures.

"In this case, it's the storm of storms. Their temperature goes to extremes we may have never seen before. Their capillaries rupture from powerful blood pressure. This can cause blood in the eyes.

"It's apparently so rapid and so intense that the victim dies within minutes. After the thyroid storm set in, each of these victims died within an hour. So it appears that the virus is attacking cells in the thyroid gland, setting off this response.

"Now women are known to have an extremely strong immune response thanks to estrogen; that's why they suffer from thyroid disease more frequently than men. To be more specific, five times more often. So when the virus starts reproducing in the thyroid gland, these dames' immune systems start attacking the gland itself, which in turn causes it to produce incredible quantities of hormones.

"The only woman who has come down with symptoms but hasn't died is a lady over fifty. She's already reached menopause, so her immune system has slowed down because she doesn't have as much estrogen. We also suspect that girls under eight would be less vulnerable because they haven't started producing high levels of estrogen yet."

"So what do we do to stop it?" Karen asked.

"Well, we know that none of these women we've investigated so far has had any thyroid problem before, so we think we can exclusively blame the virus for the thyroid storm. We also know that for every five women who get the symptoms, only one man will, so we could have a lot of male carriers out there who don't even know they have it.

"Also, there are no symptoms at all until the thyroid storm starts, so it is difficult to know who might be infected until it is too late. We don't have any treatment for the virus, specifically. If the body can't fight off the virus by itself, it might become necessary to kill the thyroid gland so that they can survive.

"Unfortunately, since it comes on so fast, it's not likely that we *could* treat anyone in time and even once their symptoms were being treated, there's of course nothing to do about the virus itself."

Karen said, "So basically what you're telling us is that we know a lot more about it, but we're still screwed."

Doctor Compton said, "Thanks to Doctor Giordano's team, we can test to see if someone is infected, but it is a long process and couldn't be done on a mass scale yet." He paused, "Basically it comes down to this: a vaccine must be developed, and it must be developed soon."

Doctor Giordano said, "There is another option, actually."

Every head turned to him.

"What would that be?" Karen asked.

Everyone was staring at Doctor Giordano in expectation. He knew his idea was radical. Intuitively, he knew the virus was incredibly dangerous. The fact that it was an RNA virus and would mutate so quickly; the structure of its protective layer, or capsid; the evidence that it had been transferred through various pathways already . . . it was the perfect virus. So perfect, in fact, that he wondered if it had been *engineered* that way.

So he proposed his idea, "The virus causes the immune system to attack the thyroid gland in most women and some men. Thyroid storm starts, and in less than an hour the person is dead. So why don't we treat the thyroid storm before it starts?"

"How?"

"Iodine."

"Radioactive iodine?"

"Yes. We kill the thyroid gland even before the virus has a chance to attack it."

"Why not just give out PTU[7] or Tapazole pills?"

"Because they can cause agranulocytosis[8]: the virus would run amok. At this point, killing the thyroid gland would present zero risk."

"But we would have to know exactly whom the virus would strike next."

"I think it's safe to say it will attack *everyone* next. Anyone in the Baltimore area should be treated."

---

7   Propylthiouracil, or PTU, is a drug used to treat Graves disease and hyperthyroidism. It reduces the amount of thyroid hormone produced by the thyroid gland. It is known to cause serious liver injury, including failure and death.

8   Agranulocytosis is a lowering of white blood cell count (to less than five percent of the normal level), resulting in severe suppression of the immune system and extreme risk of infection.

"You want to put two million people on hormones for the rest of their lives?" Karen exclaimed.

"Yes," Doctor Giordano said. "I do."

"I want to kill this virus," she swore, "not wave the white flag of surrender!"

"But think of what this could become. If it gets away from us, which I think it might do, consider the stakes. How can we possibly work on containing it if we're busy digging mass graves? I just have a gut feeling that this will totally overwhelm us—and fast. Sure, we gotta find a cure, but right now we have the chance to save two million lives. We cannot blink at the chance."

"*Digging mass graves?*" Karen repeated his words dubiously. "Guy, I think you must be getting a little less sleep than you're used to. We're nowhere near that point. Now I agree, proactively treating with iodine could be a solution if it gets out of control, but not now. We have to be rational."

"We should tell the people what's happening and let them choose."

Karen started shaking her head, "No, noooo—"

"We need to give them the option."

"No, Guy, no. Just be calm, let's find the cure, and stop it dead. That's it." She sighed, "With Towson under quarantine, we'll control it."

## Towson, Maryland

Wesley's mother was still under observation at the hospital. Wesley was at the grocery store to pick up a four pack of puddings and other comfort foods she liked, as well as a sandwich for himself.

When he had arrived at the store, it had been nearly empty. Now, as he waited for the woman at the deli to finish wrapping his sandwich, he saw an increasing number of people running up the aisles. The lady handed him the sandwich and he said, "Thanks." When he turned around to grip his cart, a frantic man pushed it out of his hands and ran away with it. Wesley shouted at the man at first, shocked, but then gaped in disbelief as he saw that the canned goods aisle directly adjacent from him had filled with people who were feverishly emptying the shelves. He looked back at the lady at the deli, "Are you guys having a sale?"

She shrugged incredulously.

Almost in a haze, Wesley walked from the deli towards the dairy section. He asked a woman who shoved past him what was going on, but she didn't respond. When he reached dairy, he noticed that the refrigerators that held the milk were empty. Every last bottle of every kind of milk had been taken.

An older man jogged up beside him, his arms full of goods. He swore in aggravation, "The milk's gone already?"

Wesley said, "Yeah . . . can you tell me what's going on?"

"You haven't heard?" the man panted.

"No."

"Towson is being quarantined. Nobody in or out." He nodded, "Makes you wish you had stocked up like those doomsday wackos, doesn't it?" He said, "Good luck, my friend." And with that he took off.


## China Academy of Sciences


"My proposal is that we go to Antarctica and find this dinosaur DNA."

"Ah, I see. Only that. A simple stroll down to Antarctica and 'Oh look! Dinosaur DNA!' and we pick it up and show the world."

"Something along those lines, yes." Doctor Ming-Zhen felt his superior's eyes upon him, studying him contemplatively.

Zhang finally said, "I am under great pressure by the State to remove you from the Academy."

"I understand," Doctor Ming-Zhen replied calmly.

"If I asked you to resign, would you do so?"

"Certainly I would do anything you asked."

"The State is keen to redeem China from the disgrace of these overwhelming accusations of fraudulence."

Doctor Ming-Zhen looked down, sensing his fate. He would have to resign; his career was certainly over. What would he do to support his family? His daughter was only six years old.

Zhang clenched his jaw and said firmly, his face almost trembling, "But I would be caught dead before I allow you to fall unjustly." He stood and nodded to Doctor Ming-Zhen, "Your resignation is forbidden. You will lead our effort to fight these accusations, and we will fight them to the death." He straightened his shirt, "Tomorrow I will speak with some friends in the Party to see what might be done to assist us in this effort."

Doctor Ming-Zhen stood and offered a quick nod, "Thank you, *Xiàozhǎng*."

"The skull inside that dinosaur fossil was an extraordinary discovery, and you deserve all possible credit for your honesty. Any other would have buried it forever. You have my utmost respect, sir."

He was overcome with appreciation. He swallowed a frog in his throat, and managed a "Thank you."

Zhang nodded with compassion, then, with a wave of his hand, said, "Now be gone. You have work to do."


*Xiàozhǎng* Zhang needed to do little persuading with his friends in the Party: Doctor Ming-Zhen's ambitions for Antarctica drew the government's immediate blessing, and funding for the research flowed generously. Any opportunity to save face in the debacle was welcome by everyone.

Almost immediately he was officially adopted as China's champion, the one to restore the nation's fortunes in science and best the nation's detractors. He was featured prominently in all government media, and a special space on the internet was established to follow his exploits, like a twenty-four hour reality TV series.

Cameras followed him everywhere, he was called upon for constant interviews, and he was even placed in ribbon-cutting ceremonies for grand public projects and other events.

Thus, the solemn, unassuming Doctor Ming-Zhen ultimately found himself in the nearly unbearable conditions of the Antarctic, sent there as his country's unwitting hero.

# Paradeisia
## Poseidon's Platter

After they had returned to the surface with the wretch Jinkins had called "Andrews," Jinkins had insisted they all go to the restaurant where he would explain. Andrews was left at the island's hospital.

Despite the circumstances, the restaurant awed them. It consisted of many tiers of tables centered around a circular stone grill where flames licked the food that four chefs cooked. A giant glass wall offered an incredible view of an aquarium full of sea creatures. The semi-circular wall that surrounded the rest of the interior featured coral reefs with bubbles blowing upwards, clams that opened and shut, and fish that peeked out from crevices. The ceiling looked like the underside of the surface of the sea and it undulated and shined as if waves were passing across.

"We need know what's really going on here, Jinkins. And we need to know now," Henry said. He was no longer angry: now he sounded tense, uneasy. They were all sitting around a large flat table shaped like a giant shell half. The kinkajou was wandering from plate to plate, sampling everyone's sweetest foods.

Jinkins said, "Andrews will be fine, and I do mean," he nodded as if to convince himself, "fully recovered. Our hospital here is state-of-the-art."

"Jinkins!" Lady Shrewsbury said, slapping her hand down on the table. "At this juncture we do not care about the state-of-the-art facilities! We care about what happened to that poor devil! Will you please elucidate, for heaven's sake?"

Jinkins hesitated.

"Now wouldn't be a moment too soon!"

Jinkins looked down at his plate and took a long breath. He removed his pith helmet and placed it on the table. "Andrews was part of the first group that went down after we built the portal. They landed and did a little exploration. It was supposed to be just for an hour or so. They were very careful. Took samples of the air, the water, that kind of thing. Scientific data. But when it was time to go back up, Andrews was gone."

"They looked and called for him. They did everything they could.

There was no sign of him. So they went back down over and over again, searching everywhere. It became a monumental effort.

"He was a real explorer, Andrews. We decided he had wandered off on his own to do his own research. He would come back, we thought." Jinkins sighed, "That was three years ago. I suppose he finally did come back."

After a long silence at the table, one of the board members spoke, "Well it doesn't sound that serious to me. The man wandered off, probably ate something that didn't agree with him. Been wandering around the last three years and finally spotted somebody."

Jinkins said enthusiastically, "Precisely! See? It's very sad of course, but nothing like what you all had been thinking. And now the story has ended better than I thought. He's alive and will likely recover!"

Henry interrupted Jinkins' joviality, "Recover or not, how did he survive down there for *three* years all by himself? Is there really anything to eat?"

"There are fish," Jinkins said. "He could have eaten fish."

Lady Shrewsbury said, "The man doesn't even know his own name, for goodness sake. How could he possibly have had the discipline to catch fish, especially if he'd eaten something toxic already?"

"Are there any edible plants?" someone asked.

"We've found yellow tomato plants. And they're gigantic, too. Over thirty feet high with hundreds of tomatoes each."

"Now *that's* very interesting." another of the board contributed. "Do you know what's causing them to grow that way?"

"Well, Doctor Pearce analyzed the tomato's genes, and it turns out they are very unlike what we eat here on the surface. They are very old; a very ancient breed unpolluted by modern science. Since tomatoes back when Columbus arrived were actually very small and yellow, our scientists have theorized that the increased carbon dioxide and atmospheric pressure accounts for their huge size. Some day we think it's possible we could feed the guests from things grown down there."

"Getting back to guests, when were we originally scheduled to open?" Henry asked.

"Ah! Well, actually we would be scheduled to open before long, and I do very mean soon," Jinkins said, twiddling his thumbs.

"When, precisely, is 'very soon?'"

Suddenly, Jinkins' phone rang. He looked relieved at the distraction. He pulled it out of a giant holster on his waist. It looked like a giant radio from World War II. Answering, he listened to the voice on the other end briefly. Then he hung up, saying, "Doctor Pearce insists I go see him at the hospital at once. It's about Andrews."

Henry stood, "I'll go as well. The rest of you may turn in if you wish; it's getting late."

Jinkins added, "Yes, turn in, or you can go take a turn around Atlantis Bay. It's very pleasant in the evenings."

Henry said, "Aubrey."

Taken totally by surprise, she replied, "Huh?"

"Get my things ready for the morning."

## Paradeisia Hospital

"How is it that you didn't notice this before?" Henry demanded, staring in perplexity at the man lying on the operating table before them.

"We didn't notice before because he was never in the dark before," the doctor replied. Doctor James Pearce was originally from one of the near islands; Trinidad. He had a very solemn-looking face with a neatly trimmed white mustache.

The three of them, including Jinkins, were standing in an operating room where Andrews lay anesthetized. The room was dark except for some soft lighting illuminating a counter on one side.

"But what is it?" Jinkins asked impatiently. "And by 'what is it' I mean what relevance does this have?"

Doctor Pearce folded his arms, "It has all the relevance in the world, I think. The man's been missing for how many years, he comes back, and now he has this. How do we explain that?" He motioned down to Andrews' arm where, glowing with a soft green tint from within the skin was a marking:

# ודדחשוטעבו

Jinkins was between Henry and the doctor and he looked back and forth between the two of them, "It's quite simple, I'd say. He had this before he came to Paradeisia, some newfangled glowing tattoo."

The doctor objected, "Look closer. It's made of tiny dots of light. I extracted one. It's over here." He walked them over to a petri dish on the counter. Barely visible was a tiny translucent ball smaller than the point of a pen. "As soon as I removed it, the light went out. It seems to have been powered by his body, maybe his warmth. Or, more likely, bacteria."

"Well that doesn't prove anything. I still say he could have had it before he came." Jinkins snorted. "I mean if you're trying to say that somehow he received it when he was down the portal, why that's preposterous. How could that possibly have happened?" Jinkins wiped his forehead of a sweat he had developed.

"There's still a lot we don't know about what's down there," Doctor Pearce said quietly with a nervous glance at Henry.

Henry had just been standing there, his hand on his chin, looking deeply contemplative. Finally he interrupted, "Let's drop it, gentlemen."

The other two stared at him.

"It's late. There's no reason to speculate at this hour. Let's go to bed now and you can begin to pursue your theory in the morning, doctor. Some things are better addressed after a good night's sleep."

The doctor nodded and Jinkins, looking relieved, agreed with a, "Yes, yes, let's get some sleep. And I suppose you won't be going to China after all, eh Potter? Now that you've seen what's down the portal?"

"I will be going to China. But I'll only stay overnight." He turned to the physician, "Thank you doctor. You have my number if you have something worth telling me."

Jinkins simply shrugged and followed Henry as he walked out of the room.

Henry stopped to use the restroom in the hospital before he left, so Jinkins was long-gone by the time he stepped out through the sliding glass doors into the still-warm night air. As he jogged down the steps to the road where a Jeep waited, he felt a tap on his shoulder. He swung around.

"Mr. Potter," said the person standing there.

Henry replied, "Yes?"

He was a stocky man with short-trimmed hair, a goatee and large eyebrows. He wore a tropically patterned loose polo and big shorts. An expensive-looking watch ornamented his wrist, but he had simple sandals on his feet. He took one last puff of his cigarette before flicking it onto the pavement, stomping it out. He held out his hand, "I'm Scott Nimitz, Operations Supervisor."

"Good to meet you," said Henry, looking less than thrilled. "And what is your role this drama?"

"There are sixteen of us along with four forecasters. We work the command center at headquarters—in the FlyRail Hub on the top of the mountain. We're there twenty-four hours a day. We have video feeds of almost everywhere on the island."

"Interesting," Henry said.

"And that's what I wanted to talk with you about. I was bored, you know, watching Poseidon's Platter when you guys were having your meal. Word's gone around that you're now the man in charge."

Henry said, "Indeed I am. There will be a formal announcement."

"I'm not a brown-noser or anything like that. I just think there are some things you should know if you're going to make this place a success, you know."

"I'm all ears," Henry said.

"Operationally this place is the bomb. Runs like clockwork. We get the occasional computer glitches—but who doesn't have those. But I'm more worried about other things. Now don't get me wrong, Jinkins is a good guy. He's a nice man, you know. We all love him. But I think he kind of . . . he's been in denial about some stuff. In operations, we hear most of what goes on here. In other departments you know how it is, the right hand doesn't know what the left is doing. But in ops we're the brain, the mind. There's not much that doesn't pass through."

"Yes," Henry said, apparently getting impatient. "So what is it that you want to tell me?"

"Andrews disappeared three years ago like Jinkins told you." Nimitz said. "But Andrews isn't the only one who's gone missing. He was just the only one to go missing when he was down the portal."

"How many people *have* gone missing?" Henry said.

"Including Andrews . . ." Nimitz hesitated. "Eleven."

Henry's eyebrows rose. "Eleven. And he's the only one who's come back?"

Nimitz nodded, concern creasing his face.

"Is there any pattern that you've noticed?"

"They were all young, but no children were taken."

"Taken?"

"Yes, I think they were taken."

"Hmm," Henry said, looking skeptical. "Had they all gone down the shaft previously?"

"No. Just people from all over the island, working all kinds of jobs. But Andrews was the first to disappear. Nobody disappeared that I know of until after the portal was complete. Of course, we didn't have nearly as many people working here back then."

"And what is the working population now?"

"Seventy-five thousand, give or take."

"Well then, eleven disappearances doesn't sound all that extraordinary. Doesn't it seem likely that they disappeared for legitimate reasons; for example, just walked off the job and went home? Or perhaps localized crimes?"

"I wouldn't rule out localized crimes. But of course we have a security force here, a kind of police force, and they haven't resolved anything," Nimitz said.

"And most of the workforce comes from the surrounding areas?"

"We have a good mix. Most of them don't work for Paradeisia; they're from the developers. A lot of Caribbean islanders. A lot of Asians. Plenty from the States and South America. A bunch of Cubans. We even have a lot from Europe. It's like Babel around here."

Henry stuck out a hand to shake, "Well, thank you for the information, I—"

But Nimitz was shaking his head. "Mr. Potter, the disappearances are one thing. But there's something else that I wanted to tell you about; something that makes me even more nervous."

Henry dropped his hand to his side and said, "And that is?"

"Sightings."

# Antarctica

A giant dome that allowed light in but kept the wind out had taken shape over the site, an inhospitable glacier far inland. If nothing else, the effort would produce strides in making Antarctica habitable— habitable being a very broad term.

In the 1970's, the lowest temperature on earth had been measured nearby, a mind-numbing -128.6 degrees Fahrenheit, and the dome did not succeed in warming the place much: it was more useful at keeping the sudden, furious winds at bay.

Passing him with a loud engine was a snow tractor pulling a passenger trailer laden with eager, camera-snapping tourists; another load of the press. They had been summoned from all over the world to witness this. The camera crew for the government's reality show had followed him around for two years now. It was a necessary evil, just like the physical maladies he had suffered since his arrival.

He had been daily afflicted by bloody and chapped lips, chafing dry skin, eye twitches, and nose bleeds. But he was grateful for those paltry annoyances. In the beginning, it had been much worse.

For the first few weeks, he had lost his appetite, he couldn't sleep, he frequently vomited, his joints ached, and his ears hurt. He had lost about eight pounds since he came. But the astonishing thing was, his symptoms were no worse than for anyone else new to this part of the Antarctic. Mankind was not meant to come here.

The site on the glacier was at a high elevation so oxygen was scarce. Even now, almost a month into his residence, he breathed heavily as he walked towards the dome exit. When he was inside the dome like he was now, he wore gloves, boots, and a snowsuit complete with a hood.

The door of the dome was the size of a highway tunnel entrance, and as he approached the air became crisper, dryer. The sky was a brilliant, cloudless blue, and he could see the speck which he knew to be a thirty-foot twin propeller plane as it approached.

He walked out to the strip, his boots crunching the packed snow beneath them. Then he waited for the turboprop to land, taking in the horizon's distant craggy peaks which never failed to inspire awe no matter how many times he saw them.

The plane finally bounced down on its skis. They never shut off the propellers when they landed. Instead it was as brief a stay as possible, then a quick takeoff; otherwise the engines would freeze. It took some time for the crew to open the hatch and a stair to be driven up, but, finally, the people he was waiting for emerged.

He had found Antarctica to be surprisingly mountainous, and beautiful. He vividly recalled his first helicopter flight from a ship flotilla to China's coastal research station, named Zhongshan. The pilot had steered them directly through a magnificent archway over the deep navy of the churning sea. It was a giant monument created by the collapsing glacier, with warm, orange sunlight glistening off one side while contrasting blue dimly glowed in the shadow of the other.

Ahead, he could see the waves crashing against the white shore where the myriad of tiny penguins endlessly waddled up and down in front of giant ice-cliffs. There were sea lions, too, basking in the sun or sliding down icebergs, trying to catch one of the swimming penguins.

Established in 1980 and intended as a long-term endeavor, Zonghshan had consisted of only several small structures and housed a mere sixty people at most. Now, a veritable city had been erected in its place to support Ming-Zhen's research effort, making one forget how very remote and isolated it actually was.

From Zhongshan, he remembered a near three-hour-plane ride to the inland site. Aircraft could reach the site only five months out of the year. During this period, from October to February, the sun shined twenty-four hours a day. This was the Antarctic summer—averaging - 22 degrees. Antarctica was the driest land mass on earth in terms of precipitation—a desert, in fact.[9] The snow had piled up in huge glaciers over many years. The glaciers slowly moved out to the coast and broke off into the sea.

---

9    Near the coast, the Antarctic ice caps were replenished by snow above and sea below, but in the interior, the lack of precipitation meant that movement of the glacial ice diminished to less than three inches a year in some areas. The ice there could be very old, over a million years, if it had been there that long. At Lake Vostok, the ice moved twelve feet a year from west to east, meaning that ice there would take 70,000 years to entirely cross it.

His seat was jarring, his breath formed little puffs, and the turboprop engines rattled the plane like a tin can, but when he stood up to look over the pilot's shoulder, the view out the windshield was spectacular. Over land, the mountains were endless stone peaks covered by ice. He marveled at the clarity of the air. The sun somehow seemed closer than he was used to and the snow below was blinding as it sparkled with its reflection.

The landscape of ancient Antarctica, complete with lakes and, it was suspected, even rivers, was below the ice cap. The largest of these bodies of water was Lake Vostok, the site they had chosen. East and slightly south of the center of the continent, it was the size of Lake Ontario. The average temperature of the water was probably -3 degrees, but it wasn't frozen; the immense pressure applied above it and geothermal warming that occurred somewhere in the lowest part of the lake prevented that.

And the lake was indeed deep: the third deepest in the world. Although covered with over two miles of glacial ice, Lake Vostok was visible from space because, in contrast to the surrounding area, the ice above it was almost perfectly flat. Having been covered since the poles froze, it was now as it had been thirty million years ago (or however old it was). It was a time capsule.

To Doctor Ming-Zhen, this was intriguing enough. But there were two even more provocative features to the lake. One was that radar showed there to be an island of some sort in the center. The other was a "magnetic anomaly" measuring sixty-five by forty-six miles.

When his plane landed, he had been greeted by a charismatic, large man with celebrity-worthy white teeth, a thick beard, and big gloves. He exclaimed warmly, "Welcome to the dead zone! I am Ivan Toskovic. Good to meet you after so long."

Doctor Ming-Zhen's stoic demeanor caused the other to slap him across the back and laugh heartily, "Smile, my friend! I am not Ivan the Terrible!"

As they entered the dome and boarded the transport, Doctor Toskovic explained that in 2012, he had been a young researcher at the Russian Vostok station to the east. Recently he had been seduced out his professorship in Saint Petersburg to head up operations here for the Chinese, chosen due to his experience.

"In 2012 we did not have nice big dome," he said, making a sweeping motion as they entered the giant structure. The dome's chief purpose, as Doctor Toskovic explained, was to make the drill operable through the Antarctic winter. Its secondary purpose was keeping its inhabitants from freezing to death, "although," he said with a wink, "some days we lose one or two."

The vehicle whirred down a well-used track in the snow from the entrance to the residential area, a large cluster of rectangular, windowless metal boxes surrounding a large community building. There, they disembarked and Doctor Toskovic introduced him to the cafeteria, a bustling hall with metal tables and noisy chairs. "You like food from cans?" Doctor Toskovic asked him. "Good, here you eat like prince!" As they sat down for a meal of soup and fresh rice, Doctor Ming-Zhen noticed a tattoo on Toskovic's arm.

# ודדחשוטעבו

"What does your tattoo say?" he inquired.

Doctor Toskovic grinned mysteriously, "It only means I know more than you. My little 'badge of honor.'" Then he proceeded to detail the Russian experience with Lake Vostok, a history that Doctor Ming-Zhen already knew to be fraught with peril.

Despite protests from all over the world because of fears of contamination, the Russians had spent twenty-four years drilling through the two miles of glacier towards the lake, yet their borehole was smaller than six inches wide. By the time they neared the surface in 2012, they were averaging only about five feet a day, a dismally slow rate. It was at this time that the scientific community was stunned by horrifying news. The Russian team had disappeared.

There had been three days of radio silence with no one hearing from them, and the worst was feared. Scientists warned of the danger: the pressure difference could have sent a powerful geyser up through the hole. As the days dragged on to five and then seven, the internet was ablaze with speculation, especially among conspiracy theorists. Had an unknown bacteria swarmed up from the lake to infect them? Had they been removed by some government agency that did not want them to reach the lake? Had they been abducted by space aliens with a secret base hidden in the lake (the magnetic anomaly)?

"Of course there was nothing to any of these rumors," Doctor Toskovic laughed. "We were so busy and excited that we couldn't bother to answer radio."

When Doctor Ming-Zhen heard this, he was leery. How could they be so busy that even one person could not bother to answer increasingly distressed calls over seven days?

At any rate, the Russian team did succeed in reaching the water, and a geyser did not kill anyone; in fact, the up flow from the pressure actually helped them to acquire samples. They were able to obtain these from water that froze inside the borehole several hundred feet up from the lake surface.

Doctor Toskovic himself carried the samples to Saint Petersburg, the voyage so long that it wasn't until 2013 that they were able to experiment with them. What they ultimately discovered baffled the imagination.

They found DNA, DNA representing thousands of species.

Most of these species were bacteria, but eukaryotes (single-celled organisms with a nucleus) and over one hundred multi-celled organisms were found, four of which were associated with mollusks and fish (in such roles as aiding in digestion).[10] Amazingly, it was said a species entirely unknown to science had also been found, although nothing more on this subject was ever mentioned.

It was believed that the DNA could not have survived millions of years merely drifting in the lake. Therefore the alternative was that the samples represented a living biology that presently occupied it, leading one of the excited Russian scientists to make the extraordinary claim that "living fish" might be found there. The statement was quickly

---

10  The Saint Petersburg scientists' findings were corroborated by a study from Bowling Green State University which examined ice samples that had been bored above the lake by an international team in 1998. Though the ice was not extracted from fresh lake water as in the Russian study, nor was it from nearly as deep, it was from lake water that it was believed had glaciated above its surface. In the study, genetic traces of many types of microorganisms were discovered, including one which was known to inhabit the bowels of fish.

retracted, but the damage was done: doubt was cast on the findings and the entire team suffered the consequences. The scientific community used the press to seriously question all of the findings, saying the DNA samples were modern contaminants, and eventually all of the Russians were shamed into silence.

Doctor Toskovic disclosed to Doctor Ming-Zhen that he himself had found his role as a scientist castigated since then; at conferences he was shunned, and he found it difficult to publish papers in respected journals. Research money or partners were suddenly scarce. Thus he spent most of his time in Saint Petersburg lecturing rather than doing any practical research. And he had never returned to Antarctica until now. He was eager for the chance to redeem himself.

"You and I, we are alike, I think," Doctor Toskovic said, his face serious. "We both make discoveries, they don't like, call fraud, career fall to pieces. Now we have chance to show them truth."

After dinner, they left the hall to walk down an aisle of barracks to Doctor Ming-Zhen's new "home-away-from-home," as Doctor Toskovic called it.

His quarters were six feet by six feet, but he was relieved to see he did not have to share a bunk. There was a single, twin-sized cot, a lightweight desk, and a metal chair. As far as enjoying the comforts of home, though, Doctor Toskovic summed it up best: "You like bed of nails? Good! Here you sleep like infant!"

Doctor Toskovic left him to settle into his quarters for the night. The bathroom was in a building about thirty steps from his quarters, so his trip was not a pleasant one. Then he slipped under the bedding with most of his layers still on and found the cot to be just about as comfortable as Doctor Toskovic had promised: jagged wire pressed into his back. He would have slept on the floor (his bed at home was almost as hard as the floor), but that would have been colder.

As he tried to sleep that first night, he thought of what the Russian had said. It was true: they were alike. They were both on a mission of redemption. And Doctor Ming-Zhen had learned his lesson: this time he wanted the scientific community to be without doubt that if he discovered anything, it was 100% legitimate.

That is why he was here. There would be no robot submersible: a person had to enter the lake and witness it with his own eyes. This was the only way to remove all doubt.

It was also 100% dangerous.

In the cold darkness, he felt very alone and missed his family. He felt a pang of guilt. A very straightforward man, he didn't agonize over the choices he made. But this one had become a thorn in his flesh almost the moment he decided to go. Anyone who was not very intimate with his wife would never have known that she was troubled: she did not scold or criticize him, she simply had moments where she could no longer restrain her internal, emotional turmoil and she would stare into space as a silent tear navigated her cheek. She was not ignorant of the tremendous risks, and although she had supported his initial efforts to redeem himself, she had not realized then that this would ultimately place him in a life-jeopardizing submersible in Antarctica.

It was the very danger, however, which made it a matter of duty, he thought. He could not send people down there if he was unwilling to go himself. After all, this mission was the brainchild of his conception.

There had doubtless been a contest to see who would be the first on the moon. Lake Vostok was no less remote, and, depending upon what, if anything, was discovered there, the man who first entered it would be immortalized.

He was suddenly very nauseous. As much as he detested the idea of braving the frigid air, as his stomach churned and his mouth filled with saliva, he knew it was inevitable. He kicked off the blankets and ran out the door, blinking in the light and realizing that it was still totally sunny out. He remembered that there were twenty-four hour days here this time of year—

As the vomit showered from his mouth, he realized how advantageous the increased light must be to his camera crew who had appeared just in time to record this memory for him.

That first unpleasant night now a month behind him, he watched as the door of the plane opened and his family blinked as they stepped out into the frosty air. His daughter, Li, pointed and waved to him from the top of the staircase. Made rotund by an apparent suitcase-full of pants and coats, she struggled to make her way down the steps.

His wife, Boa, held her by the hand, but when they finally reached the ground, Li could be contained no longer and broke free from her mother to run into his arms. This girl was the only thing in the world that caused Doctor Ming-Zhen to fully break from his stoicism and smile from ear to ear.

Hugging his daughter with one arm, he drew Bao close with the other. She had a broad face, short neck, and upturned eyebrows. Her thick, graying hair protruded from under a large cap, and her cheeks were rosy with the cold. Tears streamed down her face, but she said nothing.

"I told you I would come to you in Zhongshan," he scolded, then kissed her forehead. "It is much colder here than the coast."

"I could not wait, not one minute more," she replied softly, her voice breaking. Her tears had already frozen on her eyelashes.

He squeezed his family happily. "Let's get back on the plane before you turn into snowmen."

The trip to the coastal Zhongshan station and the two-night stay there with his wife and daughter would have been one of the happiest times of his life had it not been shadowed by the fact that, as soon as the visit was over, he would return to Vostok and make the descent two miles under the ice. When he waved goodbye as their helicopter rose into the sky, he wished beyond anything that he had listened to his parents and chosen a major other than Paleontology.

As it was, he returned to miserable Vostok and was greeted by the ever-cheerful Doctor Toskovic and, to his dismay, the camera crew. It was now evening. He would go to bed. The next morning would be the descent.

The drilling station had a tower that was almost ninety feet tall. It was at the center of the giant dome, 250 feet in diameter and a hundred feet high. Nearby were giant storage tanks and a huge pile of ice. A power station near the rim of the dome generated the electricity which powered the thermal drill (and everything else).

With this drill they had bored a tunnel twenty-six inches wide—a mere nine inches wider than the average man, and two miles long. They had sealed the water at the bottom with a pressurizing chamber. And, long before the drilling was done, they had built the five titanium submersibles that, at least in theory, met all the qualifications of the mission.

Now, Doctor Ming-Zhen was trapped in one, and he was descending down the shaft whether he wanted to or not.

"Four thousand feet," the voice of a controller came over the speakers in the submersible.

When he raised his face, Doctor Ming-Zhen could just barely see the shaft going all the way up to the dark opening where camera flashes were still erupting. In a few minutes, this last glimpse of civilization would vanish. The light from the surface that glowed through the white snow wall was diminishing quickly the lower he went, but there was also a change in its composition. It was becoming more opaque and had a bluish hue that grew deeper with the descent.

"Six thousand feet."

Doctor Ming-Zhen knew that the lake far below him had fifty times the amount of oxygen found in today's waters, something which would be consistent with what was known about prehistoric earth's atmosphere. This seemed to be yet another indicator of the lake's ancient age.

"Eight thousand feet."

One of the reasons he had chosen the Antarctic as opposed to the Arctic was that no nation had any effectual claim on the place. Finder's keepers.

"Ten thousand feet."

As he reached a depth at which there was no light, he switched on the exterior lights. The height of the tunnel was shockingly dramatic now that it was illuminated from the inside.

"Twelve thousand feet."

Finally, the submersible came to a stop with a slight bounce as the steel cable vacillated taut. From below he heard the grinding sound of what he knew to be the pressurizing chamber opening. When that stopped, the submarine gradually lowered into the chamber and outside the bubble he could see only metal. There was a clamping sound as the hooks at the ends of the Y-split on the cable were released.

"I am in the chamber. Prepare for radio silence," he said.

"See you on the other side," Doctor Toskovic's voice came over the speakers.

He watched as the cable spun around on its way out the pressurizing chamber and up the tunnel. He felt very much alone as the concave hatch twisted shut above him.

He hit a button to begin the sanitizing process. To ensure no contaminants made it into the lake from the submarines, they were self-cleaning. First, jets of boiling hot water were released to soak the outer skin, followed by a chemical bath. This process took only five minutes.

At the last minute, he remembered the stick of gum he had brought and slipped it into his mouth. Chewing rapidly, he waited for the five thousand pounds per square inch of water pressure.

With a loud grating noise and a blast, the water shot in from below, blasting his round viewport with a violent spray. He could hear very tiny creaks as the vessel was gradually fully subjected to the force of the lake water. A sudden sharp pain jolted his inner ears: he chewed harder until they popped.

Finally, the pressure was equalized and the door on the side slowly opened. He engaged the propulsion and the craft slowly slid to the side and out of the chamber. Once fully in the water, he allowed the top of the sub to lower so he was laying horizontal.

The circumferential exterior lights illuminated a slowly swirling cloud of white specs that stretched out for about twenty or thirty feet, but beyond that was total and overpowering blackness.

He pushed a button to capture a water sample in one of the twenty small storage compartments. As he peered at the white dots as they brushed up against the bubble, he could see with his naked eye what they were: near-microscopic shrimp. They were moving. With tiny arms and tails, they were sifting through the water, though their movement was certainly more at the mercy of the currents than of their own volition.

He could scarcely breathe, he was so mystified. *There is a living biology here.* Before he came to Antarctica, he assumed that if there had been anything alive down here, it would have been some single-celled bacteria. Certainly not crustaceans.

He knew that, on the earth above, brine shrimp like these were at the bottom of a very long and very large food chain. But, doubtless, there could be nothing larger than these tiny shrimp in these conditions.

Almost with a sense of foreboding, he gazed farther out into the darkness, as far as the lights shone. *What else might be beyond, in the black unknown?* He desperately wished he could communicate to the surface, but of course that was impossible.

He knew Doctor Toskovic's submersible would be coming, so he decided to pilot his farther away from the chamber to avoid any collision. The whir of the electric motors was somehow comforting as he maneuvered down and out into the deep. On a screen underneath the glass, a pinging dot showed the location of the pressurizing chamber moving off from the center.

In this darkness he would certainly have no way of knowing where the exit was if the beacon failed.

He grew alarmed as he noticed the beacon moving faster than it should have been. Looking out through the bubble, he could see that he was not really moving independently of the shrimp, but that they were all heading in the same direction, in the same current. He quickly reversed the propulsion. This slowed his vessel somewhat, with the shrimp rushing on past—but it only worked momentarily. Before he could even think, the craft swung around and he could sense that he was traveling at a great rate of speed. Extremely anxious, he fumbled with the joysticks to try to escape the current, but this only succeeded in causing the submarine to spiral wildly. The beacon drifted away from center ever more swiftly and his heart began to pound in his chest as he felt both a panic overcoming him as well as an onslaught of claustrophobia.

In desperation, he cried out, "Command! Can you hear me?" But of course his suppressed, logical mind knew that they could not. He was in the grip of total terror, and he was hurling into the abyss.

## Cognitive LifeScience Corporation
## Laboratory G

The laboratory had a white tiled ceiling with fluorescent lights. All the walls except one were lined with counters and on those were bunches of plastic bins, a slew of scientific instruments, and a solitary microscope. Jutting out from the back wall were giant rectangular gray boxes with metallic frames. In the middle of the room was a broad, totally empty stainless steel table. This is what Abael saw as he stared into the large glass windows from his wheelchair in the sterile hallway.

A ding at an elevator down the hall sounded and the doors opened. A man in a white lab coat emerged carrying a foot-wide semitransparent bin that was sealed shut. The contents of the bin were indistinguishable, but blood was smeared all over the inside. When the man saw Abael, he smiled as he approached, "What brings you to our little house of horrors today, Mr. Fiedler?"

"I wanted to know that you're doing well."

Now in front of Abael, the man said, "You didn't have to come all the way down here; I would have answered the phone." He lowered the bin down to Abael's level, "Could you hold this a second?"

"Certainly," Abael replied, taking the bin in his lap. "You know how enamored I am with your work. Call it a fetish."

The man held the back of his hand up to a reader by the door and a click sounded. He pushed the door open and held it for Abael, who motorized himself in. When they were both inside, the other man took the bin and set it on the steel table. Then he gathered some supplies from the nearby counter: several rectangular green plates, a long and very sharp looking knife, a ruler and a tray. He took a roll of thin plastic and spread a few sheets of it on the stainless steel table. Finally, he snapped on a pair of blue latex gloves, and he was ready.

He opened the bin, revealing a bloody, globular brain. His movements rapid but adept, he lifted the organ out and placed it on the tray.

"May I hold it?" Abael asked.

The other man paused, looking uneasy. "Why would you want to do that?"

"Now, Gary, I told you how fascinated I am with your work. I want to get as intimate with it as possible."

Doctor Gary Riley took a deep breath, "I really don't think—"

Suddenly angry, Abael snapped, "Do I need to remind you who's paying your salary?"

Gary nervously shrugged his shoulders, "If you want to hold it, I guess you can hold it." He went to the glove dispenser and pulled some out, but when he tried to hand them to Abael, the man just shook his head. So Gary took the brain and placed it in Abael's waiting hands.

Abael ran his fingers over the folds of the tissue. The blood was trickling onto his lap, but he didn't seem to mind. "Amazing how heavy it is. What was so special about this one?"

"She had progeria. It's deathly-rapid aging. They rarely live past their teens."

Abael suddenly looked less enthusiastic. He handed the organ back to Gary with a wry smile. "I think I prefer less imperfect specimens."

Gary placed the brain back on the tray. Abael's eager gaze made Gary feel very self-conscious as he grasped the knife and began cutting the organ methodically as if he were slicing a loaf of bread. He took each of the slices and spread it out on one of the green plates.

The rest of the process was like clockwork. He would feed the trays to the huge box-shaped robot behind him. This would in turn further divide the brain into slices only several microns in width and spread each of these onto a new plate. Then another robot would utilize a process called *in situ* hybridization to explore every last sample for a certain gene sequence by highlighting them with RNA dye. Then another robot, this one equipped with digital microscopes, would take photographs of each slide, quantifying the amount of gene expression within each area. All of this data would be stored through tremendous computer power and further analyzed by scientists.

Gary's only question was "why?"

Day in and day out he worked at Cognitive Lifescience. Each day, samples were delivered by nondescript white vans. Day after day he performed the analysis, and day after day he wondered what it was all for.

When he had come to Cognitive LifeScience, he was instructed that the work was a matter of national security and that he couldn't disclose the details to anyone. A miniscule RFID (radio frequency identification) chip had been inserted under the skin of his left hand. To access the lab, or any of the computers in it, he had to press his hand against a sensor. At first, he found this unnerving, but eventually he came to appreciate the convenience of not having to type in passwords.

Everyone at Cognitive LifeScience was working on behalf of the mysterious program, but none of them admitted to actually understanding what it was about. And, given everything he had seen so far, it was impossible to piece it together either. Discrete searches on the computers had not provided him with any meat. All he knew was that when you heard the word *Preseption*, you did whatever you were told.

That was the name of the project. Preseption.

At any hour of night or day, he would receive calls from anonymous people on a secured phone Cognitive provided. Most of them were questions: "What would this do?" "Was there a gene for that?" "Have you ever heard of such-and-such?" "How much data was there on this?"

Some of the calls, however, were directives. "You'll be working on this now." "You'll be looking for the gene for that now." "Find out where this is."

From time to time, he received calls and visits from Abael himself. Those were mostly to ask, "Is everything going okay? Is there anything you need?"

Gary's problem was that it just wasn't very gratifying to work for a big "why." But Cognitive paid so well (incredibly well, in fact) that Gary wasn't motivated enough to look elsewhere for more fulfilling work.

And that was mysterious in itself. If this program was of importance to national security and so secretive, why did they not take any steps to determine how loyal he was to the nation? They just gave him big fat checks. It seemed to Gary that people engaged in such supposedly top secret, national security-type work shouldn't be doing it simply for the money. They should be doing it for love of country.

And yet, here he was. And he hadn't heard from China or Russia yet, so apparently Preseption was still a well-kept secret. Either that or, and this is what he really suspected, the whole thing simply wasn't that important after all.

Abael's voice sounded behind him, "Do you ever receive extra samples? I mean samples you don't use?"

"Well, I don't know where the samples come from. But I'm sure they are very expensive, so there wouldn't be extras."

"I see," Abael said, frustrated. "What about extra pieces? You know, parts of the brain you don't use."

"We use all of it."

"Oh. Well, do let me know if something extra does turn up."

Gary didn't think he would let Abael know even if one *did* turn up, but he said, "Sure."

"Gary, I truly appreciate the work you're doing here. I know you are kind of in the dark about its purpose, but I can assure you it's of prime importance to the nation."

"So I've been told."

"The world is going to change dramatically. You will soon understand just how pivotal your work has been."

"I wouldn't mind knowing now."

Abael's eyes dropped down to Gary's crotch, which he pointedly stared at, "I'd need to know the extent of your loyalty." He then gazed directly into Gary's eyes. Seductive. "What are you willing to do for your nation?" He raised his hand to touch Gary's thigh.

Gary fidgeted uncomfortably. "Uh . . . ."

Abael's eyes grew cold. He dropped his hand. "I'm sorry we couldn't come to an understanding."

Gary didn't say anything.

"Do let me know if you come up with any extra samples."

"Sure," Gary replied.

"Help me with the door, will you?"

"Sure," Gary said, jumping to go hold it open. He couldn't get there fast enough.

When he passed Gary on the way out the door, Abael stopped. Staring straight ahead, he said, "You know, I usually get what I want." Then he raised his eyes to look at Gary with an aura of possession, as if he owned him, "It's part of the deal."

"What deal?"

He smiled wickedly, "Oh, being the President's right hand man." Then the motor whirred as his wheelchair propelled him forward.

As Abael wheeled out and down the hallway towards the elevator, Gary felt a strange, sick feeling building inside him. Abael was beginning to seem like a psycho, and a scary one at that. Besides the veiled threat, his request for the extra tissues was troubling, to say the least. What could he possibly want with them?

Beyond sickening him, Abael's visit left Gary with a question. Where *did* the samples come from? He wanted to know more about what this was all about and what he was contributing to. If he found the source of the samples, perhaps he could discover more of the truth. But without the truth, he had no reason to stick around.

Anyway, in a few hours he would be home, and a few hours after that, he would be doing what he truly lived for these days.

## Cairo International Airport

She held out her hand, "I am glad to finally meet you in person, Doctor Katz." She had long well-defined eyebrows that were perfectly arched over large, brown eyes, highlighted by purple eye shadow. Her loose, airy top and pants were not enough to disguise her attractive figure, and the head scarf she wore only enhanced the mystique of her beauty.

No matter how attractive she was, though, to Doctor David Katz, she was off-limits. He was a widower with three children, and not looking. But aside from that, the fact that he was a Jew just off the plane from Israel and that she was a betrothed Muslim in Egypt was more than enough to prevent a relationship.

Doctor Katz thought, as he often did in these situations, that it was odd how people from different countries frequently had to resort to English if neither of them knew the other's language. *It was Babel.*

Shaking her hand, he smiled, "No more email! Thank you for picking me up, Miss Fayed."

"Call me Layla," she said seriously.

He was the head of Middle Eastern and African History at Tel Aviv University, a position he had only recently, lamentably accepted after the sudden death of his mentor.

Doctor Katz had happened across Layla's blog via an internet search for "mummy DNA." She was an amateur historian studying at the Cairo University and had authored reams of well-documented data on the pharaohs; especially about Akhenaten. On her blog, she frequently diverged from the official Egyptian Ministry of Antiquity talking points and even criticized the ministry's head for what she called "self-aggrandizing tactics." This freedom of expression was very rare for Egyptian scholars, particularly those who didn't want to kill their careers.

Especially intriguing to Doctor Katz was one article in which she outlined why she believed the notorious KV55 mummy could not possibly be Akhenaten, as the Ministry said, and created a different family tree for Tutankhamen than the Ministry's.

Doctor Katz prided himself on being open-minded. That is why he had emailed her and a frequent dialogue had begun; anything that challenged the status quo attracted his attention.

Beautiful young women also attracted his attention, and his work as a professor at a university full of them was usually enough to satisfy his appetite—and had frequently been enough to get him into trouble with his late wife of five years. Of course, he never did anything more than look, but he didn't think his wife had ever believed him when he had declared himself innocent.

His wife certainly had not shared his fascination with the past as his students did. The most he had ever got out of her when he had tried to share his excitement was a sigh; usually she had rebuked him to "save his lectures for the university."

In addition to lecturing, he spent a great deal of time with his students at archeological digs or visiting his connections at museums and colleges to chase down answers to little mysteries he discovered. In the evenings, he was generally found with his students at their usual haunts; bars, clubs and even their dormitories.

The truth was, Doctor Katz was hip; he couldn't help it. To emphasize the point, he wore a bandana on his head, a chain around his neck with a silver star of David, and loose-fitting clothes. He was never clean-shaven, preferring to look more on the adventurous side.

Through all their internet exchanges, he had somehow been imagining some mole-faced, older woman with glasses, a head covering, and a big drape-like kaftan. That's why he was surprised to see now that Layla was young, brilliant and appraising him with her gorgeous eyes.

She said, "A taxi will take us to the museum. There I will show you my discovery."

As they walked, Doctor Katz sensed Layla's eyes look him over again, and narrow. She wasn't impressed. Despite her youth, she apparently didn't appreciate his casual appearance the way his students did. She probably took it to indicate incompetence.

He had faced this kind of prejudice over and over again among elderly scholars, and every time had proven it baseless. How ironic that now he faced the same skepticism from a youthful beauty. Doctor Katz was nothing if not competent, and he would prove it to her.

When they slipped into the back seat of a taxi, Layla asked the driver, "Do you speak English?"

In English, he said, "No," and shook his head.

"In Arabic, she instructed him to take them to the Cairo Museum.

As they rode in the taxi, Layla slipped some documents out of a briefcase and got down to business. It was a chilly day in Cairo, but fortunately it wasn't too chilly for the windows to be open: the driver's odor was foul.

The KV55 tomb was discovered in 1907 in the same area of the Valley of the Kings as the Ramesses II, Tutankhamen and other notorious pharaohs' tombs. The mummy inside KV55 had never been successfully identified, however. Several possibilities for an identity were put forward, but there had never been any way to conclusively decide who it was.

When DNA analysis was finally performed on it, as well as a number of mummies found in nearby KV35, some supposed facts were presented by the Ministry. First was that KV55 was Akhenaten, the pharaoh famous for introducing worship of a single god, Aten, to the Egyptians. This religion lasted only as long as Akhenaten did, and there was a great deal of mystery surrounding what happened to his notoriously beautiful wife, Nefertiti. Some said that she ruled after Akhenaten died. Some said that another person from the family, "Smenkhare" perhaps, had seized the throne. Everyone agreed, however, that Tutankhamen ruled after this brief period of uncertainty.

Layla showed him the Ministry's version of Tutankhamen's family

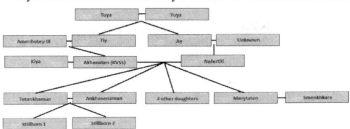

line:

Amenhotep III and Tiye bore Akhenaten who then fathered Tutankhamun with Nefertiti (his cousin).

She had reasoned that, given obvious allele generational jumps, the DNA showed that the stillborn fetuses could not have been maternally grandfathered by the KV55 mummy, which the Ministry proposed was Akhenaten. (An allele was an alternative form—by mutation—of a gene located in a certain place on a certain chromosome.)

She showed him her own version of the family tree:

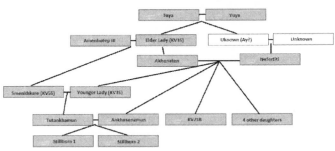

Amenhotep III and the mummy known as the "elder lady" in tomb KV35 had borne Akhenaten who then, with Nefertiti (his cousin), bore the mummy known as the "younger lady" in KV35. Smenkhare, who very likely was the KV55 mummy, fathered Tutankhamen through this "younger lady."

If Layla's version was accurate, it would mean that the Akhenaten mummy was still missing. Since virtually every record of his existence was defaced, destroyed, or disassembled by subsequent Pharaohs, this was not surprising.

At least Doctor Katz wasn't surprised. That is, he wasn't until she dropped the bombshell.

"I asked you to come, Doctor Katz, because you are the only one I trust," she said.

"I hope I am worthy of it. You said you've made a very big discovery and I had to come down here right away."

"Yes."

"So what was this discovery?"

"Akhenaten's mummy is in the museum basement. It was there all along."

He just stared at her, dumbfounded.

She said, "He was hidden. They didn't want anyone to see him."

"Why?"

"The same reason all the Pharaohs tried to erase his memory."

"What reason is that?"

"Look at these pictures. See if you notice anything strange."

She showed him a series of paintings of Akhenaten and his family, and a photograph of one small statue.

"I've seen all these before," Doctor Katz said. "You mean besides his feminine shape? Nothing looks strange to me."

"The strange thing is that Akhenaten is huge. Look how much taller he is than Nefertiti, even when they are seated. And look at this little statue of Akhenaten with his daughter on his lap. That's not his daughter at all. That's his *wife*."

Doctor Katz reexamined the images. He protested, "But Pharaohs are usually pictured taller than those around them in ancient Egyptian art."

"Yes, but not *this* much taller. And look at this, even his chief general Horemheb was a giant," she pulled out another image.

"Layla," he chided. "You must know that artwork is rarely proportionate. If aliens from outer space ever receive images from today's media, they would think all our women look like wasps."

She rolled her eyes so quickly it was barely discernible, "Yes, but *look at him.* If this was proportionate, he would be three to four meters tall at least! This isn't a simple exaggeration. This is a representation of fact."

"So you're saying he was a giant?"

"No, he was more than just a giant," she said emphatically.

"What do you mean?"

"I'll show you his mummy. You can see for yourself."

## 24 Oakland Street

"Daddy, I saw eyes."

The words made Doctor Gary Riley's heart skip a beat. It was his little two-year-old, Jeffery, standing by the leather office chair and looking up at him. The little guy had just come from his room and he had said the words matter-of-factually, without an iota of enthusiasm.

Gary collected himself. Jeffery was smart for his age, a certified genius by MENSA, in fact, but genius or not, like all two-year-old's, you couldn't know for sure what he was saying. Gary inquired, "What did you see?"

"Daddy, I saw eyes."

It sounded like "eyes," but it could have been "lights." Maybe Jeffery was talking about the sun. "You saw lights?"

"Yes Daddy, I saw eyes."

Jeffery's bedroom was on the second floor, so Gary wasn't concerned about a window peeker. But out of an abundance of caution, he stood and said, "Show me."

Come see," Jeffery exclaimed, leading the way. He was excited now, if only because his father was following him.

When they reached the room, Jeffery pointed out the window, where the edge of the sun was visible just disappearing under the horizon. "See eyes."

"Oh, that's the sun setting. It isn't an eye; it's just the sun going away for the day."

"Sun going away! Eyes go away?"

"Yes. The sun is going away, but it's just a light. It's not eyes."

"Eyes run away!"

Gary scratched his neck and yawned. Storytelling. "I'm going back to my office. I'm still busy working."

"Going your office? Okay! See you later, Daddy!"

Gary knew that "later" meant two minutes, max.

That's the way the entire evening had been. Jeffery had been in again, out again, in again, out again. And his wife Stacy wasn't getting home for another three-and-a-half hours. Gary hadn't done much of anything for the gene project he was supposed to deliver in the morning.

Fortunately, it was almost little Jeffery's bedtime.

And then, with little Jeffery in bed, he could do what he really wanted to do, what he had been thinking about all day. What he thought about very nearly all the time these days.

Just a few more minutes . . . .

## 24 Oakland Street

Investigators were crawling over every nook and cranny of the house. Police were swarming outside with flashlights. A K9 unit had arrived and the dogs were barking with excitement.

But Gary Riley sat on his couch with his head between his hands, his hair disheveled from repeatedly running his fingers through it. His wife, Stacy, was beside him, her eyes red, her mascara smeared on her cheeks. FBI special agent, Jarred Kessler, sat on the coffee table in front of them. He was inquiring, "Did you notice anything suspicious, tonight or maybe before?"

Gary looked up, shaking his head with his hands covering his mouth, "*Oh my* . . . . Why didn't I listen?"

"Listen to what?" the agent asked.

"Tonight, Jeffery told me that he saw eyes. I asked him to show me, and he pointed outside his window. But the sun was setting. *I thought he said 'lights.'*" Stacy stared at her husband's face with disbelief. She didn't say anything, but her absolute hate for him was obvious.

"What time did he say he saw eyes?" the agent asked.

"It was about 7:30."

"Okay, so he said he saw eyes at 7:30. Then you put him to bed at 8:00. You went to work on your computer, and that's what you were doing when your wife came home at 11:10. She went into the bedroom and saw that your son was not there. You called 911. That's right?"

Gary nodded grimly, "Yes."

The agent continued, "Now, I noticed that if I opened a door or window, your alarm chimes. Did you hear a chime at all between 8:00 and 11:30?"

"No. But the alarm was set on 'stay.' It would have gone off had anything opened."

"Were you listening to any music or watching TV?"

"No, just working on the computer. I had a big report due tomorrow. But the alarm is loud, I would have heard it even if I had headphones on."

Abruptly, the agent said, "Well, that's all I have for you now. I'll be in touch." He stood and extended a hand.

Gary just looked up at him sadly and mustered an appreciative nod.


Special Agent Jarred Kessler stepped out the door and down a long lawn of grass to the police cruiser where Captain Trey Wiggins leaned.

"So what did you find?" Wiggins asked.

"Nothing."

"Nothing?"

"Yeah, nothing. This case is not solvable."

"Oh, c'mon, Jarred. You're just getting lazy."

Jarred looked the captain in the eye, "The kid is two. Nobody kidnaps a two-year-old except in child custody cases. No window was broken and the kid's bedroom is on the second floor. So the only way anyone could have gotten in is by opening a door and strolling in. But the alarm was set, and if one of the doors or windows had opened, it would have sounded and the dad would have heard it. Plus, the dad was sitting in the room right next to where the kid was sleeping, and he didn't hear a thing."

Wiggins didn't look impressed. "What if the creep snuck in and was waiting before?"

"How did he get out of the house? The alarm would have gone off." Jarred shook his head, "Oh, and the kid's pj's were on the bed under his blanket, laid out like he had just been wearing them."

Wiggins clapped Jarred on the back, "This is easy. The dad killed him and hid the body."

"I don't think so. It didn't feel that way."

"You'll see. Just keep digging."

Jarred looked up at the night sky. The stars were clear as crystal. He shook his head, "No, it wasn't the dad. It was something else." Then he slipped a folded paper out of his pocket and opened it up. He had found it in the child's bedroom, and it made the hair on his neck stand on end when he saw it.

"*What is that*?" Wiggins intoned in a low voice.

"I found it in the boy's room. He must have drawn it."

Wiggins looked Jarred in the eye, squinting, "Kid had nightmares?"

Jarred looked back down at the crayon markings, "I hope so." But he thought, "When you have eliminated the impossible, whatever remains, however improbable, must be the truth."


That night, Gary went to sleep on a futon in his office: Stacy didn't want him anywhere near her, as usual. As he lay down, staring up at the dark ceiling, he thought to himself about the secret he had kept. He had not told Special Agent Jarred Kessler the entire truth about what had happened that night. And if Stacy knew the entire truth, she probably would want him in hell, not merely on the futon.


# Flight


The next morning they were supposed to have flown out at five o'clock.

But they were delayed.

As soon as Aubrey followed Henry and Maggie aboard the aircraft, they were greeted by Jinkins in his safari garb. An old-fashioned and well-worn suitcase was sitting at his feet where he stood in the lounge. Lorraine was also there, and at the sight of Henry's displeasure, immediately explained that she had allowed Jinkins aboard when he claimed to have been invited.

Jinkins himself also chimed in, "I truly thought that since you couldn't come on the tour you'd enjoy having me to consult for you in China."

"What could possibly have given you that impression?" Henry blustered.

"Someone," he replied with a frown. Then his face lit up with relief and he said, "And by 'someone' I mean her." He pointed behind Henry.

A strong voice answered from where he pointed, "It was indeed I who requested him, Henry." Lady Shrewsbury was standing there wearing an enormous straw hat and frock. "I am going to continue enjoying what the island has to offer, but Jinkins will generously be donating his time to you in China."

Henry said, "I would very much prefer that he *not* be so generous."

She barked, "Indeed he will! It will be up to you to decide whether to utilize his counsel." When Henry began to protest, Lady Shrewsbury raised her eyebrows and said, "I'm quite through listening to your grievances, Mr. Potter. You make me feel like Moses with the tribe in the desert, and I'm not nearly that old yet. Now, go on your Mandarin holiday if you insist, but do not dilly-dally. I'd like to see you apply yourself to something more productive than burning jet fuel."

After they took off, Henry informed Aubrey that she would be spending her time flipping pages of a contract he was signing. They sat in his office together on opposite sides of his desk. Aubrey skimmed some of the pages, but it was just nauseous legalese, so she was very relieved when the door swung open. Jinkins stood there smiling agreeably, and said, "I need to tell you something, Mr. Potter, if you have a minute."

"I don't have a minute."

"It's of great importance, sir."

"It can't be as important as this contract. Remind me later."

Aubrey felt sorry for the older man and would have rather spent her time with him, but she was a prisoner in Henry's office it seemed. She wondered why he needed someone to flip pages for him. He had clearly grown too accustomed to being waited on hand and foot.

Just when she couldn't stand the boredom any longer, Henry suddenly shocked her by saying, "Would you like to know why we are going to China?"

Aubrey blurted, "Yes! And what's this contract about? It's as long as the Bible!"

"It's about the machines that are hopefully going to staff Paradeisia."

"What machines?"

Henry drew a breath and said, "Genetically engineered machines."

Aubrey's eyes narrowed. "What are those?"

Henry shrugged, and explained, "Economical sources of labor have been exhausted. This has been a growing problem for every company I know. The Chinese have adopted a western lifestyle much like the Japanese; and, much like the Japanese, wages in China and the rest of Asia for production-line work has increased beyond cost-benefit ratios. Africa was expected to become the cheap labor pool for the West and for the East, but civil upheavals and disease have continued to make commerce relatively risky in certain parts, and the developed parts have the same labor problems we do. Where there is peace, cheap labor is simply not available. People won't do what they consider to be menial work.

"China has already been in the designer babies business for a long time now—in fact, they beat the west to the punch  When it was new and relatively cheap there, many US babies were 'made in China." But designer babies were only a stepping stone towards the efforts to develop designer personnel, so to speak."

"Now of course it would be ethically irresponsible to grow babies and have them work jobs. Even if, technically, you created them, it would still be considered slavery. So there isn't a genetics lab anywhere in the world that hasn't been searching for the 'self' gene. To create workers that are capable of most everything humans are but do not have self-awareness, a desire for self-fulfillment or genuine emotions. Everyone knew the 'self' gene had to be discovered.

"Well China found the self gene first, and now their genetically engineered bipedals are going to revolutionize the world economy, I believe.

"Instead of *finding* low-wage workers, corporations are already *growing* them. Unlike robots or other machines which demand constant repair and inevitably require replacement, genetically engineered workers should be good for at least forty years, probably closer to sixty, need nothing more than nourishment and seven hours of sleep, repair themselves in most cases, are capable of creative response, and are able to perform relatively complex tasks repeatedly without tiring or wearing.

"Best of all, they are reproduced; not built. In other words, once you line up the genes you want, it is virtually free labor.

"China has created machines that can be trained in a multitude of tasks as well as ones that specialized in creative response, such as rescue agents, greeters, and personal attendants. The programming of the machines is not at all similar to computers. No software code is uploaded; nor is a machine immediately ready for its new occupation upon birth. They are learners.

"China has been able to instill some instincts through rapid reproduction and a keen understanding of epigenetics, but the majority of their abilities are taught. At an early age, positive/negative response circuits are installed inside the brains of each machine. When a machine does something good, it is rewarded with a tiny shock to pleasure nodes. When one does something bad, it is reprimanded with a negative signal. This is technology that was successfully experimented on in rats as early as the 1990s.

"Initially, the genetically engineered machines were grown in women hired as child bearers. Soon after the project began, however, China grew machines for the sole purpose of birthing more machines.

"China now has a massive, machine-bearing factory in Shanghai where hundreds of specimens are produced daily.

"I have never used this technology before because it wasn't perfect yet, but now I have read that it is ready for primetime and I am hoping to save Paradeisia with it. The labor costs on the island as they stand now are unsustainable, particularly if we don't meet the attendance goals we'll need to meet. But, based on data Maggie obtained for me, from merchandise producers to greeters to ride operators to housekeepers to chefs to store clerks, over eighty percent of Paradeisia's labor force could be these genetically engineered machines."

Aubrey instantly disapproved of this idea. It sounded freakish. "So you'd have a bunch of Frankensteins crawling around all over the island?"

He smiled at her patronizingly, "No. The customer-facing ones would look just like people."

"If they look just like people, doesn't that make them people?"

"Certainly not. With the 'self'' gene removed, they don't even know they exist."

"They don't have to know they exist to be people."

"Don't be ridiculous. From what I understand, they are entirely dependent upon us to function. Their DNA makes them look somewhat human—more so in some cases than in others, but otherwise they are not what I would even call 'animals.' They can't feed themselves. Many of them can't talk. Most of them don't have the creative intelligence of an ape. They are classified as an entirely new species under a different genus than humans. And even if they were people, which they are not, but even if they were; *we* created them. Doesn't that give us the right to determine their fate?"

"You created them? So now you're God?"

"There is no God."

"Well you didn't create them out of nothing, did you?"

"The entire universe didn't come from nothing."

"And these things were made from the parts of other creatures. So that means you didn't create them, you *assembled* them."

"Created, assembled, whatever you want to call it. They're ours, made for our own purposes, just like anything mankind makes."

Aubrey said, "Are we going to see these things in China?"

"Yes, that's why we're on our way."

"Well I hope they *do* look like freaks. Then you won't buy them."

"That would depend," Henry grinned, "on the price."

## CDC

Karen was standing at the head of a huge conference table that had a vast screen built into its surface. An officer in uniform and several other well-dressed people stood around the table with her.

Unlike her usual aggressive stance, she now appeared somber, even defeated, as she said, "You all know the President hasn't had a cabinet meeting in forever. We've all functioned well enough without them, and we all meet individually as we find the time or need. But I think you'd agree, it's long overdue, especially with the situation we're facing. I asked him first. He refused. So that's why I've asked you here.

"As you all know by now, a virus of unknown origin has been on the loose, and it has been kicking us in the balls. I secured an executive order to quarantine Towson as things were heating up. To get that accomplished, I had to pull teeth.

"I will be sending the President a new executive order request. This one goes far beyond what any of us imagined might be required when this thing first began. My next request will have repercussions for the entire nation, perhaps for years to come—regardless of the outcome of our fight against this virus. So I'll need each and every one of you to be on the same page with me when I present the new order.

"Now, before we get into that, I have General Fox here to report on the quarantine situation so far." She nodded to the uniformed man.

General Fox, a solemn-looking man with thick eyebrows and a large bald head, motioned to the screen where a map of Towson was displayed, "Right now, we've sealed Towson in on I-83 on the west and 695 on the north. We've sealed the south on West/East Northern Parkway. And Route 542 closes off the east. That's an area of seventeen square miles. We have eyes watching every inch of that perimeter. I guarantee you, if anyone has sneaked through, they're invisible.

"We've had just shy of thirty thousand cases outside the Towson quarantine area. Every new case outside of Towson—all thirty thousand, and anyone who is connected with them by Epidemic Intelligence Services—is brought into Towson.

"Of Towson residents, there have been 12,000 fatalities that appear to be directly from the virus. He paused, seemingly to digest his own words.

Someone said, "You're saying that this virus has killed 12,000 people?"

"No, I said the body count from Towson is 12,000. The body count of those brought into our quarantine zone is 17,500."

Karen said, "To do the math for those of you who want to turn this into a numbers game, the total is 27,852 . Eighty-five percent of those are female."

The cabinet members around the table were dumbfounded.

Finally, someone said, "How could twenty-eight thousand people die like that and we haven't even heard there was a major problem? I mean I know I'm only Secretary of Commerce, but. . ."

Karen said, "I think you could ask the President that question. The fact that he isn't even here speaks volumes."

"But Karen, *you* could have called us."

"*I am calling you!* Right now! This thing has happened in a matter of days. On Monday we discovered it was an unknown virus. On Wednesday we had quarantined the hospital. Then, before we know it, five are dead. Towson is quarantined. All hell broke loose. It's been a week-and-a-half since this thing began. A—" she cursed, "—week-and-a-half and twenty-eight thousand dead."

Lisa Ching, the Secretary of Agriculture and a close friend of Karen's, said, "We don't need to cast blame here. Karen has clearly done the best she could have with the resources she's had. Let's just see how to move forward, shall we?"

Karen nodded appreciatively. Karen paused to allow them to further digest the information. Then turning to the General, she said, "General Fox, will you please tell them about the camp situation inside Towson."

General Fox said, "We have a camp established where we're housing and feeding anyone who is homeless as a result of confinement. But the camp is overcrowded and we're running out of room to erect new tents. We are starting a new camp on the golf course at Towson's country club but that's not going to last long. In short, we cannot sustain this. We don't have room in Towson for the scale of this disaster."

Karen said, "Doctor Compton, fill them in on the hospital situation, will you?"

There was silence. She looked around, but he wasn't there.

Terrific, she thought, my greatest ally has fled the battle.

Doctor Giordano volunteered, "I can tell them."

She exhaled, "Beggars can't be chooser. Go ahead."

Doctor Giordano said, "Every new case that happens outside of Towson is brought in. About sixty-five percent of new cases result in fatality. We have been stacking and cremating the bodies in the stadium across the street from St. Joseph's Medical Center. The hospital originally had 305 beds. Now we have taken over the Center for the Arts and a large portion of the university nearby. Many of the staff from St. Joseph's walked off the job when this first began to get serious, and all around the area word's gotten out. Nurses and doctors are leaving in droves. The U.S. Army doctors are filling in at St. Joseph's, but it's becoming exceedingly impractical. We don't have room, even with the buildings we've taken over, to deal with this."

Karen said, "Tell them about the geography of the virus, if you can."

Doctor Giordano said, "The virus has infiltrated the entire Baltimore area, including the suburbs. There have been a couple hundred cases in the D.C. region. Beyond those zones, we haven't traced a single case."

Karen said, "The gestation period for this seems to be about four or five days. The problem is that, by the time any symptom develops, you are minutes from death if it's going to kill you. Then there's the fact that men are carriers but only one in six even shows a symptom, but most women die within less than a week of contracting it. So, with Towson quarantined, that's 70,000 in isolation. But it's still spreading in Baltimore, as he said. So we quarantine the million in the Baltimore area and we stop this thing dead. We trace anyone who has left the area and we bring them back to Baltimore. If we have to, we shut down air traffic. Everywhere. But if we quarantine Baltimore, we get the facilities we need, the space we need. We bring all the sick into the city. Baltimore dies, but the nation is saved.

"The fact is that all the interviews, all the fact-gathering hasn't done a thing for us. We still don't have a clue who's going to drop dead in the next five minutes. So we have to shut it down here and we have to shut it down now. I need your support on this. Can I count on it?"

There was a moment of silence. General Fox asked, "How do you propose we execute such a quarantine? Confining over a million people to that large an area is not something we are prepared to do. People would get out."

"You're telling me that with heat-seeking technologies and all the resources of the military we couldn't accomplish this?"

"I'm telling you that we don't have the manpower."

## Lake Vostok

Doctor Ming-Zhen had gained the composure to think of releasing the controls. This eventually stopped the dizzying spinning of the vessel, but he was still hurling into the unknown with the cloud of shrimp.

Oddly, the water had seemed to grow less black: he could detect a source of ambient light somewhere ahead. The current was slowing, but he jumped in the vest that held him when a craggy projection of ice passed right by the view port.

With dismay, he saw the dot on the screen blink one last time before disappearing out of range. He knew the range to be five miles. It was incredible to think he had been carried that far this quickly. He remembered reading somewhere that, because the ice was not the same thickness from west to east over the lake, varying pressures could cause currents. They certainly had never anticipated currents this strong, however.

It was then that he noticed how warm he was. Looking at the screen, he saw the temperature: 67 degrees—a far cry from the -3 degrees they had anticipated. Indeed, the submersible was equipped to warm him, but nobody would have thought in a million years that a *cooling* function would be necessary. He tugged at the neck of his wetsuit uncomfortably.

He could tell he was almost free-floating now, and the current was minimal. The shrimp cloud was beginning to disperse away from him (or perhaps he was moving away from the cloud). This led to an increasing clarity in the water.

Fiddling with the controls, he was able to level the submarine and propel forward, through the shrimp. As he neared the edge of the cloud, he saw the outlines of giant ice structures that protruded down into the water from the ceiling.

Looking up to the craggy, inverted mountains of ice, he noticed that the water did not touch the ice everywhere: there were areas where he could see the bottoms of waves. There must be pockets of air.

He engaged a thruster to steer down to avoid one of the structures, and when he leveled the vehicle and looked up again, what he saw made him draw a breath in awe.

Frozen within the next monolithic ice formation was the dark outline of a gigantic creature. A large, tapering tail, four gigantic flippers, a huge body, and an incredibly long neck which extended out of view. He immediately recognized it. This was an elasmosaurus, the ancient Loch-Ness monster. The largest fossil found had been almost fifty feet long.

He could hardly believe what he was seeing. Here he was, witness to a more perfectly preserved ancient species than any paleontologist could dream of, but he was trapped two miles under ice with very remote odds of returning. Frozen as perfectly as it appeared to be, this specimen could surely provide DNA, and answer more questions than science had even thought to ask. He was filled with a surreal sense of wonder, and yet despair quickly overcame him.

He looked down at the screen again. There was no beacon. Naturally, nobody had thought a compass would be necessary, so he did not even know what direction he was facing. How could he possibly get back to the pressure chamber? The submersible had power for no more than fifty-seven hours and could travel at a maximum of five miles per hour. After that, life support wouldn't be possible, let alone propulsion.

He remembered Doctor Toskovic's compass. *Where was Doctor Toskovic?*

Doctor Ming-Zhen looked up. He froze in immediate terror.

A giant, dead-looking, green eye was outside the viewport. It was certainly not dead, though, because it twitched as it examined his submersible. The eye was part of an eight-foot, flat-shaped head with sharp teeth protruding out from the jaw. The teeth at the end of the snout were especially jagged and long. He traced the head back to a neck, and this neck he followed up and around to the ice. The frozen elasmosaur in the ice was not frozen at all; its body was silhouetted *behind* the ice, and it was moving. The flippers were sifting very slowly through the water, and now they propelled the body slowly downward.

As he looked at the elasmosaur's head, he was overcome with the impression that this was a terrifying animal; not at all what he, or anyone else, had imagined. The skin was a dull green color, patterned with diamonds. Undulating frills of vibrant crimson flared out from the back of the head and all the way down the neck, from the top of the body, and the tail.

With the flippers paddling slowly to keep the body motionless, the extraordinarily long neck propelled the head around his submersible, coiling like a snake. While horrifying, this was also astonishing to him because he knew that recent research on fossils from the creature had concluded the neck to be about as flexible as a giraffe's. Of course, there was also recent research that had concluded that dinosaur vertebrae were much farther apart than science had long assumed, and although elasmosaurs were not dinosaurs, it could still—he stopped his mind short. *What difference did it make now?  Here was the animal in the flesh.*

He felt his submersible jolt alarmingly as the creature spiraled its neck around it to clench it tight.  The head was poised above the viewport bubble, and the mouth slowly opened, revealing the full array of teeth and a long, forked tongue.

Hoping against hope that the titanium and acrylic glass would hold against this onslaught, Doctor Ming-Zhen wondered why the beast would, by all appearances, be trying to *eat* his submersible.  By fossil's stomach contents, elasmosaurs were known to eat fish, clams, snails, crabs, and squid.  *Squid.*  The submarine looked like a squid.

The giant jaws clamped down on the viewport, and a grating sound erupted as the teeth scraped along the acrylic glass, chiseling long lines on its surface.

What could he do to make the submersible look less like a squid?

Looking puzzled, if that was possible for its hideous face, the elasmosaur pulled back and surveyed its prize.  *Maybe it would just go away.*  Cocking its head to peer closely with one of its dead-green eyes, Doctor Ming-Zhen had the distinct impression the creature was looking directly at *him.*

It knows I'm in here.

He tried to be totally motionless, but it was to no avail, because the mouth came down firmly on the bubble again, this time from a different angle.  The teeth scraped horizontally across as the beast seemed to be trying to pry the submersible open by brute force.  *It's intelligent,*

Doctor Ming-Zhen thought...*and tenacious.* He struggled to think of something he could do to stop it, and the only thing that came to mind was to switch off the lights.

Unfortunately, the only way to turn *all* the lights off, including those in the cabin, was to shut the submersible down.

He hesitated. What if he couldn't get it back on?

A metallic groan from the middle of the vessel made him ignore his reluctance and quickly disengage the power.


## Lake Vostok


Totally in the dark and with no sound of the whirring of the thrusters or life support, he could see nothing and hear only his own breathing. Doctor Ming-Zhen waited, but there was no sound.

He didn't know how long he should wait. If the lights flicked back on, would that agitate the giant elasmosaur enough to leave, or entice it further? Should he wait until he was ready to pass out from lack of oxygen in the hopes it would slip away from boredom?

Suddenly, he saw a white light that slowly orbited his submersible, going out of view on one side and then reappearing on the other. The light grew brighter, and he squinted as he tried to make it out. Was this some kind of tiny bioluminecsent creature, he wondered.

Then, as it grew larger, he realized what it was: Doctor Toskovic's submersible, about two thousand feet away. With his own submersible flipping end over end, Doctor Toskovic's appeared to be only an orbiting speck.

He immediately engaged the power. Stabilizing his submersible, he began to search for the light. It took only seconds to spot the other one again, and his outside lights clearly illuminated the form of the elasmosaur as it steadily glided towards this new target.

"Toskovic, do you hear me?" he shouted over the radio. "Can you hear me, Doctor Toskovic?" There was no reply. Not sure what to do, he propelled his vessel forward, after the elasmosaur. As they drew nearer the other submarine, the elasmosaur suddenly swooped downward, away from both of them. Paddling fast, it did not take long for the creature to disappear into darkness. Perplexed, Doctor Ming-Zhen looked back up to the other vessel.

He called over the radio, "Toskovic, do you hear me? Do you hear—"

A broken voice came over the speakers, "Zhou? Are – out—."

"Toskovic, I am here, Toskovic can you hear me?"

"Ah! There you are sneaky weasel. Can you see me?"

"Yes, I am approaching."

"I did not know we came to play hide and go to seek."

Doctor Ming-Zhen smiled. Any relief to the tension was welcome. He said, "You just saved my life."

"How?"

"Did you see the sea monster?"

"I saw something very large."

"It was an elasmosaur."

There was a moment of silence, then, "That is amazing. We should follow this monster."

Doctor Ming-Zhen was surprised by this suggestion, and it immediately confounded him. Having Doctor Toskovic here gave him a new sense of security, but the elasmosaur had already proven to be extremely dangerous. "Is your compass working?" he asked.

"The one on my neck?" Doctor Toskovic asked. "I left it behind."

The shaft was on the west corner of the lake. Without the compass, they had no way of knowing which way that was.

He didn't think that following the elasmosaur to a deeper depth was the safest thing to do, although if they reached the bottom they might be able to get a feel for which way to go.

Doctor Toskovic said, "Let's follow the elasmosaur. We came here to find life, right?"

"It is very dangerous. It attacked my submarine."

"These submarines are titanium. There is no way it could cause any damage."

"It scratched the viewport," Doctor Ming-Zhen said. He was now nearing the other sub, which was turned away from him so he could not see Doctor Toskovic's head inside the bubble.

"The viewports are five inches thick. Little scratch on exterior is no harm."

Doctor Ming-Zhen considered his words. Upon close examination, he could see that the teeth had barely scratched the surface. Perhaps he had allowed himself to panic unnecessarily. He had been in no true danger. The idea that the elasmosaur could penetrate this machine was, in all likelihood, ridiculous.

Doctor Toskovic asked, "Have you lost nerves?"

"Perhaps," Doctor Ming-Zhen said, "But I have a wife and daughter. I have the right to lose my nerve."

"That is fair, but let me remind you, if we descend to the bottom, we can gauge the depth. If we can gauge the depth, we can determine what part of the lake we are in. So, you are in charge. What do we do?"

Doctor Ming-Zhen considered. They were both fairly familiar with the topography of the lake, so if they could find a landmark, or figure out which way the depth decreased, perhaps they could navigate back to the shaft. There was an island at the middle-north edge of the lake. If they could find that, certainly they would know which way was west. Also, there was a valley in the middle of the lake with a depth of 3,000 feet. On the west side, the depth was 700 feet, and on the east side the depth was 1,500 feet. Gauging the depth could tell them which side of the lake they were in. Doctor Ming-Zhen took a deep breath and looked at the picture of his family. "Let's go down," he said.

The average depth of the lake was fifteen hundred feet. They were descending at about two feet a second, so it would take them about ten minutes to reach the bottom, depending upon which side they were in.

The subs had been equipped with enough oxygen for fifty-six hours. The readout told him he had fifty-four hours left.

Midway through the descent, he collected a sample, though he couldn't see anything alive in the water. As the bottom gradually came into view, Doctor Ming-Zhen saw that it was gray and flat.

Doctor Toskovic said, "Okey dokey, we are for sure in middle of lake."

"But the depth here is 700 feet: the middle of the lake has a valley with a depth of 3,000 feet."

"You are mistaken, my friend. There is *ridge* in the middle with depth of 700 feet. The west side of the lake is shallower at 1,300 feet and the east side is deeper, 2,600 feet."

"I thought the west side was 1,500 feet and the east side is 2,000."

"The maximum depth is 3,000 feet, my friend," Doctor Toskovic sighed. "But even so, perhaps we have different sources for our information. We will see which one was right. Let's go this way," Doctor Toskovic's submersible rotated perpendicularly to Doctor Ming-Zhen's. "It looks like the ground slopes up this way."

Doctor Ming-Zhen couldn't disagree with that, so he followed the Russian.

Doctor Toskovic asked, "Do you agree that the island is in the middle of the lake?"

"Yes."

"So if we find the island, and I think we will this way, then we know we are in the middle of the lake."

Soon they were traveling along about six feet from the bottom. Their lights provided a maximum of forty feet of visibility ahead of them, and Doctor Ming-Zhen kept a wary eye out for the elasmosaur. Somehow, the soft whirring sound of the engine was reassuring.

It wasn't long before something ahead on the ground glinted with the reflection of their lights. Doctor Toskovic must not have seen it because he didn't say anything, but as they approached, Doctor Ming-Zhen slowed and lowered his vessel to get a closer look. It was a small, shiny object, gold in color, but he couldn't see it well enough to figure out what it was. He utilized a remotely controlled camera to zoom in on the object, and was astonished to realize that it was a half-buried pocket watch. *What was a pocket watch doing at the bottom of Lake Vostok?*

Zooming in a little more, he examined it more closely. No, it wasn't a watch. He stopped breathing with shock.

It was Doctor Toskovic's compass.

Doctor Toskovic's submarine had stopped now, too. His voice came over the speakers, "Why did you stop, my friend?"

Doctor Ming-Zhen's mind was reeling. It was a complete and total impossibility that the compass be here. Doctor Toskovic said he had left it at the surface. Maybe he didn't want to admit he had lost it. But if so, how *had* he lost it? There was no way for anything inside the submersibles to get *outside* the titanium walls. This was beyond the ability of his mind to process.

"My friend?" Doctor Toskovic's voice prodded.

Something inside him told Doctor Ming-Zhen that he should keep this discovery a secret. So he quickly maneuvered away from the compass and said, "I had to scratch an itch. No problem."

There was silence, and Doctor Ming-Zhen feared his lie would face scrutiny.

Several seconds passed, then Doctor Toskovic said, "We have limited power and oxygen, you know. Best we not waste it on little itches, eh?" He laughed.

Traveling on through the blackness, Doctor Ming-Zhen wished he would have sucked the compass into a storage container. Although he couldn't bring anything from the containers into the sub, he might have been able to see which direction they were going.

Before long, there was a distraction to his thoughts. Ahead, at the edge of the beams from their headlights, a pair of tiny points of light appeared, gleaming blue through the water. "Do you see the lights?" Doctor Ming-Zhen asked.

"I see them. Do you know what they are?"

"No. They look like eyes," he replied.

As they drew closer, more pairs of lights became visible hugging the floor of the lake. They seemed to move slowly from side to side, with new ones suddenly blinking on at such a rapid rate that within minutes there were hundreds of them. Closer and larger, it was apparent that they were triangular in shape, and each pair was at the front edge of a round dome. Spreading out from underneath each dome was a crop of fourteen grotesque, insect-like legs tipped by sharp-looking claws.

Doctor Ming-Zhen slowed his speed. Each of the creatures was no more than two feet long, but he wasn't sure if they were dangerous or if they could swim up from the ground. "Do you know what they are?" he asked.

"Yes, I think they are giant isopods, bottom feeding crustaceans," Doctor Toskovic said. "But you would never see this many. There must be much food that drops down for them to eat."

"Are they dangerous?" Doctor Ming-Zhen asked.

A laugh erupted over the speakers. "No, my friend," Doctor Toskovic chuckled, "They wouldn't eat you unless you were in nice little bite-sized pieces."

Doctor Ming-Zhen found Doctor Toskovic's casual, nonchalant attitude irritating. The Russian had a good excuse to be so worry-free: *he* hadn't been attacked by a sea monster.

As the submarines passed over them, the giant isopods watched them eerily with their highly reflective eyes, almost as if they were silent guardians of some forbidden territory.

They passed over the isopods. Beyond was a beautiful, ambient, and blue luminescence. Doctor Ming-Zhen was awestruck: he had never really asked the question the first time, but how could there be any light down here at all? This lake should be totally black.

Before long, he received the answer. They found themselves entering a smack of hundreds of jellyfish, each of them glowing blue. The creatures silently sifted the water, and were not too dense for the men to pilot their submersibles through.

"I think I catch one," Doctor Toskovic said.

"No. They could get sucked into the engine and clog it up."

"I think you spent too much time studying dead animals, my friend. Simply because something is alive does not make it dangerous."

"We really should focus on getting back to the shaft. We can modify the subs to deal with the current and come back down again to collect more samples. Clearly, this lake is hosting an abundance of life, and it isn't going anywhere."

"Is that what you think? All this life is trapped in Lake Vostok?"

"Well, yes," Doctor Ming-Zhen said, befuddled at the question. Of course the life was trapped in this lake. That was why they had come: to see if there was evidence of life trapped here after eons of years. It only so happened that there was life itself instead of its remnants.

"That is theory and you stick it to it." Doctor Toskovic said in an amused tone.

Annoyed, Doctor Ming-Zhen said, "Yes. But why? What do you think?"

"I think that there is more than meets eyes about this place, my friend."

"How?"

"Well, giant isopod, for example . . . ."

"What about them?"

"Suffice it to say they should not be here. Nor should jellies. Not even one."

"Why is that?"

"We shall see, my friend. We shall see."

Doctor Ming-Zhen wished the Russian would just say what it was he was thinking. This condescension did not seem at all like him. In the month Doctor Ming-Zhen had known Doctor Toskovic, he had been gregarious, easygoing. Certainly never condescending.

And, besides, Doctor Ming-Zhen was in charge. Doctor Toskovic should be showing more deference.

Now the Russian's submersible slowed to a stop, forcing Doctor Ming-Zhen to stop also. A small, clear canister extended from the body of the sub, towards one of the unsuspecting jellyfish.

"I said no. We do not have time for this," Doctor Ming-Zhen protested.

"It will take only minute," Doctor Toskovic said.

The canister was far too small to accommodate the creature, but that didn't seem to bother Doctor Toskovic.

Doctor Ming-Zhen warned, "Make this quick. We don't want to run out of oxygen."

"Anything you say, my friend." Doctor Toskovic's voice had an odd, stoic tone.

With the creature struggling to free itself, suction gradually pulled the jellyfish's tentacles into the canister. The suction kept pulling, until the bell was plastered on top. Finally, the bell ripped and the rest of the parts were vacuumed in. The canister retracted back into the sub. Doctor Toskovic said, "Nothing to it."

"You killed it," Doctor Ming-Zhen muttered.

"I like to kill," Doctor Toskovic's voice said without an iota of emotion.


Continuing along the bottom, Doctor Ming-Zhen noticed that the grade of the slope was becoming steeper. He said, "We must be approaching the wall of the lake," he said.

"Yes, I think so also. Or island."

That seemed too much to hope for. If they found the island, they would certainly know which way to turn from there in order to go south.

Sporadic rocky bulges protruded out from the sediment on the bottom, increasing in frequency until they reached a wall of tiered boulders. Sponges grew all over them.

They followed the tiers upwards for about ten minutes until they could see ice. Doctor Toskovic said, "You stay here to provide point of reference. I will go around and see if this is the island."

"It's very unlikely this is the isl—"

The Russian's voice sounded impatient, unconcerned, "Wait here. I will return."

Doctor Ming-Zhen did not appreciate Doctor Toskovic's attitude, but the idea did seem logical: a point of reference would provide them with a better idea of the topography. Doctor Ming-Zhen said, "Okay, go on."

Despite the galling persona that Doctor Toskovic was adopting underwater, Doctor Ming-Zhen felt anxious watching his submarine disappear around the bend of a rocky outcropping. He definitely did not want to be caught alone if the elasmosaur returned.

## FBI Field Office, Baltimore

Special Agent Jarred Kessler sat at his desk. He had just come off the phone with Stacy Riley.

She was angry.

She was aggravated with the FBI for "not doing enough" to find their son. And Jarred internally agreed he had not done enough, but this wasn't because of lack of effort. There was simply nothing to follow. They had tried everything they could:

The only fingerprints in the house they found were from Gary and Stacy. No unexpected shred of DNA appeared anywhere, not even on the boy's pajamas that had been left behind. They had combed all around the house for evidence of murder, or for a sign that someone had been trying to hide the body. They had searched all the computers and cell phones Gary and Stacy owned for anything suspicious. There was nothing that related to the crime. Even if the dad was guilty, they had found nothing which could possibly peg him. And the drawing, though terrifying, provided nothing actionable.

Instinctively, Jarred knew it wasn't the father. After dealing with hundreds of missing persons cases, he could smell guilt. He knew that this guy wasn't guilty. Yes, they had found evidence that Gary Riley had his own dirty secret, but it wasn't something Jarred wanted to roil the FBI up in, and was certainly not related to the disappearance.

It was as if the child had vanished into thin air.

Jarred found himself mulling over the last words that Gary had heard his son speak, words that now rang with the terror of an omen: *I saw eyes. Daddy, I saw eyes.* It seemed to Jarred that perhaps innocent little Jeffery had seen his captors even before he was taken. But why had he said he saw "eyes?" Was his vocabulary so limited that he couldn't say he had seen a person? And if he had seen someone, how had this person been on the second floor?

He was suddenly interrupted by Todd Humphries, a fellow Special Agent. He was the comedian of the office. "Did you hear the strange case that hit the national alert?"

"No?"

"Yeah, it's a missing child case."

"Okay."

"Same as all the missing children cases: a child is missing," Todd had a dopey grin. "But with this one, there's a catch."

"What's that?"

"The child was never born! The guy claims that his wife was pregnant and then 'poof' the baby was gone."

"So he thinks the baby just disappeared into thin air?" Jarred asked.

"I guess. What a nut."

Slowly, Jarred agreed, "Yeah..." But inside, the machination of his mind began to churn. Perhaps it was only desperation, but Jarred thought the case sounded a little too familiar to ignore. *A sudden, inexplicable vanishing with no trace?* He stood up and, despite the look of dubiety on his friend's face, asked, "What region did it come out of?"

# Jet

Aubrey had fallen asleep on the desk. They had been working all day and were now crossing the arctic at night. Henry pulled out a screen and entered a term in a search box:

### glowing tattoo

Dozens of entries came up. It was apparent that glowing tattoos were readily available. So, there was no cause for alarm in the Andrews' case, Henry thought.

He slipped the screen back into his brief case and turned to gaze at the starlight out the window. On the ground below, he could see a vast white nothingness bathed in the moonlight. It was beautiful in a cold, lonely sort of way.

Suddenly, a bright flash from high in the atmosphere illuminated the landscape for an instant. Then Henry spotted something with a long tail streaking through the air. A meteor. It was hard to judge distance and size, but it looked like it must be large given the long trail of what was visibly blazing hot fire. Henry watched it plummet all the way down to the white earth, where it was no longer visible. Henry spun his chair back around and looked at Aubrey.

She was a gorgeous girl. The most beautiful girl he had ever seen, in fact.

He allowed his eyes to linger. Feeling guilty for staring at a sleeping woman, he looked back down at his papers.

It was amazing to Henry that in legal matters paper was still a prerequisite at times. Everything else was digital.

His eyes drifted back to her, and he suddenly felt some compassion for her, sleeping on the hard surface as she was. Deciding to ask Maggie to wake her and take her to bed, he opened the door to the office and strode down the hall, past the board room and the public salon to the crew quarters. Lorraine was there sleeping, a bottle in her lap. The alcohol was out of control. But her addiction reminded him of someone very dear from years past; that's why he tolerated it . . . and he felt sorry for the woman. Who would give her work in that condition?

She would surely become destitute.

Maggie was also there, sleeping. The only other people on the aircraft would have been Jinkins and the pilots. Most planes flew themselves these days but Henry insisted on having pilots, *just in case*.

Henry peered into the cockpit through the door that Lorraine usually left open. The instrument panel glowed many different colors, but outside the windshield he could see a cloud approaching. There was turbulence as they entered. Sporadic bursts of lightning ignited the cloud with a pale glow. Henry stepped into the cabin and addressed one of the pilots, "Uneventful flight, Michael?"

The pilot turned to greet him, "Yes, sir. I hope it's more interesting back there."

"Everyone is sleeping," Henry replied.

They emerged on the other side and the turbulence ebbed. Henry could see more clouds approaching, the billowing tops gray in the moonlight. And the clouds were transforming, quickly; blotches of shadow were swiftly shifting and undulating. The lightning burst from within the clouds, yet the shadows remained, growing ever larger.

Henry rested his hand on the back of the pilot's chair as he leaned forward. Those were not shadows, but dim shapes gliding in the air towards the plane. The hair on Henry's neck bristled. It was clear they were not planes or birds or anything else that should be in the sky. Henry blinked and looked closer. There was no doubt. They were heading directly for the aircraft. Henry addressed the pilot: "Michael?"

"I see them, Mr. Potter. But they're not registering on our system," he replied.

Michael shook his copilot awake. "What do you make of that, Drew?"

Drew, groggy and a little disoriented, made an effort to focus on the figures in the distance. Finally, he said, "Whatever they are, they're turning."

It was true: the objects had changed trajectory. Michael said, "Looks like they're heading away south."

Drew said, "Well that's a relief. Aircraft without lights or communications are never good."

Henry walked back to his office where Aubrey was still sleeping. He stood there, pondering what to do for a few moments. Then he knelt down and lowered his face towards hers to wake her. Her eyes were closed, but it almost appeared that she was smiling. Was she awake?

"Aubrey?" He tapped her.

She was sleeping very soundly.

He jostled her, and she began to rouse. In a half-sleep, she said, "I'm so tired."

"Stand up," he commanded.

She didn't move.

He pulled on her arm, "Time to go to bed." She stood slowly, and, her eyes half-open, slid her hands up to hold his neck. Having her hold him like that gave him an unfamiliar, warm sensation.

"Aubrey," he said awkwardly. She had buried her face in his chest. With nothing else to do, he lifted her easily and carried her down the hall to his private suite to lay her on his bed. She was snoring immediately. He paused for a moment at the door before he closed it and left her to sleep. *She really was tired.*

Then he went to his office and pulled his wallet out from his suit coat. From deep in the recesses of a fold, he flipped out a picture of a beautiful young woman. Wearing an elegant dress with a deep v-neck and a diamond necklace, she was standing next to a man who had apparently been deliberately blacked out. Henry contemplatively gazed at the photograph for a time before pressing it to his lips in a brief kiss.

# Shanghai

It was almost three o'clock PM local time when they arrived in Shanghai.

A limo sent by Genetic Labor Solutions picked Henry, Jinkins, Maggie and Aubrey up from the busy airport and drove them to the company's headquarters. The traffic was horrific, but the towering glass skyscrapers of Shanghai were impressive.

The entrance to the GLS compound was foreboding. A tall wall with barbed wire was interrupted by a gate with a security booth. The gate opened automatically for the limo. Inside, Aubrey could see that it was a monstrous sprawling complex comprised of mostly older concrete buildings, but also a lot of very new glass ones. Nearest the gate was a twenty-floor, spiraling office tower.

As the limo pulled up under a huge portico jutting out from the office tower, a group of executives in suits waved and welcomed them as they stepped out, greeting them all with limp handshakes. They were then led into the lobby of the building, which was sleek and modern. From the lobby it was a quick walk to the elevator. Aubrey was surprised to see that buttons were missing; four, thirteen and fourteen. She whispered to Jinkins, "Why are floors missing?"

Amused, he replied, "Those numbers are bad luck."

They rode all the way to the top; floor "seventeen."

Once they stepped out, an expansive view of the surrounding city awed them. Their hosts guided them to an area recessed into the glossy floor and edged by a giant screen. A row of round armchairs was against the circumference. When they had all taken seats, the lights dimmed and a bass drumbeat and aggressive cello music began.

The screen was black until a series of white sentences appeared and flashed toward them, a deep voice intoning each:

IMAGINE A WORLD

WITH 40% HIGHER EFFICIENCY

WHERE ACCIDENTS ALMOST NEVER HAPPEN

WHERE FACTORIES OPERATE 24 HOURS A DAY

7 DAYS A WEEK

BUT NOT A SINGLE PERSON

WORKS THERE.

WELCOME TO THE WORLD OF

GENETIC LABOUR SOLUTIONS.

WELCOME

BIOBOT

The screen flashed white and the chiseled face of a man in a closed-necked white shirt appeared. He stared into the camera and, expressionless, said, "I am Biobot, the world's first genetically manufactured industrial robot. I may be customized to virtually any task. I require almost no maintenance. I use no electricity. And I have no wish but to service your business.

"Here are some examples of what Biobot can do for you: Biobot can work your factory floor."

A scene of a humming manufacturing plant was displayed.

"Biobot can perform routine maintenance."
A jet hangar was shown with scaffolding around a plane.

"Biobot can answer your telephone."
A busy call center.

"Biobot can make your deliveries."
A freight van speeding down the highway.

"Biobot can service your rooms."
A pristine hotel bed was on-screen.

"Biobot can cook your vegetables."
A bustling restaurant kitchen was displayed, then it was back to the face of the man. He said, "There is virtually no limit to what Biobot can do." His lips formed a robotic smile, "So the only question is, 'what may I do for you?'"

The screen faded out and one of the executives rose to stand before them. "Before we proceed, would any of you like a drink?" A busboy supporting a tray of many stemmed glasses of sparkling amber champagne strode up. The executive raised a glass and took a sip. He placed the glass on the tray and said, "Thank you, Biobot." The man smiled proudly, "This is our miracle of science. This is Biobot," he motioned to the server.

Jinkins said skeptically, "So these 'Biobots' are capable of restaurant service?"

"Indeed, they are."

Jinkins shook his head, "I don't believe it. How are we to know that this isn't a person posing as a Biobot?"

The executive said, "Believe it," and took one of the glasses off the tray. He then astounded everyone by pouring the glass onto the busboy's head. The busboy didn't flinch. "Smile," he commanded. The busboy's lips curved into a grin, though its teeth were not exposed. The champagne dripped from its chin onto its vest. The man explained, "The computer monitors every Biobot's location. If it strays from assigned parameters, the Biobot receives a negative signal in its brain. After it completes a task according to how it was trained, it receives a positive signal.

"The Biobots can be switched off," the man said. He lifted the tray from the busboy's shoulder and, touching its hand, said, "Shutdown." The Biobot immediately lowered itself to the floor and lay on its back, closing its eyes. The man quickly touched its hand again and said, "Start up." The Biobot raised itself to its feet and the man handed it the tray. "Biobot, offer them drinks," the executive ordered, pointing to the group.

After the Biobot made the rounds with the tray, Henry commented, "I knew of everything you could do, but I confess this is truly astonishing to see in person. Very well done. You have my congratulations."

The executive nodded gratefully.

"Now, you have factories, I believe. May we see one?"

"Certainly. Let us go at once."

Aubrey was stunned when they entered the glass-walled room overlooking the factory floor. The Biobots laboring over the apparatus were all apparently very young. They did not have legs, but sat on small, round stools and robotically moved fabric over sewing machines with their tiny hands.

Henry was gazing down at them approvingly, and their hosts smiled proudly. "Factory is twenty percent more efficient," one of them boasted. "Ninety percent less accident than at traditional factory."

Jinkins had broken into a sweat and began tugging at his collar nervously. Although he didn't say anything, Aubrey could easily tell he was growing very uncomfortable with what they saw.

"So these are more specialized than the restaurant busboy you showed us earlier," Henry said.

"Correct, we specialize Biobot for all tasks."

Finding herself really agitated by the spectacle of what, for all appearances, were legless children working a factory floor, Aubrey banged her hand on the glass, startling everyone in the entourage. Henry shot her a warning glance, but not before several of the Biobots raised their eyes to her. They all flinched in unison, as if stung, and quickly resumed their work.

Another executive host explained, "Perhaps the best feature of these production-line Biobots is that computers monitor their movements and instantly correct any erratic behavior. This means there's no chance yours would be wasting your time or money. So, have you seen all you wanted to see? We could show you our erotic dance Biobots. I think they could be very beneficial to your island."

At this, Jinkins exclaimed, "Paradeisia is a family destination! That would be entirely out of place!"

Looking irritated, Henry said to their hosts, "We have no need for adult entertainments, yet. But," he smiled, "We'll see what the market demands."


Once Henry had seen his fill of the Biobots, they were back in the limo. "So, where are we staying tonight, Aubrey?" Henry asked.

Nobody had told her to book a hotel. She said, "Uh . . ."

Henry frowned, "Please tell me you booked accommodations."

"Nobody told me to do that."

Henry rubbed his face with one hand, "Maggie?"

"I apologize, Mr. Potter. I mentioned something to her but I'm afraid she forgot."

Aubrey shot Maggie a glance. Why had she just thrown her under the bus like that? Aubrey started to defend herself, "You didn't say—"

Henry interrupted, "Ladies! Let's get on the internet, shall we?"

Maggie was able to book some rooms at the Starline Regal Shanghai. As their limo took off for the hotel, Aubrey was silent and just stared out the window. She was angry. She was angry with Maggie, but even more than that she couldn't believe what she had just seen at GLS. *Genetic Labor Solutions. Yeah, right*, she thought. *More like Slave Labor Solutions.* Worst of all, she couldn't believe that Henry was pursuing these "Biobots" as a viable labor source. He really was without morals.

Henry asked, "What's the matter, Aubrey?"

She didn't say a word but continued to gaze at the passing traffic.

"You're forgiven for not booking the hotel."

She didn't respond.

"It's the Biobots, isn't it?"

She nodded.

"They're not human. You can't think of them that way. They're machines—animals, at best."

"Animals!?" Jinkins piped incredulously.

Aubrey just shook her head.

"I know it's hard for *you* to understand. But they wouldn't even exist had they not been built. They can't even survive without the nourishment that's provided for them."

Aubrey said, "I'm sure plantation owners told themselves that every day! What we saw in that factory were *little kids!*"

"I'll admit, they do look like children. But that's only because they share some genetic material with humans. That's nothing extraordinary. 98% of our genes are common with other animals! What you saw were simply Biobots at the *beginning* of their shelf lives with another fifty-plus years of service to offer."

"Haven't you heard of child labor? Isn't that the kind of thing Nike got in trouble for?"

"That is completely irrelevant here. You're comparing apples and oranges."

Maggie interjected, looking apologetic to Henry, "Aubrey, really. You shouldn't interf—"

Henry raised his hand, "It's all right, Maggie. I asked her."

Aubrey turned from the window and said, "This is slavery. Genetically glorified slavery."

"Five hundred *Fortune* Five Hundred companies disagree with you. Even the U.N. disagrees with you."

"Well the U.N. can go to—"

"Aubrey!" Maggie warned.

Aubrey spun back to the window and placed her chin back on her fist.

Jinkins, nervously wringing his hands, mustered a complaint, "Mr. Potter . . . It's not what I envisioned."

"In the Out of Africa area of Paradeisia, didn't you purchase genetically modified animals from a company called Convergent Genetic Science? It's hypocritical of you to criticize me when your hands are already bloody, don't you think?"

"That's entirely different. Convergent sells animals that have been made tamer and safer. They do not sell modified *humans*."

"Did you ever think to ask if the animals were given any genes that came only from humans? It's a likely possibility. But as I've said before, human genes do not make a thing human. We share genes with most every creature on earth, but that doesn't make any of them humans!"

"Human or not, I cannot conceive of those things wandering around my island like an army of zombies."

"I suppose you can conceive of bankruptcy, then?" Henry went for the jugular, "I suppose you can conceive of every other company in the world making use of them while Paradeisia sinks under a burden of high wages, healthcare and benefits? If we do not employ Biobots, Mr. Jinkins, Paradeisia will die."

There was a moment of silence as the limo drove along. Aubrey thought Jinkins had succumbed, but then, still looking down into his lap, he intoned, "Better dead and buried than standing on the back of slavery."

"*Slavery*? You too?" Henry shouted incredulously. "This kind of absolute ignorance genuinely astounds me. Ignorance, or stupidity, I'm frankly not sure which it is." Henry leaned forward, "I mean, have you totally lost your mind?"

Jinkins said, "Mr. Potter, I want to be diplomatic, I really do, but rest assured I will oppose this. I will oppose it to the bitter end."

Aubrey chimed happily, "Me too."

Henry leaned back in the seat and smugged, "Well, that's the bright

spot in this situation. Neither the kangaroo nor the pouch has a say."
As he sat there, grinning in victory, suddenly Henry's phone rang.

When the call was over, Henry looked at Jinkins with annoyance, "Well, we have yet another happy thought to ponder. Your prodigal son, Jinkins, has disappeared. Again."

Aubrey asked, "What prodigal son?"

Impatiently, Henry snapped, "Of course Andrews. He's vanished."

## Cognitive LifeScience Corporation

After the disappearance of their son on his watch, Gary needed something to distract him from constant feelings of desperation and self-loathing. So he turned to the other unexplained mystery in his life; what was he doing at Cognitive? While the FBI worked on his case he set about solving this question with a fervency born of loss and grief.

With this in mind, he was waiting when the delivery came this time.

It was a nondescript *E* series white van. The driver wore a blue uniform and ball cap. Gary couldn't make out any badge. As soon as the van squeaked to a stop, the delivery man jumped out with an acknowledging nod to Gary. He went to the back and opened up the double doors. After a moment or two, he returned with a package in his arms to follow Gary into the facility. As they walked toward the refrigerator, Gary casually asked, "How long have you been making these deliveries?"

"Four years, boss."

That was the same amount of time Gary had worked for Cognitive LifeScience. "Like your job?"

"Pays the bills . . . ."

"What was the name of your company, again?"

"Biocertica."

"You make a lot of deliveries?"

"All day long."

"Any pickups?"

"Nope."

"No pickups at all?"

"None."

They entered the walk-in fridge together and the man placed the box on a shelf. Then he took out an electronic pad which he had Gary sign. As the man turned to leave, Gary asked him one more question, "Do you know who brings in the samples? I mean, have you ever seen any coming in?"

The man stopped and faced Gary, his posture defensive, "Doc, I don't know anything about the samples. I load up the van and I deliver them. That's all." Then he added, "And I'm smart enough to keep my nose in my own crap."

## FBI Field Office, Baltimore

Special Agent Kessler was at his boss's desk, saying, "I made calls for every missing person alert we have."

"You mean everyone at our office?"

"No, I mean everyone in the FBI."

His boss sat back in his squeaky chair, "You've got to be kidding. 2,500 people go missing every day."

"Yeah, but you know most of them are child custody cases or the senile. Once you take out the superfluous ones, it's not that many. Only about a hundred kids are verified as kidnapped by creeps every year."

"Yes, that's true."

"Legitimate disappearances have come up 400% over the past three years. Nobody noticed because nobody was separating the legitimates from the divorces and silver alerts. I thinned the herd down to about 500 active cases that I thought fit my bill. We spoke with someone from each of the families."

"You know, Jarred, we don't have a 'special agent of the year' award . . . ."

Jarred said, "I know. But listen; here's the rub:" he paused. "In almost every one of these cases, the missing person had an anomaly. Some had special traits, such as the case I'm working. He was a two-year-old genius. But many of the missing people had diseases. A lot of them had psychological problems. But they were all *rare*." Kessler continued, "My question is, what is it that makes this uniqueness valuable? Especially the sick ones. Why would anyone *want* a deadly disease?"

His boss said, "That is a *very* good question." He tilted his head, "And precisely why I think you might be taking this a bit too far. Aren't you just grasping at straws, here, Jarred? This seems like quite a stretch. I mean how many of the missing people have some rare characteristic like you're talking about?"

"479."

"You know it's very easy to get caught up in conspiracy theories if you look to hard enough."

"This is no theory. This is an epidemic of the lost."

## Biocertica

Lightning flashed to illuminate the oak-lined road Gary was driving. It was probably going to rain before the sun came out. He was on a street near an imposing windowless building surrounded by a parking lot. It was about three floors tall, as wide as a city block, entirely concrete and brown. The structure's only distinguishing features were the two blacked out glass doors at the front.

It was plain and depressing, not a building anyone would be proud to work at. The only positive thing that could be said about the place was that the paint looked new. Well, that and the fact that the parking lot was home to several sparkling BMW's, Audi's, and even a Rolls Royce.

He switched off his headlights and pulled his SUV up over the curb and onto an area clear of brush where he had a view of the loading dock at the back of the structure.

This had been the only address he could find for "Biocertica." He figured that if they had any illicit pickups, they would happen at night. So here he was, waiting in the dark.

For a long time, nothing happened and he alternated between

wondering what he was doing there and if he should go home. He hadn't told Stacy where he was going. He knew she would probably tell him to stay home and it would turn into an argument. Whenever they spoke anymore, that's what it was; an argument. Every time.

Finally, at three twenty-seven, there was movement. A black Mercedes cargo van pulled into the parking lot and slowly drove around to the back of the building. It backed up almost to the dock, which was much taller than the floor of the van. Two men emerged from the front doors and stepped around to open the van's rear cargo bay. They hopped up inside together, and, after a bit, Gary saw a long black box being pushed out. The men appeared again and grasped handles on each side. As they extracted it fully, Gary got a good view. It was the size of a coffin.

The figures carried it up a ramp to the top of the dock and set it down. One of them pushed a button on an intercom at a door which opened after only a short time.

A middle-aged, overweight woman holding a screen came out. She motioned to the box. One of the men unsnapped some latches and flipped open the lid. He moved his arms into the box and grappled something inside—Gary couldn't see what.

When the man pulled his arms up out of the box, Gary almost jumped at what he saw. The man had jerked a child upright by his hair. The child's large eyes belied a state of shocked terror.

He was a very young boy, maybe only two or three.

To a man who had lost his son only weeks before, the scene was mind-numbing. The pieces suddenly came together for him. He had found an answer here that he wasn't looking for. This was the explanation to his son's disappearance. *Jeffery was kidnapped by Biocertica. This facility was where his little boy's short life had ended.*

How had he not thought of this? He had been in the business of using biological samples for years. He knew how expensive they were and how difficult it was to procure the right ones. And yet, day in and day out, the perfect samples arrived at Cognitive LifeScience. Samples that aligned with whatever the secret Preseption project required. How else could they obtain so many samples of such a specific nature?

*What had made him so blind?* Was it the money? Had a deep, dark part of his mind immunized him against the fact that the samples rolling in were too good to be true?

He wasn't the only one running samples at Cognitive—far from it. *Hundreds* of scientists were at the facility running *hundreds* of samples. *His own child, his little boy could have been sent to the very building where he worked.* Gary lowered his head, putting his face in his hands. *How many other families had lost someone precious; someone who had ended up in bloody pieces on his lab table?*

When he looked up again, the woman was holding her screen out and comparing a portrait image on it to the little boy in the clutches of the man before her.

She nodded her approval and the boy was shoved back into the box, the lid slammed shut, and the latches locked. As the men lifted the box to carry it through the door, Gary's feelings of regret were now transforming into a hot rage.

He opened his glove box and slipped out a handgun. He relished the feel of it. Resting the gun on his lap, he quickly pulled up Jarred Kessler on his speed dial.

There were a couple of rings, but a sleepy sounding answer came. "This is Jarred."

"I know what happened to Jeffery. I need help *now*."

The reply he received stunned him: "Don't call me. I'm off the case."

"But I found—"

"The case is closed."

And the line went dead.

## Towson, Maryland

The good news for Wesley Peterson was that his test results had come through and he had been cleared to leave Towson.

The bad news was that his mother couldn't be cleared. They couldn't clear her because they couldn't run the test on her. They couldn't run the test on her because she was only one of thousands of infected and possibly infected.

They had evicted his mother from the hospital because it was overrun; high-risk and emergency patients had taken precedence. Because his mother couldn't leave Towson, they were sleeping in a large U.S. Army tent at Robert E. Lee Park, a forested wilderness area. They shared the tent with thirteen other people, all of them men; and even with all those bodies it was still freezing. They had been promised that this crowded state of affairs was only temporary as the Army erected more tents. But as more trees were cleared and more tents went up, it seemed those were immediately being filled by a constant stream of new refugees.

In the tent, there was only one electric outlet in the form of an extension cord, and competition was fierce with electric toothbrushes, cell phones, shavers, and other essentials sucking power. When Wesley was lucky enough to have his cell phone charged, getting call through wasn't possible. The lines were too busy.

Aggravating the situation further were signs everywhere with a Red Cross number to call for missing persons. But of course with no working phones, getting through was hopeless.

There was only one TV that he knew of in the entire camp, and it was watched religiously by a crowd of hundreds day and night. The irony was that the reporters couldn't get inside Towson to find out what was going on, but all the quarantined who were already inside Towson didn't know what was going on either.

Wesley got most of his news by word-of-mouth. So far, most of what he had learned was nothing more than camp gossip. For example, a group of environmentalists had decided the Army shouldn't be bulldozing the trees, even though there was no space otherwise, and had staged a tree-hugging protest. This lasted for days with the camp administrator reluctant to infringe on any constitutional rights, fearing legal repercussions. Finally, someone in the Army had decided enough was enough and had the protesters forcefully removed and placed in internment.

Now, tents stretched over the hills everywhere within sight, and still it seemed that room was running out.

The lavatory situation was awful. Comprised of rows of portables in the mud, the lines were long and the stench was unbearable.

Showers were rationed, and getting a spot at one of the plastic sinks for dental hygiene was a nightmare. It was so bad that fights broke out.

Recently, a constant, billowing smoke had appeared in the east and ash had begun to rain down on them like a constant snow, only it was gray and foul.

The worst, however, was the boredom. People were left with nothing to do but idle around the camp. Gas was not available in Towson any longer, so anyone who was lucky enough to have access to a car couldn't use it. Certain areas of the town were blocked off by soldiers and Humvees anyway.

One thing appeared certain; they weren't getting out any time soon. That is, Wesley could get out any time he wished, of course, due to his negative test result. But his mother was stuck here, and he wouldn't leave her without a very good reason.

So Wesley and his mother were now sitting in the tent playing with a deck of the cards somebody had given them at the hospital.

"I just don't understand why they can't bother to do something about those port-a-potties. The last one I used looked like it was almost full. Why don't they open up some of the local businesses for us?"

"Nobody is working at those businesses. They probably don't have the keys."

"Well, the only good thing I can say is thank heavens it's mostly men in this camp or the lines to the washrooms would be much longer." She placed her discards down and said, "You think the government has everything under control and a plan for every contingency, and then something like this happens. We're all packed in here like rats and there's not even a decent washroom!"

"I'm sure they're doing the best they can, mom."

"And what is that huge cloud of smoke? I think the city's on fire and they're not telling us. Now that they've got everyone trapped here including the firefighters, the fire is probably going to sweep through and kill all of us!"

"Mom, really."

"Well if they've let things get this bad I certainly won't place my bets on the hopes they won't get any worse! This is nothing less than full-fledged incompetence. I'm sure that if they hadn't bungled this crisis, we could all be sleeping soundly in our beds." She slapped down her cards, "I win again. Full house."

Suddenly the tent flap was opened from the outside and a masked man in uniform stepped in. "Wesley Peterson?" he said loudly.

Wesley stood up, "Here."

"Follow me, sir."


# Lake Vostok


Doctor Ming-Zhen waited thirty minutes. The screen told him he had fifty hours of oxygen left.

He jumped when he heard a voice on the speaker, "Ivan the terrible is back!" Then Doctor Toskovic's sub whooshed past him, "This is the island for sure. I went all the way around."

"That is good news. Now we know which way to go."

"Yes, this way." Doctor Toskovic's sub continued straight, with the rocky wall to his left.

Doctor Ming-Zhen started to follow, but then paused. "But isn't the island on the north coast? We would need to go the other way to reach the west side of the lake."

"No, my friend," Doctor Toskovic said in the unfriendliest way possible. "Island is on south coast."

Doctor Ming-Zhen thought very hard, trying to bring the topographical map into focus in his mind. For some reason, he couldn't, but he was pretty sure that the island was on the north side. *Yes, the island was on the north, the drill shaft on the west corner, and the magnetic anomaly was on the east.* He said, "No, I believe the island is on the north."

"Trauma from monster has made you forget. Island is on south, without doubt. And, remember, you were mistaken about depth in middle."

Doctor Ming-Zhen had to admit that he was having trouble remembering the details of the topographic map, but he was not able to separate the island from the north coast in his mind. On the other hand, what Doctor Toskovic said was true: he had been wrong about the middle of the lake. Perhaps he wasn't thinking clearly. He asked, "Are you absolutely certain?"

"Yes. I would bet life on it."

"Well, you certainly *are* betting your life on it because we probably will run out of oxygen if you are wrong."

"I would bet both our lives on it, my friend."

Doctor Ming-Zhen said, "All right. Let's proceed."

For some time they traveled in silence, the craggy cliff on their left grading into a gradual slope, the oxygen monitor ticking off the hours. 49. 48. 47. 46. 45....

Doctor Ming-Zhen was still wary of encountering the elasmosaur again, so he kept a careful eye out, monitoring not only the view outside the bubble, but also the monitors with video of other angles.

As they traveled, he wondered what had caused the tremendous current that pushed them so far from the borehole. He knew that one side of the lake had a larger mass of ice weighing down on it, while on the other end the ice was somewhat thinner. Could the difference in weight and pressure be causing currents?

That could be part of the cause, but that did not seem to explain a current that had been so strong and so long as to push them halfway across a 160 mile lake. Perhaps the real answer was that the geothermal activity was stronger than anyone had suspected. That would also explain why the water was relatively warm.

Doctor Toskovic's voice interrupted his train of thought, "Did I tell you what made me become scientist?"

"I don't believe so."

"I was ten years old. My family went to ski with friend of my father's in the Caucasus Mountains. His friend was scientist, an Evolutionary Biologist. We had been hiking below the snow line when we came across one hand-sized shell. It wasn't fossilized, just one half of shell mostly buried in the ground. My father's friend dug it up and told us, 'This doesn't belong here.' My father asked him, 'Why not?' He said, 'Because these mountains formed in the Pleistocene, the most recent epoch. This shell is from brachiopod. That is marine organism, from ocean salt water. These mountains were not under an ocean since they were formed.' So he carried shell all the way back down the mountain and threw it into Black Sea.

"As child, this did not seem right. How could he take shell that was there in the ground, say it shouldn't be there, and take it where he thought it belonged? It was not honest. I told my father it wasn't right, but he said, 'My friend is good scientist. He knows.

"But I argued with my father. I begged him to let us return to the mountain so we could look for more shells. But my father would not listen. I pleaded, I even cried.

'My father told me I was thinking too hard, I was going mad.

'But I knew it was they who were mad. I knew I could do better. I could be better scientist. I could prove to them. Instead of changing the evidence to fit my way of thinking, I could learn from the evidence I found. That is why I became scientist after he die. Not to be possessed by science, as my father's friend was, but to possess it.

"I devoted my life to study. Endless hours in the night, reading, researching. Do you know how many PhD's I have?"

Doctor Ming-Zhen said, "No."

"*Five*. I have *five* PhD's. There have scarcely been hours in my life when I have not toiled for the sake of science.

"Eventually, of course, I came here, to Antarctica. We captured the water from the lake. We took it to St. Petersburg. We studied it. We found organisms in the water. We told the world, the lake has organisms, a living biology. And the world told us, 'That doesn't belong there. You are wrong. You don't know what you are doing. You are fraud.'

"So I said to myself, should I have done what my father's friend did? Should I have said, 'This doesn't belong here,' and thrown it into the sea, just to fit with their unenlightened worldview?

"But then I received call from China. You were launching an expedition. You needed expert. There was hope that I could redeem myself.

"So here we are. We have seen vast living biology. It has exceeded my wildest expectation. And when I return to surface, I will bring enough evidence to prove to them that I was right all along. I will laugh at them, for their simplicity of mind not to listen to me. I will receive all glory. I will not be mad. They were mad all along."

Doctor Ming-Zhen was troubled by Doctor Toskovic's phrasing. He had been so welcoming, so inviting before. Now he sounded almost like a megalomaniac.

Doctor Ming-Zhen momentarily entertained the persuasion that it might become necessary to abandon Doctor Toskovic and try to return to the surface himself.

This was not to be an exploratory mission, anyway. They had only come to be certain the equipment worked and to take a sample or two of the water. That was all. Just those two things and then they were to return. When Apollo 11 landed on the moon, they didn't attempt an ambitious tour. They just picked up a few samples, planted a flag, and left.

The oxygen monitor beeped. Thirty-five hours left.

## CDC

A deep, sick feeling was billowing within Karen Harigold. She was accustomed to being in charge. She was always the one with the answers. Things were always under control on her watch. And yet, here she was, asking them to lend their support to quarantine the entire Baltimore area—an area with over a one point five million people . . . and she wasn't even sure if it was the right thing to do. The crises had grown so fast and so out of control that she truthfully wasn't sure that anything could stop it.

Of course, years of theory and emergency preparedness studies had proposed that this might be the case. The Clinton administration had run a simulation that started a pandemic in Chicago. The simulation predicted that it would be impossible to contain it: that it would spread to the rest of the nation regardless of quarantine efforts or other measures. The only thing that could be done was to try to manage it as well as possible as it ran its course.

But that was for a disease which left merely thirty percent of the infected dead. This was far more serious.

By closing off Baltimore, they could be condemning those million-and-a-half people whether the disease claimed them or not. Inside, it would be anarchy. Besides the virus, the lack of security would transform the place into a living hell overnight. If they'd had so much trouble sustaining the situation in Towson, how honest was it to believe they could handle a population twenty times as large?

And then, of course, there would be the dismal repercussions to the rest of the nation. Once they made a quarantine of Baltimore public, travel would grind to a stop. Many people would probably quit showing up to work for fear of getting sick. There would be a run on the banks. The country would quickly come to a terrified standstill.

The longer it lasted, the more doubtful it would be that America's economy could sustain the blow. As Secretary of Health, she was about to preside over the health crisis that could cripple the nation.

How had it come to this so quickly?

Suddenly, a calm voice sounded from behind her.

"I have very bad news."

She spun the chair around. Standing there, silhouetted in the light pouring through the doorway, was the President.

# Lake Vostok

"Look at this," Doctor Toskovic suddenly said. "Yet another example."

Towards the right was a disconcertingly large gray shape easing through the water. Doctor Ming-Zhen's body froze with fear. "Do you know what it is?" he asked.

"I believe so, yes. We must get closer to be sure."

"No, no!" Doctor Ming-Zhen said, almost desperately. He calmed his voice, "Let's not get closer until we're certain it is harmless. Or even if we know it's harmless."

"Oh, but it looks like at least thirty feet long. It is definitely harmless."

"How can that be?"

"With sharks," he said, "bigger is usually safer. That looks like basking shark."

Doctor Ming-Zhen's tension eased. Basking sharks were certainly not dangerous.

"You know what basking sharks eat?"

Of course he knew what basking sharks ate. Anyone knew that. Did Toskovic think he was in primary? He was a scientist, after all. "Plankton," Doctor Ming-Zhen said.

"Correct," Doctor Toskovic's voice sounded as if he was teaching a class.

Doctor Ming-Zhen seethed silently.

Instead of stopping so Doctor Toskovic could take a sample of the shark, they continued on along the shoreline, much to Doctor Ming-Zhen's relief. Apparently Toskovic had finally found a sample that was indisputably too big for his canisters.

"The basking shark is one more piece of puzzle," Doctor Toskovic said.

Doctor Ming-Zhen rolled his eyes. This was undoubtedly another attempt to show off by Toskovic, PhD, PhD, PhD, PhD, PhD. But he was curious, and couldn't resist asking, "What puzzle?"

"What do giant isopods, jellyfish, and basking sharks have in common?"

Doctor Ming-Zhen racked his mind. He was getting very tired of feeling like a spare wheel on the brain bike.

Doctor Toskovic said, "They are all marine animals. They all live in salt water, not fresh water."

It was so patently obvious, Doctor Ming-Zhen wanted to pound his fists against the wall of his sub. He didn't dare, of course, so instead he just clenched them.

He had to admit, though, it was an important observation. This was supposed to be a freshwater lake. It was inexplicable that oceanic creatures could be here. With a sigh, Doctor Ming-Zhen thought, *Doctor Toskovic probably already has an explanation for that, too.* He asked "How could this be a salt water lake?"

"You are very curious, my friend. Such a curious friend, you are."

This time, Doctor Ming-Zhen did punch the wall of the sub. It hurt. Then he chastised himself. Why was he allowing this to upset him? He was miles under the ice with barely a prayer of returning alive. The least of his worries should be a silly game of riddles by a suddenly patronizing research partner.

Doctor Ming-Zhen checked the oxygen monitor. Thirty-four hours left.

"Are you wondering why I am so enlightened, yet?" Doctor

Toskovic asked. Without waiting for a reply, he said, "I will tell you. Something happened the first time we were drilling to Lake Vostok all those years ago. Something happened that illuminated me. It gave me the power to know I was right and to wait until now when I could prove it." There was a pause, and Doctor Ming-Zhen thought that Doctor Toskovic had become distracted. But then his voice continued, "I know you heard the story about our seven days of radio silence."

Cautiously, Doctor Ming-Zhen replied, "Yes, I heard about the radio silence." He recalled that when he had asked Doctor Toskovic about it before, a month ago, the Russian had laughed it off; said his team was so busy with the drilling equipment they had neglected to answer.

"We knew we were very close, very close to reaching the lake. We were filled with anticipation . . . . We had worked so hard for this, suffered so long for this, and now, we were about to achieve it. We would soon have water from the lake, we were sure.

"But we were stopped. One of the scientists came inside to us and said he had seen something.

"We all ran outside. I could barely see it, but far in the distance, just on top of the white ice, was—"

There was silence. Then, Doctor Toskovic's voice, sounding eager and awestruck, said, "There it is."

Doctor Ming-Zhen did not see anything except the endless dark water. Then he noticed that Doctor Toskovic's submersible had nearly come to a stop and all its lights were out.

"Switch off your lights."

"I can't, not without turning off the sub."

"Yes, you can. It's in the menu on the touchpad, under diagnostics."

Doctor Ming-Zhen looked at the touchpad and searched under the DIAGNOSTICS menu. Sure enough, there it was: "ALL LIGHTS OFF."

He tapped this and immediately he was engulfed in blackness. As his eyes adjusted, though, he began to see shafts of light that erupted in all directions from a vast expanse far in the distance. It was surreal, like seeing moonlight streaming through clouds. Size was difficult to determine, but by any measure the illuminated area was vast: farther across than he could even see. The source seemed to be deep within a funneling valley.

"How did you know this was here?" Doctor Ming-Zhen accused.

"Coral."

"What coral?"

"There is little coral growing on the rocks down there. Coral does not grow without light. There had to be a source of light somewhere . . . and there it is." Then, Doctor Toskovic's voice, sounding hollow, almost like someone else, asked, "What do you think this is, my curious friend?"

Doctor Ming-Zhen was thinking that it was probably geothermal; that the light was from lava erupting at the base of the funnel. But if that were the case, he thought there should be smoke billowing up through the water, and there wasn't. As he stared, a continuous stream of innumerable small, glinting shapes flowed up among the shafts of light. It was like a giant, shimmering fountain of water within the water. It was beautiful.

The front end of the stream suddenly changed trajectory and snaked around to aim directly towards them. As this happened, Doctor Ming-Zhen realized that they were fish: thousands and thousands of schooling fish.

Then he realized that Doctor Toskovic's submersible was gone. No, it wasn't gone, he could just make it out ahead, approaching the light.

He would have told him to stop, but Doctor Ming-Zhen realized that he himself was moving towards it. Although his controls were set to idle, the submersible was being gradually carried along. He thought with alarm, *I'm being sucked into this light, just as powerless as Toskovic's jellyfish.* He engaged his reverse thrusters, but they were powerless against the surge.

The school of fish swung around like a lasso in the hand of a cowboy. As he was drawn closer to them, he could see their little bodies flickering as they struggled against the current.

Doctor Toskovic's voice said, "We are being drawn in." Far from sounding worried, his tone was actually entranced. "I believe that this, my friend, is our mysterious 'magnetic anomaly.'"

*So this is what he wanted,* Doctor Ming-Zhen thought. *He wanted to see the magnetic anomaly. He never cared about getting back.* The lake was 160 miles long. To get back to the right side, at their max speed, would take thirty-two hours. The oxygen monitor read 33.

But that was irrelevant now, because they were being drawn into a mysterious "magnetic anomaly," and there was no telling what that might mean. Scientists had assumed it was just a thin spot of the earth's crust. Clearly, there was more to it than that.

"It's the tide," Doctor Toskovic said. "The tide is drawing us in."

Indeed, whatever was drawing them in was exerting an ever more powerful force, and their speed as they approached the light increased dramatically the closer they came. Doctor Ming-Zhen struggled to think of something to do, anything he could do. But his mind was blank. He had been down here twenty-three hours with no sleep and no food. He realized for the first time that he was exhausted; that his whole body ached.

And it was Doctor Toskovic's fault.

He had lied to Doctor Ming-Zhen; said the island was on the south side, just so they could go the wrong way and see this anomaly. He was filled with a terrible rage at the Russian. They might have made it back to the borehole, but now there was no hope. Doctor Ming-Zhen was angry that his daughter was now certain to grow up without a father, his wife was to be a widow. Most of all, he was angry with himself for listening to Doctor Toskovic. All the warning signs were there: the man had lost his mind. *And I was stupid enough to follow him right into this trap.* He hated Ivan Toskovic. He wanted to see him dead.

*They would both be dead soon*, he thought. *Toskovic was not escaping this anymore than he was.* They were shooting over the funneling valley towards the gigantic source of light, ever faster.

The fish were beginning to break up and began spiraling around in the pattern of a gigantic vortex. The two submersibles were caught up in this flow, and soon they broke over the edge of dark rocks and were soaring around in a giant circle over the light source. He couldn't make out what caused it, all he could see was the light filtering through the water in giant shafts from a hole in the earth miles across.

His submarine was shooting down at alarming speed towards the craggy edge of the opening. The porous, volcanic-looking rocks approached dangerously close, and before long he was barreling past them.

He had lost track of Doctor Toskovic's submersible, but he didn't care. With any luck, it had smashed into one of the boulders. That's what he thought, and then he saw a giant projection just ahead of him.

He hoped he would miss it—until his sub suddenly jarred right towards it. In his rear monitor, he saw that Doctor Toskovic's submarine had struck his.

With the light now blinding in his face and the rock about to strike, he succumbed to a sudden sentiment. *This place is diyu, where souls go after people die. It is real.*

The submersible cracked with a horrific jolt. Doctor Ming-Zhen felt himself spinning wildly and saw flashing spots all over. Then there was another hit. Blackness closed in.


## Cairo Museum


After the spectacular Grand Egyptian Museum in Giza had opened, the Cairo Museum had become almost as much of a relic as the artifacts it contained. The old Cairo Museum wasn't on tourist shortlists anymore, so its halls were ghostly silent. The basement of the once-great edifice had become like one of the tombs in the Valley of the Kings: dark because few light bulbs worked anymore, foul with the smell of dusty antiquity, and damp from seeping pipes that had never been fixed. For these reasons, it simply wasn't the kind of place one would expect to find enticing.

Yet Doctor David Katz was spellbound. He had been to the museum before, to the ground level where tourists used to congregate like cattle. But he had never been invited into the mysterious basement where stacks and stacks of crates containing a century of archeological finds were stored. Most of the items there had never been gazed upon by anyone but the person who brought them into the modern age. Artifacts were so plentiful in Egypt, especially during the twentieth century, that nobody had time to catalog most of them. As soon as they were dug up they were tossed into boxes and hauled away into storage.

When Layla brought him down into the basement (armed with a flashlight), they had hardly gone two steps before he distracted her with some object of interest—a vase. No sooner had they examined this than he pointed to something else. Before long they were prying crates open in a cloud of dust as he indulged himself in a feeding frenzy of archeological delights. And the longer he indulged, the more enamored he became not only with the archeology, but also the female who shared the indulgence.

As he interpreted various hieroglyphics they found or flaunted his savvy on facets of Egyptian history, she was an appreciative and even admiring audience. Not only this, but she had a shared knowledge to the extent that he would begin to say something and she would nod and smile with excited comprehension before he was finished saying it. And when she disagreed with him, they became entwined in friendly, flirtatious intellectual arguments.

As the dust cleared from their most recent crate excavation, Doctor Katz was sitting on the floor holding a metallic amulet. In the shape of an eye, it had two lines extending out from the corner, one long with a spiral at the end, and the other short.

"The all-seeing eye," he said, "Otherwise known as the eye of Horus." He smiled, "But I'm sure you knew that."

"Of course," she replied. Scrunching up her nose, she said, "I don't like it."

"Oh, but it's everywhere these days. All the biggest names in entertainment use it. Have you ever seen a rock star in a photo covering one eye? They're making the all-seeing eye. Kind of a fad. But of course it isn't anything new as far as fads go. It's been found in many different ancient cultures all over the world." He paused, surveying the object, "You don't find it *mystical*?"

She shook her head, laughing, "No. I don't like it. It's scary."

"Well, this one is a precious artifact!" He looked at the piles of objects they had stacked up all around, "These are all precious artifacts. What should we do with all of these?"

She smiled, "We should probably put them back in the boxes."

"We could sell them on the internet," Doctor Katz laughed.

"That wouldn't be responsible scholarship, now would it, Doctor Katz?' she said flirtatiously.

"'David,' please," he said. "I'm not your professor."

"David," she repeated, letting the word roll of her tongue softly.

Doctor Katz said, "You know, I think you have more knowledge than most of the professors I've worked with."

"You think so?" she said, leaning back and tilting her head to the side.

"Yes, truthfully."

"Thank you," she said. "Now let's test *your* knowledge. Why only one eye?"

"What do you mean?"

"Why is there only one eye? Why not two for Horus?"

He casually leaned back, "Ah. That's simple. Because he lost his left eye in war. Did you ever hear the story of Horus? How he was conceived?"

"I think so, but go ahead." She said with amusement, "I've noticed you love to talk."

He laughed, "You know me well already, I see. The story is that Isis, his mother, gathered all the parts of her husband Osiris's body after he was killed and dismembered. She magically restored her fallen husband to life. But when he awoke, there was one major problem. He was missing a vital part. So she fashioned a golden one for him and they slept together. Through this, Horus, a sky god, was conceived."

"*Pure* gold?" she said, smirking. "Or was it an alloy?"

He grinned, "Pure, I'm sure. An alloy wouldn't suffice." Gazing at her as he was, his heart was beating with an excitement he hadn't experienced since he was really young. "Layla," he said.

"What?" her voice sounded almost hopeful.

"It's beautiful, your name," he said. At this point, it wasn't even her beauty that was truly drawing him: it was the fact that she seemed to respect and admire him for his passion in history. It was a passion they shared. He stared directly at her eyes and could see desire in them. Her head was cocked to the side exposing the beauty of her neck, glistening in the heat from her sweat.

She was ready. She wanted him. Some animalistic, carnal part of him made him aware of her need. Responding, he moved in.

Her eyes closed but her mouth didn't as he pressed his lips on hers. He rhythmically kissed her, both their mouths opening to each other, tongues restrained. Erotic desire, excitement flooded over his body. Their tongues touched, electrical lust shooting all over him. He wasn't gold, he thought, but he was just as—

The huge latch clacked loudly and then the door at the bottom of the stairs began to swing open.

# StarLine Regal Shanghai

After they were all settled in their rooms, Aubrey ventured out with Maggie to finally shop (on Henry's dime) for some new things to wear. While they were out, she noticed that Maggie was treating her with barely masked hostility.

After being snapped at for the third time, as they were stepping onto an escalator, Aubrey finally asked, "Why are you treating me like this? What's wrong with you?"

"What's wrong with *me*?" Maggie said sarcastically. "There's nothing wrong with me at all! You know why? You know why? I've been working my rear off for Henry for almost ten years. I've taken his abuse day in and day out, I've given up my life, my kids, everything just for his measly paychecks. And now I'm nice enough to give you a job and you arrive on the scene like Chelsea Come Lately and think you're going to be the cute little teacher's pet. Well I have news for you. It isn't happening. I can get rid of you just as quickly as I brought you in."

Aubrey was really hurt. She certainly wasn't doing anything to try to make Henry like her, in fact very much the opposite in her mind, and she couldn't believe that Maggie would be threatened by her at all. But also, she was angry. It was very unfair of Maggie to totally forget that she tricked Aubrey into taking this job, a job that nobody in their right mind would have taken. "Maggie—I can't believe you. You lied to me about this job. I never would have gotten on that plane had I known the truth. Lorraine told me Henry can't ever keep an assistant. You were on the hook for someone and you found the biggest sucker you knew: me! So don't act all innocent all of the sudden."

"Well if you hate the job so much, I'll help you get back home on the next flight out."

Aubrey suddenly felt dismayed.

But why?

If she was totally honest with herself, she didn't *want* to leave. She was having the adventure of a lifetime, and never would have dreamed she'd be in the Caribbean one day and Shanghai the next. So even though Maggie had not told the whole truth, she still owed her something. She placed a hand on Maggie's shoulder, "I didn't mean that, Maggie. I do appreciate the chance at this. Like you said, 'It's not International House of Bacon.' But honestly, I really haven't been trying to be teacher's pet. How could you think that I have when I've challenged him to his face? If I were him, I would hate my guts right now."

"He doesn't seem to." Maggie sighed, looking away for a moment. Then she said, "Look, the truth is I've never seen Henry take to somebody so fast. In fact, I've never seen him act like he does with you. I'm just . . . ." Suddenly she wiped away a tear, "I really have tried so hard for him. You know, secretaries get fruit baskets at Christmas, maybe even flowers from time to time. But I haven't even had a *word* from him. Not one word of appreciation. Not even one word of kindness, really. Not a card, not anything that says, "Thanks, Maggie, for sticking with me for all these years."

Aubrey moved in to hug her, "Maggie! I'm sorry."

"You know the last thing my daughter said to me before she left for college? She said, 'you've been a slave to that guy your whole life for nothing, mom!'" Maggie was sobbing. "And you know what? She's right. I really have thrown away my life. And for *what*?"

By now they had reached the top of the escalator and moved to take a seat at a cafe along a wall of windows with a view of the city.

A hand on Maggie's arm, Aubrey said, "Maggie, who paid for your daughter to go to that college? Wasn't it you with the money that this job gave you? You haven't worked for nothing! You've done it for your family. So don't ever think that it wasn't worthwhile. You taught your kids to work hard even when it's tough. Maybe they don't realize it now, but someday when they're working hard and they want to quit, they'll look back and say, 'Mom didn't quit! Mom kept going. And so can I!'"

Maggie looked up, a smile appearing through her tears, "You think so?"

"I'm sure so, Maggie."

When they returned to the hotel, Henry, to Aubrey's shock (and chagrin), asked to dine with her at one of the Hotel's restaurants. Maggie had gone up to her room, and while Aubrey wasn't particularly amused with him now, she didn't want to eat alone, and certainly couldn't afford any of the restaurants herself, so she acquiesced.

## Pearl Liang Restaurant

The meal of Asian seafood began in awkward silence, each of them sipping their soup quietly. Finally, she broke the quiet, "So why did you ask me out?"

"I did not ask you out," he said matter-of-factually.

"You asked me on a date. Isn't that asking someone out?"

"I asked you to have a meal with me. I don't qualify that as 'asking out.'"

"Okay, so why'd you ask me *to have a meal* with you?" she raised her hands in the air.

He swallowed, "Actually . . . I . . . I find myself enjoying your company, somehow." He said it as if the fact amazed even him.

Despite herself, she was pleased by his comment. With as much disinterest as she could feign, she said, "I'll take that as a compliment."

His face, which had been expressionless until now, broke into a grin, "I have no objection to that."

Emboldened by this, she said, "You haven't made it easy for me to enjoy your company, ya know."

"I'm your boss. That comes with the territory."

"It's not that you're my boss. It's your attitude. Especially about the Biobots."

He sat back, rolling his eyes, "Oh not this again."

"I don't understand how you can justify it to yourself! How can you look at those kids and not see *people*?"

"It's simple science, Aubrey. These things are not done in some secret evil labs; they are possible after years of painstaking research. Without the 'self' gene, Biobots are not aware of their own existence. They don't seek self-fulfillment, they're not proud. If you didn't give them a stimulus, they probably wouldn't do anything at all."

"How do you know that?"

"I've done extensive reading on this."

"Well, how do you know that what you're reading isn't just telling you what you want to hear?"

"These are peer-reviewed scientific journals. This has been scrutinized to death by scientists everywhere around the world. It's not Frankenstein. The 'self' gene is real and it's what makes us human. Put it in an ape and it would be a man."

"But what is your *heart* saying? What about your conscience?"

"You mean Jiminy Cricket? Since when did some hocus pocus feelings have any basis—" he interrupted himself, "This is science! Science tells us they aren't people!"

"Science can't say what only your heart can tell."

Henry sucked in a breath, eyeing her with the focus of a serpent. He said, "Now this is a situation Aubrey where you would be better off keeping your personal feelings and your work separate. If you want to pass judgment on my business affairs, you need to do so in your mind alone."

"Oh, so I'm on the job now? Having this date with you is part of my work with you? After dinner, what will it be? A lap dance?"

"Now really, that isn't fair," he said, looking up above her head despondently.

"Well either this is me on my time off and we're having an adult conversation where I can tell you how I feel, or it isn't!"

"I don't want to hear you tell me how to run my business. That's all."

"Well, the way I feel about your business is part of me. Either you appreciate me for who I am or . . . ."

He was seething. Through clenched teeth he growled, "Enough! That's enough! I want you out of my sight!" He was very loud, and the restaurant's din came to an abrupt silence, with servers and diners alike pausing to stare at him. He was standing, his palms face down on the table.

Aubrey was stunned, and embarrassed. They were both angry, but his sudden outburst seemed oddly out of place. She stared at him for a moment as the activity in the restaurant resumed. Then she said quietly, "You're a freak. And, yeah, I'll get out of your sight. I'm going home!" She stood up and spun around to walk past the host's station and out to the busy sidewalk.

# Lake Vostok

Doctor Ming-Zhen's eyes opened. His head throbbed. His mouth was incredibly dry, parched with thirst. The lights were on: he saw the white sterility of the cabin. The oxygen monitor read: *10*.

Ten minutes of oxygen left.

He looked out the bubble. The other submarine was very close and a robotic arm was fastened to one of the ubars on the side.

With a stabbing headache, it was hard for him to think, but he thought he understood. His submersible was being pulled through the water by the other one.

Doctor Toskovic was dragging him somewhere. He hoped it was back to the borehole. He was about to speak, but instead he froze in fear.

Suddenly there was a thud as, out of the blackness, a body in a wetsuit collided with the acrylic glass. Tiny fish were pecking at the skin from all sides. At first he couldn't see the face, but the hair waved softly out from the head. As the body rotated, the light fell upon the ashen visage, allowing him to see gaping eyes and an open mouth. He immediately recognized the face.

It was Ivan Toskovic.

The corpse rolled off his sub and continued to sink into the abyss. His heart was thumping in his chest uncontrollably. He took a moment to calm his breathing, wiping the sweat from his face. His hands were trembling, and he felt a strange tingling in his extremities. Without doubt, he had never been more terrified in his life. Gathering himself, he tried to think rationally.

Doctor Ming-Zhen did not know what was in the other submarine, but he knew he didn't want to meet it.

The oxygen showed: *8*.

There was light ahead, above. It took him a moment to recognize what it was: the pressurizing chamber at the bottom of the shaft. He was being taken straight towards it.

The submarine in front rose vertically. As it did, the rounded glass top gradually came into view. Inside, he saw the back of a large bulb-shaped head, hairless, with moist-looking white skin. He also saw a pair hands, each with six, long fingers, swiftly working the controls. The head was twitching back and forth as it worked with a devoted intensity and mechanical speed that was completely inhuman.

He only had a chance for a brief glimpse before the head sunk down beyond his view into the submarine and he was left with a heart-pounding terror.

6 minutes of oxygen.

Whatever was being planned in the other submarine was surely going to take place soon, and he did not want to wait to find out what that was. He anxiously eyed the pressure chamber. It was so close, he could almost have reached out from the top of his sub and touched it. If he tried to power his vessel to it, it would pull on the other one and alert whatever was inside. The pressure of the water outside prevented escape that way, plus even if he was able to leave his submarine and enter the chamber, how would he get up the shaft?

A sudden metallic bang right outside his submarine made him jump. He felt the sub vibrate with another jolting sound. Then he felt something grip his arm. It was a glossy, white hand with the same six fingers he had seen. The arm it was attached to was projecting straight out from the metal of the interior wall. And the grip was pulling him, pulling him towards the wall. He was entirely immobilized by the hand: either from terror or some other force he didn't understand.

The vest and straps that held him in place provided no resistance to his body. With horror, he watched the vest sink into and through his chest. As his arm touched the wall, he felt a cold sensation, and pressure. His arm was disappearing *into* the wall; the cold and the pressure, he realized, was the water. As his face approached the side, he recalled his training in China. A change in pressure could cause his lungs to explode. He instantly exhaled, clearing all the air from his lungs. He closed his eyes, and when he opened them, he was in the water.

He could see the long, white arm extending up towards a body, but most of it was concealed behind the other submarine so he could not see the face.

He didn't want to see the face.

The powerful hand pushed him into the other sub, and once again he passed through a wall. As soon as he was fully within the vessel, the hand released him, and he dropped to the floor.

He was not wet: it was as if he had never been in the water at all. He jumped up and took immediate action. All he had to do to get the submarine to enter the pressurizing chamber was press one command. The process was entirely automated.

He pressed it, then worked to disengage the robotic arm to release the other sub. He looked up, out the bubble, and saw the doors of the pressurizing chamber opening. He felt the thruster engaging. He was moving towards the chamber.

He climbed up to the foot holsters and fastened the vest around his chest, pressed the button to tighten. When he looked back up, he saw a face just outside the bubble staring down at him.

It was the giant face of the elasmosaur, the jagged teeth as menacing as before. This time, though, instead of the dull green color they had been the last time he saw them, the eyes now glowed white. A tremendous billowing smoke poured from its nostrils, and a white hot flame erupted from its mouth.

He felt something grip both his ankles. It was the white hands. He was pulled down out of the vest. The elasmosaur's head swept out of view and suddenly the grip on his ankles loosened. The hands jerked back, out of the submarine.

Shaking with fear, he looked again through the glass. The submarine was just under the ice, sliding into the chamber. He clambered back up and snapped himself into place. Looking out from the chamber, he could see the elasmosaur's body. The long neck circled up, and crushed in its jaws a white body surrounded by glowing embers. The elasmosaur threw it down into the deep, and blasted it with a tremendous fire. When the flame subsided, there was nothing there. The white body had vanished without a trace. The doors to the chamber closed just as the elasmosaur's face looked up seemingly to stare him straight in the eye.

The water in the chamber gradually lowered. Finally, the water was out and the spiraling valve above the sub spun open. The thruster began to rotate powerfully, vibrating him in the vest, and, slowly, the submarine began to rise. Clearing the chamber, the engine roared more and more loudly, shooting the sub up faster and faster.

Doctor Ming-Zhen breathed a long sigh of relief. He was free from Lake Vostok.


## Pearl Liang Restaurant


Henry sat there watching out the restaurant's glass. She had disappeared down the street in the crowds. He was fuming, feeling perfectly justified in his outburst. After all, she attacked *him* first. He had learned very early to react quickly to anything threatening. But as the seconds passed, his fumes began to dissipate and something made him extremely discomfited with his behavior. The longer he sat there, the more powerful the impression became and the more remorseful he grew to be, until he felt he could no longer sit idly.

He stood, and he did something he knew he had never done before.

He pursued someone he had wounded.

He was foggy on what he intended to do if he found her, but he very well suspected an apology would be in order. The thought made his heart sink. He paused. Make that *two* things he had never done before.

Aubrey.

Had he said her name aloud? He didn't know, but her name alone was enough to give him the bullocks he needed to go.

He rushed out the doors onto the busy sidewalk and looked everywhere. He called for her with a voice that sounded far more desperate than he intended.

The street was clogged with traffic and pedestrians pushed past him. There was no sign of her. He shook his head. He was just turning back to the door when he heard a voice crying out, "Henry!" To his relief, he saw her flapping her hand in the air through the crowd. *So she'd been waiting for him.* With a little more confidence, he took long strides towards her and quickened his pace until he was all but pushing people aside. Then, as neared her, he approached her slowly.

Finally standing before her, she looked up into his eyes. It was clear she had let off some steam, but the locomotive hadn't come to a complete stop. "Yes, jerk?" she said impatiently.

"Please—I'm British. Bastard is much preferred."

"Okay," she said, grinning despite herself. "Have it your way."

There was silence between them.

She broke it, "In order to redress your mistake, you must take responsibility for it, I think is what you said to Lady Shrewsbury."

He grinned sheepishly, "You have a remarkable memory." Then, with extreme difficulty, he said, "I . . . I must apologize."

She stared expectantly up at him. It was obvious she wasn't going to make it easy.

"I would be very grateful," he said, "if you wouldn't go." Then, folding his hands together to twiddle his thumbs, and drawing a breath, he said, "I'll . . . um . . . I'll give every consideration to what you've said. About the Biobots." He looked down, "I have more respect for your opinion than you know."

"That's very flattering," she said slowly, then finished rapidly, "but I'm still going."

He gazed into her eyes, "Please stay with me. I know that I can be a 'jerk' as you say. But I feel as if I need you, somehow. I'd like to find out exactly why, or how."

She bit her lip, looking touched. She sighed a very long sigh, glancing off to the side, "Okay, I guess. I'll stick around, for a while at least."

He gazed appreciatively into her eyes, "Thank you. I know I don't deserve it."

As they returned to the restaurant, he said, "Not that this has any relevance, but, how, exactly, were you planning on getting back to New York?"

She frowned in a cute sort of way, "I hadn't thought through it that far yet."

When they reached the suite, the lights were dim. The heavy door closed behind them and they stood in a small hallway. Aubrey waited there looking up at him in expectation. He slowly drew near, but then he paused. Her lips were primed and she tilted her head in anticipation, closing her eyes. He knew she expected a kiss, but he gave her a quick peck on the cheek instead.

When he pulled away, she opened her eyes. "That wasn't a very good kiss."

"I'm sorry," he flashed a quick, pasted grin.

"Why don't you try again?" she teased.

He was speechless. He had never liked kissing. It was much too intimate.

"You know you don't have to be afraid of me," she said softly.

"Whatever do you mean?"

"I'll show you," she said. She walked by him, touching his arm with the tips of her fingers. As she passed, he couldn't help deeply inhaling the scent of the fragrance she wore. She strode through the living room through the door to the bedroom. "Come," her voice came from the room.

He followed her into the darkness. She approached him and began to unbutton his shirt. She kissed his neck and down his chest, slipping off the shirt.

"Aubrey," he said, not romantically. "No." He swallowed.

"I said don't be afraid," she voiced. He could feel her breath on his skin.

He said, "No. Stop." He was firmly gripping her arms. She looked up into his eyes with hurt, confusion. He could not muster an explanation, but he knew he couldn't do this. The fear of hurting her arose from deep within him and overpowered his desire for her, severing all passion from his being.

She stood to lean into him, her head against his chest. She said his name in a breath. "Henry, I love you." Weakly, "I want you to love me."

He was stoic with his arms at his sides as he said. "Don't."

She didn't move, just held him with her arms wrapped around his naked torso. He could feel her eyelashes blinking on his skin. Then, tears.

He could not believe it. *Why wasn't she angry? This girl truly wore her heart on her sleeve, and, worst of all, she really did seem to have feelings for him.* He said, "I hope you understand. I don't . . . I don't want you to be hurt." He immediately thought he should have stated the truth: *I don't want to hurt you.* But his vanity wouldn't allow that.

With a final, deep inhalation, he pulled himself away from her. He plodded out of the suite and closed the door behind him to lean against the wall in the hallway. He struggled with the emotions wrangling in his heart. A brutal battle was taking place within him.

He went downstairs and ordered a drink from the bar. He felt sick. He shouldn't have let it get that far.

It was her fault: she was the most bafflingly appealing person he had ever met. Her gregarious personality, so opposite his own, had captivated him, and her beauty had put him in some kind of shock. He had been stupefied out of rational judgment.

"Daft, Henry. Daft," he said aloud to himself. Why had he let her lure him? What had he been thinking? He hadn't been thinking; that was the problem. He had dropped his guard.

After about fifteen minutes of careful reasoning with himself, he returned to the suite to explain the facts to her. It was in her best interest to stay away. He was sorry, but that's all there was to it. He was logical, analytical, introspective, and composed. She was emotional, unstable, and had an unnerving penchant for wild risk. Clearly there couldn't be too more incompatible people in the world. He left his undrunk beverage on the bar.

When he made it back to the suite, she wasn't there.

She must have come to the same conclusions he had, he thought with satisfaction. But when he slipped under the sheets, he discovered he was mistaken. The pillow was moist with the dampness of what must have been her tears and he was powerfully aware of her scent.

He didn't sleep. He spent the night building the case in his mind against her. By the morning, he was ready to stand her down.

## China Academy of Sciences

"I will never return to Lake Vostok," Doctor Ming-Zhen said

through clenched teeth.

Yue Zhang, his superior, replied, "It is much different now. We have much larger submarines, it's practically civilized—almost like a resort."

"I was in therapy for two years."

"Post-traumatic stress, I know. Caused you to suffer from bipolar disorder. And other mental health nuisances. But the fact that you have fully recovered shows your resilience."

"Why are you coming to me now? What has happened?"

Zhang looked down, "We saw what happened in Toskovic's submarine."

At the sound of that name, Doctor Ming-Zhen's body froze. Quietly, he said, "I thought the data was irretrievable."

"We were able to recover the data. We have video. We saw everything."

Doctor Ming-Zhen felt a rush of adrenaline from fear. The nightmarish memories began to flood back.

"Now of course, all the samples that you brought back was the proof that you needed, everyone knows that. The DNA of every creature that was in the containers, and every creature we brought up later, matched the DNA of today's animals with so little variance... You proved that there had been no major genetic change in species in thirty million years. No one disputes that. That's why the Academy's reputation was redeemed, and why your speaking schedule is so very full."

"Yes."

"You are considered the preeminent biological scientist today, the world over," he said it with packaged enthusiasm.

"I will not dispute that," Doctor Ming-Zhen said calmly.

"But no one believed your story about Toskovic. We all assumed that the trauma had been too much for you, that post-traumatic stress had given you delusions, hallucinations." Zhang looked regretful. "We are sorry now. We were wrong."

Doctor Ming-Zhen stared at him stoically.

"We have seen what actually happened. It is as you said. Everything." Zhang took a deep breath, "And what's more, we now know the complete truth, even what you did not. Toskovic—"

Doctor Ming-Zhen raised a hand. "Please. . . . do not say that name." It made his skin crawl. "And don't tell me."

"But you *should* know. Tosk—*his body* was pushed out of the submersible shortly after it descended. And you might wonder, how could the submarine have still been operating if water flooded in through the hatch?"

"Please. I want to hear nothing else."

Zhang leaned forward, "But that's just it. The hatch never opened. He was pushed out *through* it. Like a ghost. We saw it happen. And once he was in the water, he drowned. And then it appeared."

Doctor Ming-Zhen closed his eyes.

"It looked just the way you said it did. It took the controls and piloted the submarine, spoke to you in Toskovic's voice, everything."

Doctor Ming-Zhen was perspiring profusely. He imagined its long fingers reaching for him, terror gripping his chest.

"And when you reached the suction vortex, it purposefully drove his submarine into yours, knocking you unconscious. Then, free of any constraint, it collected all the samples it wanted." Zhang looked solemn, "Now we are facing a daunting challenge. We need your expertise."

"What do you mean?"

"We have taken submersibles through the vortex, to the other side. We need you to help us with the abundance of life we have discovered. And, we are afraid."

"Afraid of what?"

"We have lost some men already. We believe they have been taken by these . . . these ghosts. You are the only one who was able to resist. We need you with us. We believe that, as bizarre as this sounds, for some reason there is a power in you that they fear."

"So I'm your laboratory experiment. Your laboratory rat. You want to bring me down to find out why or if it couldn't take me."

Yue Zhang nodded grimly, "Yes. It could be said in a more amiable way, but yes that is true."

Doctor Ming-Zhen said, "I cannot do it again. Two years it took me! Two years to recover! Plus there is my wife and my child to think about! What of them? What if something happens to me? What if I *change*. Again. What if I relapse?"

"You mean the psychological issues? The hallucinations? Zhou, I appreciate your concern. But think of this. You unwittingly discovered that we are not alone on this planet, in terms of intelligence. There is more than meets the eye. This has ramifications which we must face—

extraordinary ramifications. Terrifying ramifications. *Military* ramifications. This has become a matter of national concern, international concern, really. It is your duty to your country to help us in this."

"I risked my life once already for my country. Is that not enough?"

"I will not force you," Zhang said, rising. "But there are others, my friend, who might not be so understanding." He turned to leave, but then said, "Oh, and you leave tomorrow, for the cruise?"

"Yes."

"A well-deserved holiday. Enjoy, my friend. And when you return, I hope you are prepared to serve your country once again."

# BOOK II

# VIOLATION OF PARADISE

NOW AVAILABLE

# BOOK III
# FALL OF PARADISE

AVAILABLE NOW

You may reach the author at
bcchase@preseption.com.

Follow Paradeisia on Facebook!
Facebook Paradeisia

Follow B.C.CHASE on Facebook!
Facebook B.C.CHASE

# EXCLUSIVE INTERVIEW WITH THE AUTHOR

**In the novel *Origin of Paradise*, Wesley and his wife speak with a doctor who offers to make them a "designer baby." Is this in our future?**

The novel takes place in the future, so of course this is a fictitious scenario. Science is a ways away from the kinds of things this doctor offers the characters Wesley and Sienna. Right now we still have a very limited understanding of gene expression (matching genes to their functions), and in fact in the second part of *Paradeisia*, I take the readers to a lab where I show you how gene expression is actually identified. But currently, aside from ethical or legal concerns, there are two things that I think make designer babies an impossibility for the time being. One is epigenetics. Science used to believe that your DNA was what it was: meaning what you were born with is what you died with. But now we know that this isn't true. Epigenetics is the concept that your behaviors, your environment, and the things that happen to you throughout your life can actually act on your genes, and you can then pass those traits onto future generations. For example, it has been found that children who suffered from relentless bullying when they were young produce less cortisol when they are older. Cortisol is a hormone that helps you deal with stress, but if it is very high for long periods, it can actually cause damage to your body. So the children switch off the gene which acts to produce the cortisol in order to prevent the immediate damage, but the gene is never switched back on after the bullying has ceased. And, amazingly, it appears that this trait can be passed on to the next generation, perhaps even generations. You can see epigenetics very dramatically in action when you look at two identical, or monozygotic, twins. Monozygotic twins might have been born with the same DNA, but no two twins are exactly alike. They don't have the same personalities, they don't act the same, and often they don't even look the same—especially as they get older. So what is to say that if we create a designer baby he will actually turn out the way we expected him to? His choices throughout life and what he is exposed to will have a very large impact on who he becomes ultimately, regardless of what we do genetically before he is born.

Now the second thing that makes designer babies impossible for the time being is that the more we discover about DNA, the more we realize how little we actually understand. For example, you might have heard that only 2% of our DNA is actually used, that the other 98% is noncoding, or "junk"

DNA. Well, scientists are beginning to realize that perhaps the system is more complicated than was ever imagined and that all this "junk" is in fact important. It is now believed that these noncoding regions act on the coding regions to turn some genes on or off. It has also been found that mutations exist in a noncoding region within certain tumors. So, while we don't understand how or why noncoding DNA is important, there is certainly evidence that it is very much so, and until we understand this fully it is hard for me to imagine manipulating DNA to create people of our specificity who are then going to propagate and therefore permanently spread any changes we make into the human race.

That being said, science is already making designer animals, of sorts, and successfully so. Glofish, for example, are I think zebra fish that have been changed genetically in order to give them a florescent glow using genes from a jellyfish that has this ability. They are very popular with children. Now the company that makes the fish inserted the genes into androgenic cells so that the trait would be passed on to future generations. This company patented these fish, so they are the only ones who can make them (without a license). If these fish were to be released into the wild, they could potentially spread these genes to the natural population. I would be surprised, in fact, if this has not already occurred.

In the United Kingdom, the government has endorsed the use of mitochondrial transfer to produce in vitro babies with genes from three parents. The purpose would be to eliminate certain dangerous genetic mitochondrial disease, but the effect would be designer babies, of a sort. This has created quite a stir among the doctor community there.

**Can you talk about some of the discussion with regard to evolution and paleontology that takes place in *Origin of Paradise*? Are you concerned that it will be seen as controversial, or maybe even discounted as ignorance?**

Well, without saying too much, one of the characters, the paleontologist, makes a discovery that causes him to reevaluate everything he knows about evolutionary biology, which is his area of expertise. For the purpose of narrative, I include the dramatic discovery that Doctor Ming-Zhen makes. Such a discovery has never been made, and, I believe, never will be made. I use this discovery, however, to present some ideas which contradict Darwin's theory of speciation through evolution. I do this with respect for the many scientists who have, over a century, built the case for Darwin's theory, and have been very surprised by how offensive many readers have found these novels to be. I hope to provoke thought and discussion, but I do not intend to upset anyone or specifically impugn any scientist's work. My wish is that readers take this for what it is intended to be: a spot of fun.

**One point made in *Origin* is that primates were living in the cretaceous. What is the evidence for this?**
The cretaceous primates to which Doctor Ming-Zhen is referring is the species *Purgatorius.* They are known from teeth, jaws, and tarsals (ankle bones) dating to sixty-five million years ago or earlier (according to the strata in which they are found). A Yale study on the tarsals demonstrated a large range of motion typical of arboreal species such as primates. They are, for this reason and the morphology of their teeth and jaws, referred to as early primates or primate ancestors. They are not monkeys or apes. More like lemurs. I deal extensively with this in the notes at the end of the third book.

**Tell us about the speech at the United Nations. How much of that is based on actual science?**
Virtually all of it. The only thing in that speech that is fiction is the personal tragic story by Doctor Martin with his sister. That story, however, is based in part on an experience of my own.

**What was your experience?**
One day I was driving home on a route I took very frequently. When I arrived at a turn, I had a premonition that I should veer off the usual course and take a long, circuitous route. I had to very forcibly argue with myself to take the usual route. However, there had been an incident on that road and the way was blocked. We were stuck for such a long time that I had to turn around and take the long route home anyway. I was very curious as to why or how I had that strange feeling of foreboding which proved to be true. Was it a coincidence? There is no way to go back in history and scientifically test it, much in the same way that there is no way to go back into history and scientifically test evolution. But it is very interesting to ponder, nonetheless.
To get back to your original question, though, about how much of the speech is based upon science. Much of it is derived from the research of Doctor Rupert Shelldrake. I do not lend credence to everything he says, but some of his evidence for his ideas is very compelling and scientifically rigorous.

**What motivated you to write the way you have? You are dealing with many different subjects and sciences. Where did the research come into play? Did it motivate the story?**

I am very concerned about the trajectory science is taking. In *Fall of Paradise*, I include some notes that outline my specific concern, namely that science is becoming dogmatic. With that in mind, I write with the intention of ruffling some feathers. To do this, I highlight some questions concerning what I see as some of the most dogmatic scientific disciplines. Facts do not make truth, and this reality is only made worse by the fact that it is becomingly increasingly difficult to sort facts from pretense and publicity in academia these days. Marketing experts write the press releases that, unchanged and unchallenged, make up the bulk of the science news that most of us are fed in the media. And, contrary to the high expectations of the internet as a bastion of truth, it seems that the internet is making things worse in some ways (the sites Newsy and Newser are cases in point). If *Paradeisia* has given you pause or made you feel defensive, then I consider my mission accomplished.

**What are your sources of science information?**

I use Google Scholar a great deal in order to sort through the masses of science journals. I also utilize books, magazines, and anywhere I can find data that is verifiable or can be corroborated by reputable sources. I am a frequent consumer of science news on sites such as sciencedaily.com and refer to the original research papers whenever including information gleaned from such sources in my books.

**Why the name *Paradeisia: Origin of Paradise*?**

The name *Origin of Paradise* I naturally selected as a reference to Charles Darwin's work.

# Characters

| Name | Role |
| --- | --- |
| Abael Fiedler | White House Chief of Staff |
| Adriaan Holt | Ranger, Out of Africa, Paradeisia (formerly a PH in Tanzania) |
| Amélie Babineaux | Senior Vice President, Legal Affairs, Preseption Logic Corporation |
| Andrews | Scientist at Paradeisia |
| Aubrey Vela | Waitress at International House of Bacon, becomes Henry Potters Executive Assistant |
| Bao Ming-Zhen | Wife of Zhou Ming-Zhen |
| Chao | Student of paleoanthropology at China Academy of Sciences |
| Chiang-gong | Pastor in Taiwan, Mei-xing's husband |
| Cynthia Peterson | Mother of Wesley Peterson |
| Donte | Li Ming-Zhen's boyfriend |
| Doctor Charles Stoneham | Director, Special Projects, Preseption Logic Corporation |
| Doctor David Katz | Head of Middle Eastern and African History at Tel Aviv University |
| Doctor Fatima Kamil | Chief Biologic Scientist, Egyptian Ministry of Antiquity |
| Doctor Gary Riley | Neuroscientist at Cognitive Lifescience Corporation, husband of Stacy Riley |
| Doctor Guy Giordano | Chief Scientist, USAMRIID in Ft. Detrick |

| | |
|---|---|
| Doctor Kenneth Angel | Obstetrician/Gynecologist. Wesley and Sienna Peterson's fertility doctor |
| Doctor Ivan Toskovic | Head of Chinese Antarctic drilling operation at Lake Vostok |
| Doctor John Burwell | Pathologist at St. Joseph's Medical Center, Towson, Maryland |
| Doctor Karen Harigold | Secretary of the United States Department of Health and Human Services |
| Doctor Matthew Martin | Cambridge University professor of biology |
| Doctor James Pearce | Head of Paradeisia Hospital |
| Doctor Phillip Compton | Director of the Centers for Disease Control |
| Doctor Richard Kingsley | OBGYN at St. Joseph's Medical Center, Towson, Maryland |
| Doctor Viktor Kaufmann | Chief Scientist, IntraWorld Capital Corporation |
| Doctor Zhou Ming-Zhen | Head of Department of Paleontology and Paleoanthropology of China Academy of Sciences |
| Donald | Senior Systems Administrator, Preseption Logic Corporation |
| Erika | Preseption handler, Preseption Logic Corporation |
| Fitzgerald Ignatius Jinkins | Founder/Creator, IntraWorld Capital and Paradeisia |
| General Fox | Vice Chairman of the Joint Chiefs of Staff |
| Henry Potter | CEO, IntraWorld Capital |
| Jarred Kessler | Special Agent, Federal Bureau of Investigation |
| Jeffery Riley | Son of Gary and Stacy Riley, two years old |
| Jia Ling | Student of paleontology at China Academy of Sciences |

| Kelle | Seeks revenge for death of husband and children |
|---|---|
| Kwame Aidoo | Secretary General of the United Nations |
| Lady Shrewsbury | Financier of IntraWorld Capital, Duchess of Shrewsbury |
| Lakeisha Franklin | Vice President, Legal Affairs, and Chief Counsel IntraWorld Capital |
| Layla Fayed | Student of Archeology, emphasis Historical Genetics, Cairo University |
| Li Ming-Zhen | Daughter of Zhou Ming-Zhen and Bao Ming-Zhen |
| Lisa Ching | United States Secretary of Agriculture |
| Lorraine | Flight attendant for Henry Potter |
| Maggie | Corporate Secretary for Henry Potter |
| Marco Gonzales | Vice President, Health and Security, IntraWorld Capital |
| Mei-xing | Chiang-gong's wife |
| Miranda | IT project management office director, best friend of Stacey Riley |
| Honorable Paul Hager | Former Canadian Minister of National Defense |
| President Robert Surrey | President of the United States |
| Sai Chu | Chief Financial Officer, TransWorld Capital |
| Sarah Rodriguez | Technician at St. Joseph's Medical Center, Towson, Maryland |
| Scott Nimitz | Operations Supervisor, Paradeisia |
| Sienna Peterson | Back office processor, wife of Wesley Peterson |
| Stacy Riley | Wife of Gary Riley |

| Todd Humphries | Special Agent, Federal Bureau of Investigation |
|---|---|
| Tom Chastain | Owner of a charter aircraft company, member of Gary's church |
| Tony Bridges | Director of Operations, Paradeisia |
| Trey Wiggins | Captain, Manassas Police Department |
| Wesley Peterson | School teacher, husband of Sienna Peterson |
| Yue Zhang | *Xiàozhǎng* (Head) of the China Academy of Sciences |

Made in the USA
San Bernardino, CA
05 February 2017